Get Your
Coventry Romances
Home Subscription NOW

And Get These
4 Best-Selling Novels
FREE:

LACEY
by Claudette Williams

THE ROMANTIC WIDOW
by Mollie Chappell

HELENE
by Leonora Blythe

THE HEARTBREAK TRIANGLE
by Nora Hampton

A Home Subscription! It's the easiest and most convenient way to get every one of the exciting Coventry Romance Novels! ...And you get 4 of them FREE!

You pay nothing extra for this convenience; there are no additional charges...you don't even pay for postage! Fill out and send us the handy coupon now, and we'll send you 4 exciting Coventry Romance novels absolutely FREE!

SEND NO MONEY, GET THESE
FOUR BOOKS
FREE!

━━ ━━ ━━ ━━ ━━ ━━ ━━ ━━ ━━ ━━ ━━ ━━ ━━

C0181

MAIL THIS COUPON TODAY TO:
COVENTRY HOME
SUBSCRIPTION SERVICE
6 COMMERCIAL STREET
HICKSVILLE, NEW YORK 11801

YES, please start a Coventry Romance Home Subscription in my name, and send me FREE and without obligation to buy, my 4 Coventry Romances If you do not hear from me after I have examined my 4 FREE books, please send me the 6 new Coventry Romances each month as soon as they come off the presses. I understand that I will be billed only $10.50 for all 6 books There are no shipping and handling nor any other hidden charges. There is no minimum number of monthly purchases that I have to make. In fact, I can cancel my subscription at any time. The first 4 FREE books are mine to keep as a gift, even if I do not buy any additional books.

For added convenience, your monthly subscription may be charged automatically to your credit card.

☐ Master Charge   ☐ Visa

Credit Card # _____

Expiration Date _____

Name _____
                            (Please Print)

Address _____

City _____ State _____ Zip _____

Signature _____

☐ Bill Me Direct Each Month

This offer expires March 31, 1981. Prices subject to change without notice. Publisher reserves the right to substitute alternate FREE books. Sales tax collected where required by law. Offer valid for new members only.

DINAH

Mary Ann Gibbs

FAWCETT COVENTRY • NEW YORK

DINAH

Published by Fawcett Coventry Books, a unit of CBS
Publications, the Consumer Publishing Division of CBS Inc.

Copyright © 1980 by Mary Ann Gibbs

ISBN: 0-449-50153-1

Printed in the United States of America

First Fawcett Coventry printing: January 1981

10 9 8 7 6 5 4 3 2 1

Chapter One

It was a lovely day in early summer of the year 1894 that Charles Bellingham, M.D., first set eyes on Dinah. Miss Bretton was the eldest niece of his old friend, Septimus Crichton, and had been spending the day with her uncle at Saltbech, bringing with her Major Clive Morrell, to whom she had just become engaged.

The sight of her did much to soften the petty annoyances of Dr. Bellingham's day, which had started badly with a visit from a concise and fussy little man, Dr. Bryce, recently appointed medical officer of health for the district.

If Charles had known that the rector had such guests with him he would have gone straight home, but Simmons the parlormaid opened the door to him, very correct in her black dress and long white apron with its embroidered bib and the wide streamers to her frilled cap, and said nothing about it.

Yes, she said, greeting him with a smile, the rector was in and she was sure he would be pleased to see him.

Nearly everyone had a smile for Charles Bellingham: there was a kindliness about the big, broad-shouldered man that was reflected in his gray eyes, although they could become dark with anger at times, as could the rugged face under the thatch of thick dark hair.

Simmons, however, instead of showing him directly into the study took him across the hall to the drawing room, where the holland covers had been removed from the furniture and the windows thrown up in honor of Septimus's visitors, and he stepped through into the garden where three people were having tea under the trees.

Septimus sprang up as Charles arrived, and when he would have hastily retreated came to him as quickly and took his arm to bring him forward to introduce him, while the parlormaid went for more tea and another cup for the doctor.

"I particularly want you to meet my favorite niece, Dinah Bretton," Septimus said. "And her fiancé, Major Clive Morrell. My dear Dinah, this is the friend of whom I have so often spoken on my visits to Bretton, though you have never met him before: Dr. Charles Bellingham."

Miss Bretton acknowledged the introduction with a slight smile and a bow, and the major got up to shake his hand.

"As I have only just entered the Bretton family, Dr. Bellingham," he said, with a heartiness that jarred a little, "I am not yet familiar with your name."

"You soon will be," said Dinah, her smile as she met her uncle's eyes deepening a little. "When Uncle Sep is with us we seldom hear of anyone else."

Charles said that he was afraid her uncle might allow their mutual interests to bore her and her family.

"Not at all," said Dinah lightly. "We are too devoted to Uncle Sep to be bored by him at any time, are we not, Uncle? In fact, we do not see nearly enough of him."

Charles felt that he had been put in his place and was silent, watching the sunlight as it filtered through the trees to touch the girl's face. She was like a flame, he thought, with her dark hair curling under her summer hat, a spray of poppies across its wide brim, and her thin summer dress had a poppy-red belt clasping her small waist.

And then Simmons reappeared with fresh tea and bread and butter, and as she poured out the tea for the doctor before leaving them Septimus told his friend all about the young couple, his short-sighted blue eyes behind his gold-rimmed spectacles dwelling affectionately on his niece. It appeared that the major was to leave for Malta in a few weeks' time and that Dinah was to join him early the following year. The rector evidently considered that this piece of news was the most interesting that his friend could have heard in a twelvemonth, and Charles glanced from time to time at Dinah as her uncle spoke and saw the color in her face and the light in her eyes as she looked at Clive Morrell, and wondered what she saw in such a stick of a man. Her laughter, though, as her uncle teased her, was the laughter of pure happiness, her dark eyes brimmed with it, her pretty mouth could not help smiling with every glance at her fiancé, and it was plain that neither of them had anything to say to a country sawbones.

He regretted the impulse that had led him to the rectory that afternoon, and, having swallowed a cup of tea and a wafer of bread and butter, he was searching for an excuse to leave when the station fly arrived to take Miss Bretton and the major to catch the London train.

"Shall we see you at Bretton this summer?" asked his niece as she kissed Septimus goodbye.

"I am afraid not. I have a command from Aunt Alice to spend August with her, and when I get back I shall be very much occupied in the parish, what with Harvest Suppers to attend and Ladies' Bazaars and so forth until Christmas."

"I know you cannot refuse Great-aunt A.," said Dinah, laughing. Even Charles had heard of The Honorable Alice Crichton, and had seen her when she had been staying in Saltbech, sitting in the rector's pew in church with her companion like a small gray moth beside her. The Honorable Alice was vast and imposing, with a large white expressionless face that rather reminded Charles of a buddha.

"But you will certainly see me before you leave for Malta, my love," went on Septimus. "I plan to visit Bretton in the New Year."

"That is a promise?"

"A promise, my love."

"Then I shall hold you to it, so do not try to wriggle out of it, however many ladies in the parish give bazaars." She kissed him again, turned to favor his friend with a polite little smile, before taking her fiancé off to the waiting fly.

"A strange fellow, Clive Morrell," said the rector after they had gone. "I wish I liked him, but I cannot say that he improves on acquaintance. His eyes are set too close together."

Charles was amused. "Surely that is not his fault?"

"No, but I have met several fellows with eyes like his and I have never trusted them, I do not know why. And now," he took his friend's arm and led him back to the tea table under the trees, "tell me where you have been this afternoon."

Charles resolutely put the memory of Dinah Bretton out of his mind as he told the rector of Dr. Bryce's visit.

"I took him out to Crossways Hall this afternoon," he said.

"To see Mr. Whatley? Whatever for?"

"I am afraid I suggested it to get rid of him, when he called on me this morning just before my surgery hour and wasted fifteen minutes of my time to no purpose."

"What was the trouble?"

"The recent cases of typhoid fever at Burston." Burston was a small and dirty town on the River Calder, an equally dirty river that joined the River Salte just below Saltbech. "I told him that the cases in question were now in the new fever

7

hospital outside Easterley, our largest town ten miles away, and that the hospital had been built through the generosity of certain local gentlemen appalled by the accounts they had heard of the old one, but he did not seem to be satisfied. He asked me if I was familiar with Burston and I said as familiar as I wished to be."

The rector smiled. "You must admit all the same that it is refreshing to find someone who cares enough to bother his head about Burston."

"Nobody bothers about Burston," protested Charles. "And nobody ever will."

"Unless Providence intervenes." For a man who had suffered many unmerited blows in his life, it always amazed Charles that Septimus still kept his childlike faith in Providence.

"Sometimes," he observed drily, "I think that Providence forgets such places as Burston, and I do not think that even Dr. Bryce will be able to make it more wholesome or cleaner. It is like a slut that has become so set in her ways that they have become a habit."

"Were Dr. Bryce's interests directed to the town's drains or its water supply?"

"Both. But chiefly its water supply."

"Did you not tell him that Sir James Collington owns most of the cottage property there, and that he has had the Company's water installed in most of it?"

"I did. And I also impressed on him that Sir James is very conscious of his duties as a landlord, and I thought all his cottages had earth closets regularly emptied."

"And did not that satisfy him?"

"Not a whit. He then wished to know if the Easterley Water Company had had its supplies analyzed lately, and had the water been beyond reproach. I told him that no water company's supplies could be that, but that I did not think the recent cases of typhoid at Burston were connected with either the water supply or the drainage system. They all occurred after all, as you and I know, in the poorer quarters of the town, where the women think nothing of taking buckets of water from the Calder for washing and even for drinking. The carcass of a dead dog floating a few yards away would not deter them."

"And then there is the glue factory just above the town. That does not add to its salubrious conditions," added the rector. "What did he have to say to your explanations?"

"Oh, he simply insisted that he must go and see the

chairman of the Easterley Water Company to make sure what kind of pipes had been used for the Burston water supply."

"That would not please Mr. Percy Whatley very much. Was he at home to him?"

"He was." Charles gave a wry little smile as he thought of Crossways Hall, a large and magnificent building of red brick, built in the Gothic style by the present owner's grandfather who had made a fortune out of cotton. He had watched Dr. Bryce mount the steps under a Tudor porch that would never have been built by Tudor workmen, and disappear behind the studded oak doors, opened to him by a pair of powdered flunkeys.

"I left him at the Hall and went on to see my patients in the village and beyond, and I am afraid that Dr. Bryce was very much disappointed in Mr. Whatley, because he only gave him a very few minutes and when I got back to the Hall he was waiting for me at the gates."

The rector said he hoped Dr. Bryce had not been critical of the Easterley Water Company, Mr. Whatley regarding his position as its chairman with pride and a sense of achievement. "Naturally being a Yorkshireman, he does not spend a shilling where sixpence will do, and he always makes sure there are sufficient well-breeched residents in the towns and villages where the water is installed, as otherwise he will not get a water rate. Nobody can blame him for that. He is a businessman."

"Very much so, and what is more, as I pointed out to our tiresome little officer of health on the drive back to Saltbech, both he and his neighbor Sir James are supplied with the company's water, so that he must have faith in its purity."

"That must have reassured him at all events."

"It did nothing of the kind. Apparently Mr. Whatley had replied to his remarks about the typhoid at Burston by saying at once that the Burston people were some of the dirtiest in the district, and went off into a panegyric of praise for the water company that Dr. Bryce was powerless to stop. He told him all about the magnificent reservoir they had constructed, with pipes discharging water into the riverbed below for fear of robbing farmers and their beasts by drying up the riverbed, and so on."

"I hope Dr. Bryce did not remind Mr. Whatley that had he neglected to do this the company would have been taken to task?"

"I do not think he had a chance, but when he enquired what pipes had been used he was told curtly that nothing but the best cast iron would satisfy the water company's engineer, who was particular about such things, and he was shown the door. I could not help feeling sorry for the little man. He came out with his black beard bristling with anger."

The rector laughed. "I have never had any business dealings with Mr. Whatley," he said, "and I do not wish to have any. He is a singularly hard-headed gentleman, I am told, with an enviable sense of thrift. But I have only met him socially, and I have found him hospitable enough. What did you advise Dr. Bryce to do about Burston?"

"I advised him to have bills printed in his official capacity as medical officer of health, instructing the Burston populace that all their drinking water should be boiled, having such bills displayed at prominent positions in the town—preferably outside the many public houses there. I doubt if it will do much good, but it cooled his temper a little."

"A new broom," commented the rector, "sweeping clean."

"And making a great deal of dust as he does it," grumbled Charles. "A tiresome little man. I told Benson to drop me here and take him on to the town hall and then put old Whitestar up for the day. I felt in need of your calm and good sense, Septimus."

His eyes went to the lovely old rectory across the lawn. It had been built in the reign of the third George, and it was long and low, with a roof mellowed with time, the slates having been brought by barge from the slate quarries of Wales. He thought how much more beautiful it was than the pretentious grandeur of Crossways Hall. There was no doubt that the products of centuries of culture were more pleasing to the eye than the products of cotton. He said slowly: "I must apologize for my intrusion all the same. I had no idea that your niece would be with you." He hesitated before he added, "How very lovely she is."

"Yes, Dinah is a pretty child," said Septimus with the understatement of familiarity, and then as a bell began sounding across the field that separated the rectory from the church he got up and said he must go to evensong.

"I'll walk with you as far as the gate," the doctor said. "It is time for my evening surgery."

The two men walked along the path through a field that was yellow with buttercups to where All Saints Church was situated, its bell sounding lazily as if the bellringer knew that not many would be there to attend a weekday evensong, and at the gate, where a may tree was in flower, they parted.

Charles returned to his tall house in the High Street somewhat refreshed as always by his talk with Septimus, but as he entered his consulting room he found a certain reluctance to return to work.

The memory of the small flame-like creature sitting in the shade of the rectory trees came back to haunt him, and he walked restlessly to the windows, his hands in his pockets. Outside a laburnam tree was in full bloom, hanging over his lawn like a golden parasol, and next door he could see his young partner's wife, Janet Annerley, picking some lilac from their little walled garden for her vases. Suddenly he envied Mark Annerley as he thought of his own house, bare of flowers and lacking any feminine touch.

For the first time in ten years he was tired of receiving and visiting patients, of asking what the trouble was, of peering down throats and at furred tongues. He wished he had chosen almost any profession other than medicine. A soldier's life, for instance, might have suited him—or would it? He saw himself surrounded by men of Major Morrell's caliber and decided that it would not have suited him at all.

It was absurd to look round at his dark, sparsely furnished house and think of it as being brightened by a girl from a county family, with poppies in her hat. All that sort of thing had died for him ten long years ago.

While for eighteen-year-old Dinah Bretton, sitting in a first-class railway carriage gazing adoringly at her handsome Clive, Dr. Charles Bellingham had ceased to exist, and she certainly did not anticipate ever meeting him again.

Chapter Two

Towards the end of January in the following year, Septimus Crichton left Saltbech for a week to visit his sister Helen and her husband and family at Bretton Place. There had been a heavy fall of snow in the night, and the engine, with a snowplough in front, made slow headway as it puffed its way through the frozen fields.

Christmas was behind him, with its carol singers, its feasting, the turkeys hanging in the poulterers, the York hams in the grocers', and children coming back from the country lanes with armfuls of holly, and mistletoe picked from old apple trees that grew wild in the hedges.

The Christmas tree that was always placed in the big bare hall at the rectory had fed the gardener's bonfire, its candles finished, the envelopes containing gold sovereigns beneath it distributed to the rectory servants, given as gratefully as they had been received. Septimus's wife, who had started the custom, had died two years after their marriage, and although there was no family to join in the celebrations round the tree, he continued to have it every year to keep her memory alive.

He was the youngest child of Sir Robert Crichton's first wife, and some years after she died his father had married again, Helen being the only child of the second marriage. Septimus was ten years old at that time, and joined his brothers and sisters in spoiling their pretty baby sister, a process that her charming ways encouraged.

The family of the first Lady Crichton were now very scattered, the only brother closest to Septimus being Quin, who had been in the diplomatic service until he contracted malaria, putting an end to his career. He had retired to a pleasant country house in Kent, with his cheerful wife Dulcie, and their four children, fast growing up.

Quin had announced his intention of carrying Septimus off on a holiday that year. "It is high time," he wrote, "that you freed yourself for a time from that enormous rectory and a selfish parish that has no mercy on a willing horse." They decided on a bicycling holiday in Sussex, a county that neither of them knew very well, making no itinerary but going where the mood took them and staying at small inns where they might depend on clean beds and good food. As the train rumbled on, his carriage getting colder and colder, Septimus thought of the prospect with pleasure. He had a trap to drive in the country round Saltbech, but he had recently bought a bicycle, which he found excellent and invigorating exercise.

From Quin and their holiday his thoughts traveled on to the family at Bretton, and his brother-in-law, Sir Roger Bretton, who had married Helen when she was eighteen. And in spite of her eight children she still managed at thirty-eight to look extremely young and very pretty, more like an elder sister to her eldest daughter. Dinah would be nineteen in February and the youngest child, Octavius was four. Between them came Julia, eighteen, Sophy, seventeen, the future baronet Harold, fifteen, who with his fourteen-year-old brother Johnnie was at Eton, and after them the twins, Paul and Paula, aged ten.

It was the last chance Septimus would have of seeing his god-daughter before she left for Malta in the middle of March, chaperoned on the journey by Mrs. Duncan, wife of Clive's colonel, in whose house the wedding was to take place.

Roger was a man with gambling in his blood, in his case taking the form of speculation, and at the time that Dinah became engaged he had just made one hundred thousand pounds on a lucky investment.

He did not hesitate to promise Major Morrell twenty thousand as a marriage settlement on his eldest daughter, and as soon as the major had left for Malta he proceeded, against all advice to the contrary, to re-invest his newly won fortune in a copper mine that was rather more disastrous. And although he tried to retrieve it time and again, whenever he fancied he was on to a good thing it somehow turned out to be a very bad thing indeed.

Septimus walked the two miles from Bretton Station, having refused to have the Bretton horses brought out in such wintry weather, leaving his modest luggage to be taken to Bretton Place on the carrier's cart later on.

He arrived in the afternoon of the winter's day, and the deepening blue of the evening sky made a lovely back curtain to the beautiful old mansion, with its snow-covered roof and the spreading parkland round it.

He did not know why he had a feeling of misgiving as he approached the house: he always enjoyed his visits to Bretton, and there was a present in the form of a jade brooch set in pearls that he had had made for his god-daughter in his luggage. He recalled the somewhat petulant letter from his sister Helen at Christmas, when she had been put out because Roger wished to hire a smaller house that year than the one they usually had for the London Season because it would need less servants.

"I told him not to be so stingy," she said. "After Dinah is married we shall have to have a coming-out ball for Julia, and a small house will be no good at all."

Merrington opened the door to him: Merrington never changed, and a young footman in rather shabby green livery was sent to conduct him through the entrance hall to the smoking room, where his brother-in-law was enjoying a cigar and leafing through the pages of the *Pink 'Un*.

He greeted Septimus warmly and offered him a cigar, saying that Helen and Dinah were out calling on Sir William and Lady Ferrers, newcomers to the neighborhood but relatives of Clive's uncle, old Lord Morrell.

"I believe old Morrell is as mean as he is high," Roger went on. "But as Clive is the old man's heir it is wise to look up his connections if one can."

Septimus refused the cigar and pulled out his cherrywood pipe, filling the bowl with golden flakes of tobacco from the pouch that accompanied him everywhere, and listened while the baronet plunged into an enthusiastic description of a gold mine in South Africa in which he had recently invested some money. It was, he said, a chance in a lifetime, and before many months had passed he would be a rich man, which made Septimus open his eyes a little behind his gold-rimmed spectacles.

When his sister had married Roger Bretton her family had said that she was lucky to marry into one of the older well-to-do families in Britain. The rent roll at Bretton had always been considerable, and there were many thousands of acres in the estate.

It seemed strange therefore to hear Roger talking about becoming a rich man on the strength of one investment, and he hoped he had not plunged too deeply in this miraculous new mine. He thought he seemed on edge and unlike himself, too, which might be accounted for by the weather. Roger was not a man who took kindly to being cut off from outdoor sport by heavy falls of snow.

Septimus let him run on and had just got his pipe going nicely when the door opened and his sister and her eldest daughter came into the room.

"Our duty is done!" Dinah said. "But Lady Ferrers was rather stiff and unfriendly so we made our call as short as we could and came home, with the excuse of snowy lanes to encounter and possible drifts." The cold had given her a brilliant color, and as she came to her uncle to embrace him he thought she looked prettier than ever. The crown of her small hat was composed entirely of artificial scarlet leaves, fitting snugly over her hair, and there was a knot of Parma violets, cut from one of the Bretton greenhouses, pinned into the sables that had been her father's Christmas present to her.

"Dearest Uncle Sep!" she said. "How I wish you were going to be in Malta to marry me to Clive!"

"I wish it, too." He returned her embrace with affection and then turned to greet her mother to receive her cool kiss, before she exclaimed at the atmosphere of the room.

"I told Dinah we should find you both here," she said, "but smoking room or not this is not to be endured. Ring the bell, Dinah, for Wilkins. One of those windows must be opened at once."

"Wilkins be damned," said her husband. "Move towards that bell at your peril, Dinah. You women are all the same—never content unless you have a gale of icy air blowing through your rooms. But the smoking room is not a drawing room, my dear, and I utterly refuse to have windows opened in the middle of a snowstorm."

"It is not snowing now and has not been since this morning," said his wife, while Dinah chimed in that it was a beautiful clear evening with the stars out and a small new moon on its back.

"But if they are content to be suffocated we had better leave them to enjoy it," said her mother. "At least we do not have to share it with them." She put her head in the air and swept Dinah away with her, saying that they would see them in the small drawing room at tea.

Septimus's thoughts followed the girl lovingly as the door

15

closed on her: she reminded him of Helen at that age, although she had been more frivolous and not quite as pretty. He hoped other women would forget to be spiteful about her as they so often were about the young, and only remember the time when they had been her age.

During the first evening of his visit her head had been bent over embroidering an afternoon tea-cloth, and when her father said with a sharp and unusual note of sarcasm in his voice that she must own sufficient table linen to supply a hotel, she had raised her head to smile at him and to point out that Clive was due to go on from Malta to India, where table linen was not easy to obtain.

In fact Mrs. Duncan had given her a lot of advice on what to take with her.

"It appears to be quite a common thing in India," Dinah told her uncle gravely but with a gleam of humor in her eyes, "for one's native servants to borrow table napkins from other people for one's dinner parties. Mrs. Duncan says she often came across hers on her friends' dinner tables when she was in India."

"God bless my soul." Septimus was shocked. "Who could believe it?" But Dinah only laughed and went on with her embroidery.

Septimus heard of little else but the wedding during those days at Bretton, Dinah's sisters being put out because they could not be bridesmaids, and through it all his uneasiness persisted. For one thing he had never known Roger to be so much on edge: instead of talking about the wedding he talked about his gold mine, at one moment in great spirits and saying it was the best investment he had ever made, and the next uttering such remarks as "it had better be." He was also drinking heavily.

When Septimus spoke of him to his sister, however, she only laughed and said that Roger was having one of his stingy fits.

"Not only has he utterly refused to rent a London house at all this Season," she said, "but he is being extremely unkind about the wedding. The two girls are longing to go out to Malta to be bridesmaids and Dinah would love to have them there, and Mrs. Duncan wrote to me most kindly, saying that not only the girls but that Roger and I would be welcome guests. But do you think Roger would agree to that? He says he cannot afford to take us all out there, and that Dinah must go alone with Mrs. Duncan, and that, mind you, after pouring thousands into this stupid gold mine that is going to be so wonderful. I do not know what has come over him lately. With no London house it means that Julia will have to have her coming-out ball here at Bretton, and hiring orchestras and caterers from London will be much more expensive, but it is no good telling him that. I have never known him so unkind and sharp with everyone."

But in other ways everything was the same as it had always been at Bretton: he had his usual warm welcome from the young people, he was taken out skating on the frozen lake, and he even joined the twins on their toboggan without losing his spectacles.

He returned home to his big empty rectory taking with him happy memories of his visit and of his beloved god-daughter Dinah, to whom he had presented the jade brooch just before he left.

Roger appeared to have forgotten his gold mine that morning, and drove him to the station himself, his horses wearing felt shoes on the frozen roads. The snow was gradually going now, but the frost remained, and Roger remarked that it was a pity the weather had been so hard, as they could have had a bit of shooting and Septimus could have taken home a hare or a brace of pheasants for the pot.

They parted with warmth and a promise from Septimus that he would come again before Easter, and then the train took him away to Saltbech.

When he saw in *The Times* a week or so later that the chairman of the Silver Rand Gold Mining Company in South Africa had left the country for an unknown destination, taking with him a great deal of money in exchange for a quantity of worthless share certificates, it did not occur to him that it could be the company in which Roger had been so interested.

Two days later the baronet went shooting rabbits in the frozen Bretton woods, and it was thought that he slipped and fell, because some time later his head gamekeeper found him there in the chill of a winter's afternoon, shot through the head with his gun lying in the stark undergrowth beside him.

On the day that Septimus Crichton set out for his brother-in-law's funeral, although the snow had all gone, there had been a succession of hard frosts and the wind, sweeping across the East Anglian fens, was bitterly cold.

After a hurried breakfast he allowed Mrs. Jennings to

brush his best frock coat and his best shovel hat, while the boy Tom blacked his boots until they shone.

Then his housekeeper, taking no notice of his protests, buttoned his Inverness cape round his shoulders and twisted a grey woolen comforter round his neck. "You'll need it," she told him severely. "The trains will be like ice across them fens, and if you have a foot-warmer from Saltbech it will be cold long before you change at Ely for Bretton."

At the last moment it was discovered that he had only one pair of black gloves and those had a hole in one finger, and as Mrs. Jennings sewed it up for him and tightened the buttons on both gloves, the rector being extremely impatient lest he should miss the early train, she said severely, "And let there be no nonsense this time about walking from Bretton Station. There'll be kerridges in plenty sent there today to meet the funeral guests, and I've packed a warm dressing-gown in with your night clothes, because there's no knowing how long you will stay and I know what them big houses is like. Fires in the bedrooms and corridors like ice. I've put a flask of brandy in, too, in case you feel chilled going to bed."

She furled his umbrella for him and let him go. He climbed hastily into the cab waiting outside the front door where the portmanteau had already been lifted to its roof, and prayed that the train would wait for him, the cabby having told the stationmaster that he was fetching the rector for the early train, or else that the horse would not slip and fall on the frozen roads.

Fortunately the stationmaster had held the train for him, and he was able to settle himself in a first-class carriage with a foot-warmer before starting off for Ely. But once the fear that he might miss the train was over and he was able to sit back in the carriage with that worry lifted from his mind, he found it haunted by another—that he might have done or said something on his last visit to Bretton that could have averted the tragedy.

He knew that Roger Bretton was a man who would never take advice from anyone, let alone himself, however gently it might have been given.

"Nonsense, my dear Septimus," he would have said, brushing it aside. "I know what I am doing. You are so out of touch with things down there in Saltbech that you cannot possibly know what goes on in the world outside."

And as the coroner had brought in a verdict of accidental death it was stupid to give way to the nagging thought that

18

Roger had been far too good a shot to walk through woods high with frozen undergrowth with an unbroken loaded gun in his hand. Maybe it was an accident; and nobody could have prevented it.

The frost lay in channels along the furrows in the fields, and under the hedgerows a sheeting of uneven white remained like a country-woman's washing put out to dry. As he stared out of the window he wondered how his sister would meet the prospect of being a widow.

The spoiled pet of her step-brothers and -sisters, she had not only had her own way all her life, but she had grown up with an exaggerated idea of her own importance, not helped by a butterfly nature.

She had never failed to put herself before others and he doubted if she ever would. He remembered when she had thrown over a young man to whom she was secretly engaged to marry Roger, because he had so much more to offer.

Poor Helen, so little prepared for tragedy, enjoyment closed to her now for the time that a widow's mourning demanded. What would she do, alone with Roger's children at Bretton? Would she give comfort, or constantly demand it? He could only hope that common sense would come to her aid as it had never done before.

At Ely he made his way to the restaurant and ordered a Bath bun and a pot of tea while he waited for the train that would take him on to Bretton; he did not reach the village until half past one, and the funeral was timed for two o'clock.

He sent his portmanteau up to the Place by one of the carriages that were waiting for latecomers in the stationyard, and walked briskly to the village church to restore the circulation in his legs and feet.

All the Bretton relatives who had come from a distance had stayed the night, and on the previous evening Dinah had entertained them alone, as her Mamma did not feel well enough to come downstairs to dinner.

Dinah's uncle, Sir Thomas Carey, took the head of the table, and Dinah sat in her mother's place, between her Uncle Julius Dewhurst, Dean of Southlake Cathedral, and his wife Agatha, while Honoria, the wife of Sir Thomas Carey, sat beside the dean. Prudence Bretton, the only unmarried one of Sir Roger's five sisters, sat next to bluff, good natured Horace Dutton, while his wife Amelia was on Sir Thomas's right.

After dinner while the gentlemen enjoyed her father's port,

Dinah took the ladies into the north drawing room where good fires were blazing at either end of the room, and Honoria spoke to her about her wedding.

"Is it still to take place next month in Malta, dear?" she asked.

"Mamma does not wish me to put it off," said Dinah a momentary cloud appearing on her grave young face. "Although I know Clive would understand if I did."

"Your mamma is quite right, my dear," said her Aunt Honoria decidedly.

"Don't let him off the hook at this stage, my love," added her Aunt Amelia cheerfully. "You might lose him altogether."

This statement was received in shocked silence by her sisters, Honoria, Agatha and the unmarried Prue. There were times, they felt, when Amelia could be very vulgar, but they put it down to her husband, Horace Dutton, a small country squire who fancied himself as a farmer. No doubt, they felt, in his company she must meet all sorts of the commoner types of people, such as tenant farmers and their wives, from whom she would pick up such coarse expressions.

Dinah said she thought she would run upstairs to see how her mamma did and escaped, knowning that the aunts wanted to be alone to have a good gossip, in which the Roger Brettons might be heavily criticized.

She found her mother full of complaints. The dinner that had been sent up to her boudoir was very poor: she hoped that served to the dining room had been better. She hated all the black dresses that Lovell had been getting out of her dressing room cupboards for her to select one to wear the next day, and indeed, if it had not been for Lovell altering the best of them she did not know what she would have done.

Her maid Lovell here erupted from the middle of a large mahogany wardrobe in the boudoir and gave Dinah a frosty smile as she went off to her ladyship's dressing room with a bundle of black garments over her arm and several small black bonnets in her hand. She had been Helen's maid for many years, and was heartily disliked by the younger members of her mistress's family because she was extremely inquisitive and given to telling tales.

"Well, I suppose your aunts were all tearing me to pieces?" Helen said plaintively when she was alone with her daughter.

"They were not likely to do that while I was there," said Dinah gently.

"No, I suppose not."

"Mamma," Dinah went on after a moment, "I do wonder if I ought not to write to Clive and ask him if he would mind if we postponed our wedding for a few months. It would show more respect for Papa, and I could be of use to you in helping with your correspondence. And it cannot make much difference, can it?"

"It might make a great deal of difference," said her mother. She did not forget that Clive was heir to a large estate as well as a fortune, and like her sisters-in-law she thought it would be folly to postpone the wedding. Young officers stationed abroad had plenty of time in which to flirt with pretty girls, and while he was waiting for a date to be fixed for his wedding Clive might find somebody more attractive than Dinah.

"No," her mother said firmly, "I have settled all that, my dear, and I am not discussing it with you any more. Your trousseau is ready, even to your wedding dress, your uncles have been asking me what you want for wedding presents, and you must go out to Malta next month with Mrs. Duncan as arranged. Your father would never have wished the wedding to be put off on his account. You can leave all your black dresses behind you when you go. Black does not become you—you are too dark-haired— and I hate it, anyway." She sighed. "I suppose I shall have to wear it for a time, and being fair I can carry it off better than you can—but I shall not endure it longer than is absolutely necessary, I promise you. Has Harold come yet?"

"Not yet, Mamma, but a carriage has been sent to meet the last London train, and if he is not on that he will be sure to come in the morning."

"I hope he will be in time. He has to walk with me behind the coffin, and he must learn to take his responsibilities now." She paused and then she said, "For one thing I am thankful. It looks as if your Great-aunt Alice will not be coming, or she would have been here by now. There are rooms ready for her, of course, if she should arrive at the last moment, but I hope she does not. I detest that old woman. With her beady black eyes and her round white face, she looks just like an eastern idol."

She returned to the subject of her black dresses, and as Lovell came back to try on some of the bonnets Dinah went back to the north drawing room. As she came down the great staircase into the hall, Merrington opened the front door and The Honorable Alice Crichton sailed in, accompanied by her companion, Miss Pettit, and Harold.

Chapter Three

"I found Sir Harold at the terminus," the Crichtons' formidable relative announced. "And so we traveled down together." The title that she gave her great-nephew shocked his sister momentarily into silence.

The Honorable Alice Crichton was a lady regarded by the Crichton family with respect mingled with apprehension, as she believed in speaking her mind. She was wearing a new black bonnet, purchased for the occasion, its velvet strings tied under her ample chin and forming a frame for her buddha-like countenance. The bonnet was decorated with bugles and black wheat-ears, so that with a slight alteration such as the addition of a purple rose it could be worn at church in the summer. Being extremely wealthy The Honorable Alice did not believe in wasting money. Over her vast black brocade dress she wore an even larger astrakhan coat with sable collar and cuffs, and in her black-gloved hands she carried a small, black velvet reticule and an ear-trumpet covered in black silk.

She was not deaf but liked to believe that she could not hear on occasions, which meant that often she heard things she was not meant to hear. Behind her crept Miss Pettit, gray and small, like a little mouse, her black bearskin fur smelling of camphor.

"We wondered if you would come, Aunt Alice," Dinah said, coming forward to receive a kiss before going on to shake hands with Miss Pettit and to embrace her brother, and then, surprise making her slightly incoherent she added unnecessarily, "You are staying the night of course."

"Naturally." Her Great-aunt, known to the young Brettons as Great-aunt A., gave her a grim smile. "I do not anticipate spending it in the park, my dear. But we would all like some dinner as we are tired and hungry, and as I expect you have a number of Bretton relatives here already and the gentlemen will be gathered in the library, it will be more comfortable if we have our meal in the small breakfast room, if the fire has not been allowed to go out."

The housekeeper, warned by the arrival of the old lady's maid Hannah and the luggage at the side entrance, now came hurrying with a rustle of black silk to greet The Honorable Alice and to take her and Miss Pettit to the rooms that had been prepared for them, where cheerful fires were burning.

"I have had fires burning in all the rooms for the past week, ma'am," the housekeeper told her. "So that they should all be warm and thoroughly aired."

"That is a comfort at all events," said Mrs. Crichton. "It has been very cold on the trains and we have traveled a considerable distance, *not* to be undertaken lightly at this time of year. A most unfortunate season in which to hold a funeral." Her tone accused Sir Roger of thoughtlessness at timing his death so ill. Then she added warmly, "But if it had not been for Sir Harold I do not know what we should have done. Foot-warmers and tea. He saw to it all for us, and I shall not forget it."

The fire had not been allowed to go out in the small breakfast room, and when Mrs. Crichton and her small thin companion had removed their cloaks and bonnets a hot meal awaited them there, the room cosy and comforting with the large oil lamp suspended from the ceiling and shedding a warm glow over the white tablecloth, and the fire burning briskly and cheerfully in the hearth.

Sitting beside her brother, who looked white and strained, Dinah was glad to see that after the first few minutes his hunger seemed to revive and he ate a hearty meal, listening while Dinah told him of the program for the morrow.

When it was finished Harold went upstairs to see his mother before going off to bed, while the Honorable Alice made her way with her great-niece to the north drawing room to greet the company there and to bid them good night.

"I expected to see your Uncle Septimus here," she said loudly as Dinah prepared to leave the room with her. "I hope he is coming?"

23

"Mamma had a letter from him on Sunday morning to say that he will be here tomorrow."

"He is taking the service I presume?"

"Well," Dinah hesitated. "My Uncle Julius here."

"The Dean of Southlake. Of course, I forgot that he would be here." The Honorable Alice's voice was rather more penetrating than usual. "In that case I shall have to sit in front, my dear, and I doubt even then if I shall be able to hear him, although I shall have the aid of my ear-trumpet. Your Uncle Septimus has such a fine, clear voice. I can always hear every word he says."

The door closed behind her and the silence was broken by a laugh from Horace Dutton who had broken away from the library to join the ladies. "An indomitable old lady," he said. "Quite one of the old school, in fact—the oldfashioned kind."

"Rather too oldfashioned for my liking, I am afraid," said Honoria. "If you are returning to the library, Horace, perhaps you would remind my husband that we have a long and tiring day in front of us tomorrow, and if he proposes to have a game of billiards before he retires he should not be long. I am going to bed now."

All through the following day the burden fell mostly on the shoulders of Dinah, because her mother resolutely refused to leave her room, having the early luncheon that was served to everyone else brought to her in her boudoir. The coffin had been removed to the little village church that served as a family chapel for the Brettons, and through the leaden hours of the morning Dinah was upheld by only one thought: in a month's time she would be in Malta with Clive, and this would all be behind her.

The small Norman building was already full when Septimus arrived, a subdued murmur of conversation greeting him accompanied by an almost overpowering scent of lilies and hyacinths from the wreaths in porch and chancel.

He made his way up the aisle and saw Quin looking for him, and as he slipped into the space reserved for him between him and Dulcie, Quin said: "Aunt Alice is here."

"No!" Septimus raised his eyebrows. "When did she arrive?"

"Last night," whispered Dulcie a gleam of mirth in her eyes. "She was extremely annoyed because you are not taking part in the service today, and showed it."

"But it wasn't very likely that Helen could ask me with the

dean here, my dear." Septimus did not appear to be the least bit resentful, in fact he was extremely relieved.

Dulcie put her hand on his arm. "Tell me, Sep, was Roger's death really an accident?"

"The coroner said so," he reminded her gently. "Let the dead lie in peace, Dulcie."

Dulcie would have liked to observe that Roger had been very good at lying during his lifetime, but being surrounded by Brettons she held her tongue.

"I think Dulcie is surprised—as I must confess I am a little—to see Emmeline and Edmund here today," said Quin.

"Edmund?" Septimus was equally surprised. "I wonder he could spare the time. Isn't he on the Frinton case?"

Roger's youngest sister Emmeline was married to Edmund Bromley, Q.C., who was rapidly making a name for himself as one of the foremost counsels of the day. He was at that moment acting in a case that had attracted a great deal of attention in the papers and indeed in London Society: Lord Frinton, having been accused of cheating at cards at a country house party, had taken his accuser to court in an action for slander.

"He and Emmeline are only down from London for the day," whispered Dulcie, "But Quin thinks it's odd, and so do I."

"I wondered if there was something in the wind, to bring him here," said Quin.

"In what way?"

"Can't say, can we?"

The Brettons as a family were what their friends termed "close." Although they might see little of each other during the year, when any family occasion arose, such as a wedding, a christening, or a funeral, they would gather in strength. If it should be a wedding they would comment unrestrainedly on the bride's (or bridegroom's) relations, if it should be a christening, on the delicate looks of the child and the tendency for fatal illnesses in its mother's (or father's) family, and when it was a funeral on the probable disposal of the estate of the deceased.

So that it was scarcely surprising that they had gathered in strength for Roger's funeral, filling the family pews to overflowing, all agog to learn if the rumors they had heard about the baronet's death were true, although to outsiders sternly refuting any mention of a possible suicide.

The Honorable Alice had taken up her position in the front

to the left of the aisle, on a level with that reserved for Helen and her family, Miss Pettit sitting behind. The Crichtons were thinly represented: those that were there had come out of respect for Helen, and all except Septimus and his Aunt Alice left immediately after the service, all London trains being stopped at Bretton Station that day.

To the rear of the church the friends and neighbors of Sir Roger gathered, and a certain amount of whispering went on among them, too, before the coffin was carried into the church by six stalwart tenants of the Bretton estates and emerged into the aisle, Helen in deep black with her golden hair gleaming through a thin black veil to her fashionable hat as she walked beside Harold, who still looked dazed at finding himself a baronet and the owner of Bretton at the age of fifteen, and a certain amount of sympathy for the boy caused the whispered conjectures to cease.

Dinah walked behind them with Johnnie, who had arrived that morning, and behind them Julia and Sophy, the twins staying at home with their governess Miss Stroud, and little Octavius and Nurse Blackwell.

Contrary to expectation the vicar of Bretton took the service, the dean only giving the address, speaking resonantly in what his irreverent nephews and nieces called his Cathedral Voice, and not a little irritated by the ear-trumpet that the Honorable Alice held firmly to her ear all the time he was speaking, which might have daunted a man less self-assured.

Half buried in a spate of words, carefully prepared beforehand, the gist of what he had to say was that their sympathy must go to Sir Roger's widow, who had lost an excellent husband, and to their children for an equal loss of a loving father.

Having dwelt on this for a little, he went on to say that to his friends Sir Roger had been one always ready to do a good turn, and here a few sly glances passed between those friends sitting behind the family as they remembered the occasions when the baronet had attempted to persuade them unsuccessfully to invest in some of his wildcat schemes. The good nature of the late baronet was dwelt upon also for some length before the dean went on to his grateful tenants—or those who should have been grateful, even if they were not.

"An excellent landlord," boomed the dean unctuously, and an almost audible whisper was heard from one of the tenants standing at the back that sounded remarkably like, "What about my roof?" "A careful manager of his estates," ended the dean, "in fact, my friends, the epitome of an English gentle-man."

As he finished, Mrs. Crichton put down her ear-trumpet resignedly, and later on as she emerged into the churchyard to see the coffin lowered into the family vault, she said loudly, "Couldn't hear a word he said. Mumbled so. These Cathedral clergy never will speak up. Now when my nephew Septimus speaks, I can hear every word. He has such a good clear voice and no affectation, which makes such a difference."

Her nephew Septimus, after saying goodbye to Quin and Dulcie at the churchyard gate, made his way back to the Place across the frozen park, wondering if the gold mine had ruined Roger and if he had taken the easy way out, and whether in such circumstances one could call it the act of one who was the epitome of an English gentleman. He also wondered why Edmund Bromley had not taken the train back to London but had come back to the Place with the others.

On their arrival the gentleman repaired to the library with Mr. Deakin, the lawyer, to hear the will read, while the ladies once more retired to the north drawing room, to be entertained there by Dinah and her two elder sisters in their mother's absence.

Directly Helen had arrived back from the funeral she had declared that she felt faint and would lie down in her room until tea-time, refusing offers of company. Dinah and her sisters talked quietly to their aunts while Harold and his brother played draughts in a corner of the big room, and as the hands of the French clock on the chimney-piece crawled with snail-like slowness towards half past four Dinah kept telling herself, "This time a month from now it will all be over, and I shall be on my way to Clive."

She was relieved that Great-aunt A. had also retired to her room until tea-time.

The lawyer, in the meantime, who had been waiting for the gentlemen in the library greeted them with respect and Septimus noticed that he had reserved a place for Edmund Bromley beside him at the big library table, with certain papers spread out in front of it for the great man's perusal.

They seated themselves round the table and waited, their eyes fascinated by the document, evidently a last will and testament, in Mr. Deakin's hand. When they were all settled, however, it was the Q.C. who spoke first and not his humbler neighbor.

"I am afraid that Mr. Deakin has some bad news for you all," he said. "Two days after Roger's death, he came to see me in my chambers in a state of great distress. He had that morning been to see Mr. Samuel Wright, the head of Wright's Bank in the Strand, a most reputable private bank that has, as we all know, handled the Bretton account over many years. But I think Mr. Deakin had better tell you himself what he discovered there."

Mr. Deakin glanced at him apprehensively and having received a kindly nod, proceeded:

"It seems that my late client had lately been obsessed with a gold mine—the Silver Rand Mining Company by name—and being grossly misled by its possibilities—its assets were I regret to say nil—insisted on investing all his available capital in it. You need not be reminded by me, gentlemen, how disastrous that venture has turned out to be, and with many others Sir Roger was robbed of his money by the scoundrel who fled the country."

The Q.C. added quietly: "As a result Helen and her family are left with very little means, if indeed any at all."

"But—but there was a settlement of some thousands of pounds on Helen when she married Roger." Sir Thomas Carey, a wealthy man and the possessor of a country mansion as well as a house in a fashionable quarter of London, looked enquiringly at Septimus. "I think that is so, Septimus?"

As Sir Thomas spoke with the authority of one who had at one time been Lord Mayor of London, it would have been difficult to deny it, even if it had not been true.

"At the time Helen married," agreed Septimus mildly, "my father had inherited a considerable fortune from an old relative, and he settled thirty thousand pounds of it on his youngest daughter. She was always his favorite."

"What has become of that, then?" demanded Sir Thomas, regarding Mr. Deakin suspiciously as if he might have purloined it.

"Roger invested it in a rubber plantation a few years after they were married," Edmund said dryly. "It never paid, and eventually it went bankrupt."

"Good God!" Sir Thomas controlled himself with difficulty and the dean said soothingly, "Surely we are not to understand that there will be no assets except the house and estate? That would be impossible."

28

"Quite impossible," agreed Sir Thomas. "The rent roll here is good, and all that it means is that Lady Bretton will have to live very simply for a time."

Mr. Deakin exchanged glances with the Q.C., and Edmund Bromley said: "It would be comforting if one could think that, Thomas, but unfortunately the house and estates are mortgaged for a considerable sum to Wright's Bank."

"Mortgaged? Bretton, mortgaged?" Sir Thomas, outraged, turned a delicate shade of purple. "I cannot credit it. Roger would never have lost his sense of dignity, of what was due to his family."

"The fact remains that he did lose it," said Mr. Bromley. "And he lost everything else as well."

"Do you mean that Wright's Bank will seize the property?" asked Horace Dutton, a gleam of malice in his eyes. For years his wife's sisters had treated him with scant respect, and his question was put not without hope that they might be humbled by the actions of their dead brother.

"I asked Mr. Samuel Wright to dine with me at my club one evening," went on Mr. Bromley quietly, "and after a certain time spent in reviewing the situation we hit on a solution to Helen's present problems—if she will consent to it. Mr. Wright has agreed that his bank will refrain from foreclosure on condition that this house is let to a reliable tenant almost immediately. He thinks he may have an American gentleman in mind who would be prepared to take it from April the first of this year. In the meantime the rent roll would be paid directly to the bank in order to cancel the debt. He thinks if this is done—and I agree with him here—in six years' time when Sir Harold comes of age—the estate should have become unencumbered."

"And what is Lady Bretton and her family to live upon during those six years?" asked Sir Thomas.

"There will be the rent from letting the house," said Mr. Bromley curtly. "And I am afraid that will be all, but Helen will have to find a small house somewhere where she can live economically with her family."

"A *small* house? Lady Bretton, in a *small* house?" Sir Thomas's complexion that had resumed its natural red now began to change to purple again. "Do you recollect what you are saying, Edmund? Lady Bretton cannot live in a house unsuitable for her position.

"Any house that she has must not only be large enough to accommodate her family and her servants, the nursery staff and a governess, but there will be the outdoor servants as well to be considered. She will need at the very least a carriage and one pair of horses. And then there will be her sons' fees at Eton—at least two hundred a year each. Is all this to come out of the rent for the Place?"

"Not for all that, and I agree with what you say to a certain extent, Thomas." Edmund pressed the tips of his fingers together. "Although in a woman determined to live economically for the sake of her children it might be possible, Helen is unfortunately not such a woman and with her it might prove disastrous." He continued judicially, "There is another solution, but it is one that involves all of us, and I am not sure that you will find it more to your liking. We can give homes to Lady Bretton and her family between us."

There was an unhappy silence while Septimus held his peace, studying Helen's brothers-in-law with some curiosity. He was the only Crichton present, and concluded, as Helen's other relatives had done, not without sense, that as she was a Bretton any problems that arose after Roger's death were for the Brettons to resolve.

It did not seem however as if anybody had foreseen problems quite as grave as this, and he waited for any suggestions they might have to make on the disposal of their sister-in-law and her family. There was Sir Thomas, for instance, with his country house that Honoria had boasted had at least one hundred rooms. Could not space be found there for Helen and her children?

Sir Thomas was evidently thinking upon the same lines, if not in quite such a generous way.

"I do not suppose Lady Carey would object to having the old nurseries opened up again at my place, although all our children are now of schoolroom age, of course. There are a couple of rooms in the nursery wing too that Lady Bretton could occupy, with the nurse and little Octavius in the nurseries near her. The rooms are tucked away at the top of the north wing and nobody would ever know that they were there." He looked round the table as if his offer was as generous as could be expected of him. "Yes," he said with a touch of complacency, "I think I may say that I am perfectly willing to take Lady Bretton and her youngest child. What about you, Edmund? I understand Dinah's wedding is to take place as planned in the near future. Perhaps Emmeline would not object to having Julia and Sophy? She is very fond of young people, I believe."

30

"I am sure she would enjoy having them," agreed the Q.C. "At least I will speak to her about it and see what can be done, but I think I can promise that we will take them both with pleasure."

"That leaves Harold, John and the twins," said Sir Thomas. "Have you room for the two elder boys in the deanery, Julius?"

The dean sighed and shook his head. "Much as I would like to take them in," he said, "I have to consider my family first. Even if the fees for Eton were to be paid out of the estate—as one supposes they would be—I have to think of the holidays, when Rupert will be down from Oxford with his young friends, and the girls home from their finishing school in Paris. The deanery is not as large as your place, Thomas, and sometimes Agatha's housekeeper is at her wits' end to know where to put all our guests."

"Supposing I take the boys?" suggested Horace boldly. "They are fine, strong lads, and I should be glad of their help on my farm during the school holidays. They can help keep down the pests, like shooting the rabbits that swarm everywhere."

His suggestion was ignored by all except Edmund Bromley, who gave Mr. Deakin a nod, and the lawyer wrote down Mr. Dutton's name on a sheet of paper in front of him under the rest.

"I daresay," continued Sir Thomas, "Prudence could be persuaded to take the twins—what are their names? Ah yes, Paul and Paula. They are ten years old I believe and appear to be well-behaved children. Their governess would of course accompany them. It would do Prudence good—give her something to think about besides missions and good works." And he smiled at the frosty look the dean gave him, feeling he deserved a dig after his unhelpful attitude over the two elder boys.

Then for the first time Septimus spoke.

"And what about me?" he said mildly, his short-sighted gray eyes studying them all from behind his gold-rimmed spectacles. "Which child are you allotting to me, Thomas?"

Chapter Four

All eyes were turned on Helen's brother, his prematurely white hair, gray side-whiskers and lined face making him look nearer seventy than fifty.

"*You*, my dear Septimus? I cannot imagine your housekeeper welcoming one small orphan in that great barn of a rectory. Why the child would be like a ghost creeping about in those big bare rooms."

Septimus's eyes met Sir Thomas's smilingly, and went on to his neatly trimmed beard and the heavy gold watch-chain draped across his generous stomach, and wondered what corner of his hundred rooms waited for Helen and little Octavius, and if he really believed that Lady Bretton was a woman who would be content to be pushed away out of sight in the top rooms of the north wing, as if she were a piece of lumber. His eyes traveled on to the frowning dean and the watchful face of the Q.C. as he said in his gentle way, "I was thinking of taking seven children into my rectory—with their Mamma, of course."

"Seven! And Helen!" Sir Thomas gasped and the dean put in quickly, "You are joking, of course, Septimus?"

"I have never been more serious in my life. So soon after Roger's death, with Dinah going to Malta next month, I do not think we can have the heart to split up the family among uncles and aunts, some of whom they scarcely know." A firmness crept into his voice, giving it an unfamiliar authority. "My old barn of a rectory was built for a family, and it is I who tread its rooms like a ghost. It needs voices echoing in its rooms and young feet racing up and down its old staircase, and my cook should use her talents to prepare meals for a family, instead of for one man who does not greatly care if he has only bread and cheese for supper. While as for Mrs. Jennings, severe as she may appear outwardly, she has a very soft spot in her heart for children, and I am afraid the still-room will never be safe from them."

There was silence for a moment in the room and then Edmund Bromley said: "Do you mean this, Septimus?"

"I do indeed." Septimus looked round the library table and the grave faces of the men seated there and said clearly and convincingly, "I will take them all. They are my sister's children and their Mamma shall act as my hostess while the boys can continue at Eton undisturbed. There will be no need for the fees to be found out of the estate: I will make myself responsible for their expenses including their clothes and pocket money, as I will for the rest of the family. Please do not think me ungrateful for your offers, Sir Thomas, and yours, Edmund, and yours, Horace. But Helen is a Crichton and her family are half Crichton, and I shall welcome them in my home. If Mr. Samuel Wright will permit them to remain here, and can find a good tenant to take the Place on April 1st, it should not take long to have everything the children and my sister wish to take with them to Saltbech packed and ready for the move by the last week in March."

"Then except for expressing our thanks to Septimus," said the Q.C., "there appears to be nothing more to be done except for Mr. Deakin to read the will, which, although on the face of it may appear to be a worthless document, nevertheless is a legal one, and its contents should be known."

Mr. Deakin cleared his throat and read the will, which had been made the year before soon after Dinah had become engaged to Major Morrell. The executors were named as his four brothers-in-law, and Edmund Bromley had been made guardian to Harold in case his father died before he came of age. Then came the bequests headed by an annuity of £4000 a year to his widow, and others of one thousand a year apiece to his sons and daughters, with the exception of his eldest daughter, who would already have had twenty thousand as her marriage settlement.

Here, before going on to other smaller bequests, Mr. Deakin paused as this was something he had not discussed with Mr. Bromley.

"Am I to understand, Mr. Crichton," he asked, speaking directly to Septimus, "that Miss Bretton's marriage plans are unaltered?"

"My sister will not hear of any change, and Miss Bretton sails for Malta in the middle of March as planned."

"I see." The lawyer hesitated and then, after a quick glance

33

at Mr. Bromley who once more nodded to him to go ahead, he said, "In that case I am afraid that Miss Bretton's marriage settlement cannot be paid. I do not know if any of you gentlemen have any suggestions to make on that score?"

An uncompromising silence answered him and then the Q.C. said briskly, "If it were cut to two thousand I would guarantee to find one, if you, Thomas, will find the other."

Rather grudgingly Sir Thomas agreed, indeed he could do little else with Septimus, having accepted the burden of Sir Roger's entire family, sitting opposite him, and so it was arranged.

Smaller bequests to old servants, it was decided, would be the first to be considered, and the first to be paid, and Mr. Deakin agreed to write to Major Morrell that night telling him why the whole of the settlement would not be forthcoming, with the promise that if further funds were forthcoming in the future the difference would be made good.

Edmund Bromley then said he would arrange a meeting with Mr. Samuel Wright and the tenants he had in mind for the Place, and it was decided that Septimus should break the news to the family of their removal to Saltbech after their aunts and uncles had gone.

The gentlemen joined the ladies in the north drawing room for tea, which was presided over by Dinah, as her mother had not felt well enough to come downstairs again. Her great-aunt was sitting there however, eating plum cake with relish and drinking a number of cups of tea.

The guests enjoyed the tea, which was as lavish as usual, the gentlemen with the exception of Edmund feeling that everything had been settled in a way far exceeding anything that might have been expected. Indeed, when they drove back to the station later on to catch the London train they almost felt that it had been Septimus's duty, as Lady Bretton's brother, to offer her and her children a home, and when they told their wives about it they agreed, with the exception again of Emmeline, who told her husband wistfully that she would have enjoyed having little Julia with her that summer to give the child a coming-out ball and all the parties she would be missing in Saltbech.

After they had gone and the servants had removed the tea tray, followed by Mrs. Crichton and her companion, Septimus told Roger's children what had been planned for them, explaining as simply as he could the Bretton finances that had made the move from the Place essential. They listened to

34

him quietly, in somewhat stunned silence, and he left them to mull it over among themselves while he went upstairs to face the far more difficult task of telling his sister.

He found his Aunt Alice there, and as she showed no sign of moving, he had to tell Helen of his plans for her in front of the old lady, who said nothing, looking in her black dress with her plainly parted gray hair surmounted by a strangely shaped white cap trimmed with purple, more than ever like an idol waiting for a sacrifice.

Helen, however, had plenty to say.

"It is very good of you, Septimus," she said, holding some smelling salts to her nose, "but I could not dream of accepting your hospitality. It is quite out of the question."

The Idol then spoke. "Why is it out of the question?" she asked. "Your brother has offered you and your family a home for the next six years, Helen. I would not have thought that you could have dismissed such a generous offer quite so ungraciously."

"I am not being ungracious, and of course it is very kind of Septimus," Helen said impatiently. "I never said it was not. But neither he nor that man Deakin, nor indeed Edmund, understand Mr. Samuel Wright as I do. He is a very kind man, and he would not dream of turning me out of Bretton. The thing is laughable. Of course he will allow me to live here as long as I like—until Harold comes of age, in fact. There can be no question about that."

"But Septimus has just explained to you that there is a very large debt owing to Mr. Wright's bank," said Mrs. Crichton sharply. "How do you propose to pay it off if you go on living here and spending as you have done every since you married Roger?"

"Roger always liked me to have everything I wanted, and in any case everybody has debts. There is nothing unusual in that." Helen dismissed the issue as being of no importance. "I daresay Dinah's trousseau will not be paid for in years, but I shall not have sleepless nights over it. Tradesmen have always been glad to have the Bretton custom, and they always will be."

"They might have held to that attitude while Roger was alive," said her aunt ominously. "But not now. I am afraid this is an occasion when you must make up your mind to cut your coat according to your cloth, Helen. Septimus has offered you a way out of your troubles, and if you are wise you will take it."

"And what will happen if I don't choose to take it?" demanded Helen angrily.

"Helen," said Septimus gravely, "I dislike saying this beyond anything—but the Bretton estates might have to face the prospect of bankruptcy."

"So," said his aunt triumphantly. "It is as bad as that, is it?"

"I am afraid it is, Aunt Alice."

"But"—Helen looked horrified. "I could not possibly live for the next six years in *Saltbech!* And besides, Lovell does not get on with Mrs. Jennings."

"Then dismiss Lovell," said her aunt unfeelingly. "There will be a housemaid at the rectory who will be able to do your hair for you." And then as Septimus left the room she added more kindly, "Come, Helen, my dear, I know this has been a great shock to you, though it has not been at all surprising to me. There could be only one end to Roger's incurable love for speculation. But for the sake of the children you must make up your mind to settle down for a time at Saltbech with your brother. There is nothing more to be done."

"I could *never* settle down in Saltbech," said Helen rebelliously. "It is a perfectly horrid little town, with no Society, just full of people busy doing nothing. I shall hate it, and so will Lovell. And I shall never dismiss Lovell. She has been with me for years, and I would not dream of letting a rough little country housemaid lay a finger on my hair." She began to cry. "Everybody is being very unkind to me. To lose my husband, and then, on top of that, to be turned out of my house as if I were a beggar. It is very cruel, and whatever Septimus may say about it I am sure it is not in the least necessary."

"You will think differently perhaps in the morning, my dear," said The Honorable Alice, and went downstairs to join her nephew and the Bretton children in the library.

Prudence Bretton had decided to stay on for another night, which pleased Dinah and her sisters very much. They were all very fond of their Aunt Prue: having no ties of husband or children she had visited Bretton far more often than her sisters, and what was better still, Great-aunt A. liked her.

When Prue was eighteen she had been adopted by a cousin of her mother's who had been sorry for the girl and set out to give her trips abroad and parties and balls when they were in London. Prue had been the plain one of the family, she had been gauche and shy with men, and in spite of her cousin's efforts to get her married somehow, little Prue had been far happier living alone with the old lady. So she remained her devoted and much loved companion until she died, when it was discovered that Prue had been left the large house that had been more of a home to her than Bretton, with its pleasant gardens and the old servants to keep it as it had always been kept, together with an income that was far larger than the Brettons had ever expected.

Fortunately the capital had been left in trust, so that it was free from predators: Prue was such an obliging and trusting little soul that if it had been left in her hands she would have followed Roger's advice over investments and been ruined in five years.

But she was a romantic at heart and she was extremely interested in Dinah's trousseau, and when she heard that the wedding dress was complete and at that moment hanging in the wardrobe in the dressing room that had been set aside for Dinah's wedding clothes, she asked if she might have "just one peep" at it before she went to bed.

"I know it is supposed to be bad luck for anyone to see a wedding dress before the wedding day," she said, "but you will be so far away from us all, Dinah my love, and if I can just see it, I shall be able to think of you wearing it on the all important day."

The Honorable Alice who was playing cribbage with Harold, here looked up to observe drily that she was sure Dinah had shown the dress to several people already, and when Dinah agreed that she had, added, "So that showing it to your Aunt Prudence today will not make the slightest difference. Any bad luck there may have been will have been incurred long ago."

It was perhaps the strain of the day that made the words fall so heavily on Dinah's heart. Bad luck was a horrid expression, and one that seemed bound up especially with preparations for a wedding. The bride must wear something old and something new, something gold and something blue, and she must kiss a chimney sweep for luck immediately after the ceremony. She wondered if there were any chimney sweeps in Malta. She did not like to think of kissing a chimney sweep's black face as she came out of the church on her bridegroom's arm.

Her thoughts went to her handsome Clive, and some of the sadness lifted from her young face and the sparkle came back to her eyes. Long before the end of next month she would be there with him in Malta, and life would be heaven thereafter.

In the trunks upstairs were gossamer dresses in pink and white and sprigged with blue, ball-dresses in pale-colored silks, and tailor-mades in gray and white flannel. She was glad that her mother wanted her to leave her black clothes behind, and even Prue admitted that mourning did not suit her. Black took what little color there was from her face, only the pink of her firmly folded lips giving a touch of it there. She had a firm face, thought her Aunt Prue, and a very beautiful one, and presently her lovely color would return with her happiness.

So when they retired to bed her aunt was taken into the dressing room and the wedding dress was taken out to be admired, Prue agreeing that silk was a cooler material than satin would have been in a warm climate. The white satin shoes were also admired, and the filmy veil with its tiny spray of orange blossom to fit over it at the back of Dinah's fringe, and as they left the room Prudence remarked that it must be a relief to her to know that Julia was now old enough to take her place in the family she was leaving behind. Julia and Sophy had been very helpful that day, looking after elderly Bretton cousins and talking to their aunts and uncles. She had noticed that kindly, good-natured Emmeline Bromley had been particularly struck with pretty Julia.

But Dinah was scarcely able to give her family a thought as she hung the wedding dress up again, giving a final caressing touch to its silk skirt and train as she did so. "Julia will be eighteen in April," she told her aunt lightly. "It will do her good to grow up now and behave less like a hoyden. She is out of the schoolroom now—though I suppose there will be no Coming-out ball for her, poor love."

After Prue had gone Dinah shut the dressing room door and went on into her bedroom, to admire the photograph of her beloved Clive in uniform. It stood in a silver frame on her dressing table facing towards the bed, so that it was to be the last thing she saw before she blew out her candle at night, and the first thing to greet her eyes in the morning, when the housemaid who brought her early morning tea tray drew back the curtains on a day nearer her wedding.

The photograph showed him to be a handsome young man, although last year he had been rather heavier than when the photograph had been taken. But he had had his important-looking fair moustache, and although his expression was unsmiling it was scarcely surprising, as having one's photograph taken was such a very uncomfortable business.

She wished he had been there that day: it would not have been quite so sad if he had been there.

Her maid came to help her undress and to brush out her hair: it was naturally curly and did not need the severe curling pins that were necessary for so many ladies to keep up with the fashion. And as the girl took up her black dress to hang it up in a wardrobe something fell out of the pocket and rolled across the floor.

"A half sovereign, miss," said the girl, putting it on the dressing table.

But it was not a coin, though it was the size of a half sovereign and of gold. It was a tiny gold medallion, with the figure of St. Christopher on it, and a small ring with which she could hang it on her bracelet. Her uncle had slipped it into her hand that night before she said good night to him.

"Before I forget," he said smiling, "Bellingham sent you a tiny gift to wear on your journey and to bring you safely to its end." And this was what she found wrapped in a scrap of tissue paper, with not a word enclosed with it.

It had amused her at the time, but now she held it to the light of the candles on her dressing table, and as the maid left her she sat there for a moment or two remembering the broad-shouldered man with the thoughtful eyes that had rested on her with such an interest that it had annoyed her a little. But at the same time he had given the impression of immense strength and reliability in a crisis: perhaps, she thought, that was why her uncle liked him so much. She dropped the medallion into her jewel-case and thought no more about him.

The following morning, when Septimus visited his sister he was relieved to find that she had changed her mind about her stay in Saltbech. She apologized for having seemed so ungrateful the previous evening, blamed it on the shock of hearing what he had to tell her, and thanked him for offering to have her and her family to live with him.

Her Aunt Alice, when she heard of this altered attitude wondered what Helen was up to, and gave it as her opinion that Lovell had something to do with it, in which she was correct.

Lovell had listened to what had been proposed for her mistress and her family without comment the night before when she was getting her ready for bed, but when Helen had started again on her grievances and the tragedy of leaving the Place while she sat up in bed having her breakfast on the following morning, Lovell agreed that she did not like Saltbech herself.

"Of course the rectory rooms are very bare, m'lady," she continued. "I daresay the rector would not object if we take your ladyship's piano and the best furniture from some of our rooms here. And once we are there and Bretton is let, I daresay some of your ladyship's friends will invite us to stay for the summer."

Helen thought this over while she was bathing in her dressing room next door. If the children were established at the rectory there was after all no need for her to stay there as well. Miss Stroud would be able to go on teaching Paul and Paula in the schoolroom there, there were the nurseries for Octavius and Nurse Blackwell, and no doubt there were music teachers and drawing masters who could be brought out from Easterley to teach Julia and Sophy.

Her thoughts went on to those among her friends who might take pity on her: Vi Crowborne for instance, who was one of her oldest friends. She might invite her to Crowborne Abbey for the summer.

While Lovell was brushing her hair later she said she thought she must try and answer a few of the letters of condolence she had received herself. Up to that moment she had intended leaving it entirely to her daughters, but now she went on, "Lady Crowborne, for one. She wrote me such a charming letter of sympathy. I feel I should reply to that myself."

Lovell continued to brush her hair for a few minutes in silence and then she said how fortunate it was that her mistress looked so elegant in black. "There is nothing like golden hair with mourning," she said. "It sets it off as nothing else can," and then she continued, "Lady Crowborne is one who cannot wear it at all. It makes her ladyship look ten years older. I heard from Warren, her ladyship's maid at Christmas, and she told me that Mr. Wakefield was visiting the Abbey for the festive season."

Helen moved impatiently under her hands. "I think I told you, Lovell," she said coldly, "that I never wish to hear that gentleman's name mentioned."

"Yes, m'lady. I beg your pardon, m'lady." Lovell went into the dressing room and returned with a selection of dresses which she laid out on the bed for Helen's selection, and as she looked at them Helen said:

"I wonder what happened to that tiresome wife of the colonel's?"

"I was told she returned to her mother's family residence in Perthshire, m'lady. Mr. Wakefield lives at his London club when he is not in Paris. Warren said she heard he had a beautiful apartment in Paris. Being so wealthy a gentleman, of course he can live where he likes."

"Servants' gossip." But though her tone was contemptuous Helen's wide blue eyes were thoughtful. "I hope you have found me something better to wear today. I hated that old thing you put out for me yesterday. It looked horrid."

And then when she was dressed Septimus had come to see her and was delighted to find that she had changed her mind about coming to Saltbech.

"Roger used to say that women had no notion of business matters and had far better leave them to men," she told him, touching her eyes with a morsel of lace handkerchief. "And if you and my brothers-in-law all think that by letting Bretton I shall be better off, I must give in to your superior understanding. I have never understood anything about money matters, and I do not wish to learn about them now. I am sure that in your hands, dear Septimus, what little means I have left will be perfectly safe."

Chapter Five

The girls and their two elder brothers had had their breakfast early with the twins and Miss Stroud, and they had retired to the schoolroom to discuss what they intended to take with them to the rectory. They spoke of the move with a mixture of excitement and sadness—excitement because going to live with Uncle Sep was an entirely new experience, and sadness because the thought of leaving Bretton Place for six years seemed to stretch in front of them like eternity.

"Paul and I will be sixteen by the time we come home," Paula said, tears in her eyes.

"We shall have to take our rabbits with us," said Paul, infinitely more practical. "And our ponies, and the dogs." There were two ponies of their own in the stables, and at least four sporting dogs in the outside kennels, besides Digger, a terrier and their special pet.

"There will be stables and kennels at the rectory," Sophy told them. "We are not going to a *hovel*, Paul."

But Paul remained extremely doubtful. There might not be room for four gundogs he argued, and Mrs. Jennings might object to having Digger in her rooms.

"They are not her rooms," pointed out Harold. "They are Uncle Sep's."

In the small drawing room Helen, clad in a black dress that had more style to it then yesterday's, found Septimus, Dinah, Prue and Aunt Alice. The latter, her gray hair parted as usual in the middle and strained back into a meager bun at the back, was wearing a lace cap this morning, ornamented with a bow of black velvet ribbon. Miss Pettit, more like a shadow than ever, in a gray dress with a gunmetal watch pinned to her attenuated bosom, was busy knitting some garment for her employer in gray and purple Berlin wool.

Helen was greeted kindly by her brother and abruptly by her aunt, while Dinah drew up a chair for her near the fire and sat down on a stool beside it. Prue arranged a screen so that she should not feel a draught from the door, and Miss Pettit provided a hand-screen in case the fire should scorch her face, and Helen felt like a contented cat.

She said in a low voice to her brother that she was afraid she would have to take a great many things with her to the rectory, "As we are to be with you so long, Sep dear."

"All you have to do is to make a list—or perhaps one of the girls will do it for you—and I will return just before Dinah leaves for Malta to go through it and see if I have room for everything. I am sure I shall, because as you know the rectory is large and very bare of furniture. There will certainly be plenty of space in the drawing room for your piano."

"Dear Sep," she said holding the scrap of lace once more to her eyes, "What should I have done without you? I cannot see any of the Brettons lifting a finger to help us. Although I still cannot understand why I could not have moved into the dower house, which is empty, and only needs a little doing up where the rain has come in through the roof. But I will not say anything about that, as no doubt you all decided it between you yesterday afternoon after my darling Roger was laid to rest."

The reproach of an ill-treated widow, alone in the world, was expressed in the words and in the tone in which they were uttered, and Dinah gave her uncle a look of apology which he countered with a smile. He understood his sister very well.

Septimus, Harold, Johnny and Prue were to leave after luncheon, and Helen said she would have hers in her boudoir if they would excuse her, as she felt very weak from the strain of the past few days. She had been dismayed to find that Aunt Alice intended to remain with them indefinitely.

Before she left Prue hurried upstairs to say good-bye and to say how glad she was that everything had been settled so well.

"It is very good of Septimus," she said, looking round the pretty room with its pink carpet, its flowered chintz curtains and chair covers and the big windows looking over the park. She added hesitantly then, "I suppose you never hear any news of—that poor creature?"

"Never." Helen was so decided that Prue felt she had been guilty of an indiscretion and stood abashed. "It is entirely Sep's private business and much too delicate for even me—his own sister—to enquire about. He never mentions it and neither do I."

"Very wise," agreed Prue hastily. "Poor Septimus. He has had a sad life—his wife dying so young, I mean."

"Yes, Sep has certainly experienced more tragedy in his life than many of the *Brettons*, though that would not occur to any of them. But I never speak of anything that could remind him of the past. My nature is far too considerate."

"Dear Helen. You always know exactly what to do." Prue bent to kiss her affectionately and then hurried on somewhat incoherently, "But if—that is, if you need help at the rectory—not that you will, because Mrs. Jennings is so very good—but if anything should happen—not that it will, of course—I will come at once, or you must all come to me. I only wanted to say that, Helen dear, and if Septimus had not offered you a home with him mine would have been open to you." She blew her nose, smiled damply, and went off down the magnificent staircase and through the hall, leaving the enormous fire burning there with regret as she climbed into the waiting carriage.

Left to herself, Helen smiled and began to think of the things that she would have sent to Saltbech.

On the following Sunday Mr. Samuel Wright's prospective tenant for the Place came down with his wife to look at it. They declared at once that it was just what they wanted. Mr. Spender was attached to the American embassy in London and worked there during the week: they had, his wife said, an apartment in Albemarle Street, but they needed a country house where they could entertain their friends from Friday to Tuesday.

"And oh my, oh my!" Mrs. Spender said, "If this isn't just the most perfect place." She declared the long gallery to be "cute" and asked if the portraits in the picture gallery were genuine. When assured that they were she could scarcely believe it, and said she would certainly enjoy seeing her friends' faces when they were shown Van Dycks and Rembrandts and real Gainsboroughs hanging on her walls.

Mr. Spender signed the six-year lease without question, and having been assured that the servants would all remain, and that the head gardener, Fergus, would have the gardens in perfect order by the time they took possession, they departed for London, almost as much impressed by the fact that they could order London trains to be stopped for them at Bretton Station as that they were to be the tenants of one of the finest country houses in such near proximity to London.

Presents for Dinah now began to pour in, to be added to the packing-cases stored for her in one of the coach-houses. Time passed on wings, softening the shock of their father's death, while The Honorable Alice attempted to put some measure of restraint on the furniture that Helen planned to have moved to Saltbech.

"As your tenants have seen the north drawing room with its present carpet—an Aubusson—it will not do to take it up and send it to Saltbech, where it will be much too large, and have a shabby Turkey carpet from some lumber room put down in its place."

"But there is no carpet in the rectory drawing room," protested Helen. "Only a shabby rug in front of the fireplace."

"That shabby rug, as you call it," said Aunt Alice bridling, "was a very good Persian rug that I gave your brother for a wedding present. If you want to have a carpet in there, you had better take the Brussels carpet from the large breakfast room. It will be a much better fit."

"I do not like Brussels carpets," said Helen. "They are not fashionable any longer."

"You will not find the rectory very fashionable, either," said her aunt. "So that it will not matter very much, will it?"

Helen was thankful when her aunt's prolonged visit neared its end.

On the day before she was to leave, however, something happened that was to upset many of their plans.

The second week in March was mild and warm and Dinah and Julia planned a walk in the Bretton woods to see if the windflowers were out. They were always the first to appear, a sheet of silvery white under the catkins on the willows. Just as they were about to start out, however, the afternoon post came with a letter for Dinah.

"From Malta," said Julia laughing. "I will go and gather the windflowers alone. You must stay here and read your precious letter."

"No," said Dinah, her cheeks pink however and her eyes shining. "Don't go without me, Julie. See if Sophy is still at her music lesson. If she has finished tell her to come with us. It may be the last time we will be there together. I'll read my letter while you are gone."

Julia ran off to the music room on the far side of the building where an old gentleman came out from London every Thursday to give the girls piano lessons, and Dinah sat down alone in the small drawing room to read her letter.

She was still sitting there with the letter crumpled in her hands when Julia came back to say that Sophy had just finished and was getting ready to come with them. Her sister did not answer: she was staring in front of her, the color gone from her face leaving it chalk white, and Julia ran to her and knelt beside her.

"Di! My darling Di! What has happened? Is Clive dangerously ill?"

Dinah shook her head, and dropping the letter hid her face in her hands, giving way to a shuddering sob.

Now seriously alarmed, Julia said she would fetch somebody, but a shake of the bowed head prevented her. "No, please, Julie, don't go for anyone. Just stay here for a few moments." Dinah did not take the letter from her sister as she picked it up from the floor. "Read it," she said. "Tell me what you think he wants me to do."

Julia unfolded the letter, smoothing out the creases, and read it, sitting back on her heels.

"My dear Dinah," wrote Clive Morrell, *"I need not say how shocked I have been to hear of Sir Roger Bretton's death from you and from my uncle, who tells me, as no doubt you yourself know by this time, that there is some doubt as to whether that death was an accident or might have been self-inflicted. My uncle also tells me that in making inquiries of your lawyer, Mr. Deakin, on my behalf, he finds that before your father died he all but ruined his family and bankrupted his estate, and under these distressing circumstances he thinks it might be wise to postpone our wedding plans for a time, if we do not wish to cancel them altogether. It would scarcely be the act of a gentleman to break off an engagement—such decisions are always the lady's prerogative, I believe—and I would never lay myself open to such a charge, but of course we shall have to think it over carefully, with regard to my future. My uncle as you know, has for some time allowed me a private income of one thousand a year, a sum that he generously promised to increase to two thousand when I married. But the marriage settlement promised by your father was not an ungenerous one and he naturally wished to meet it in like terms. My uncle now tells me that only a fraction of the promised settlement can be yours, by the generosity of two of your uncles. If we act against my uncle's expressed wish, I am afraid he may not only cut off my present income but no longer regard me as his heir. His title, of course, dies with him, and he is free to appoint whom he likes to inherit his fortune and estates. I have always been his favorite in this respect, and I feel that when you have considered all these things with your usual common sense your conscience will dictate to you how you should act. With, as ever, my warmest regard, C. Morrell."*

Julia read the letter through twice before she could take in its meaning and then she jumped to her feet.

"Oh the beast!" she cried. "The brute! You see of course what he is after. *He* will act the gentleman—never shall it be said that he broke off his engagement to a girl because her father has lost his money. *You* are to do that. You are to be the jilt so that he can pose as the ill-treated partner among his friends, and *you* will have the shame of it all. I never liked him, and now I hate him!" She paused in her furious striding about the room. "What are you going to do?"

"I have little alternative, have I?" said Dinah quietly. "I

shall write to him at once breaking it off. There is nothing else I can do."

"You could refuse," said Julia. "If such a man is worth keeping. You could hold him to his promise—"

"And ruin his future? His uncle has the reputation of being a mean old man, although the only time I met him he was very kind and welcomed me as if he meant it. But there is no knowing what he will be like if we go on with this wedding against his wishes."

"If Clive really loved you he would tell the old man that he could keep his horrid money!" cried Julia.

"Oh, Julie, you are too romantic I'm afraid!" There were tears in her eyes but she winked them back, and as Sophy came into the room ready to join them in their hunt for the windflowers, she got up and put the letter away in her pocket, warning Julia by a frown to say nothing.

There was at least a degree of comfort to be found in the flowers that had always been the first under the willows in the Bretton woods. These were out today, dancing in the breeze on their slender stalks, but it was hard for Dinah to appreciate them as she walked among them with her sisters. Sophy made up for her silence by her chatter about the old gentleman who had given her her piano lesson, and as she dropped behind to gather some of the flowers and a branch or two of pussy willow for the schoolroom Julia whispered fiercely: "What will happen to your trousseau? To your wedding dress?"

"I haven't thought about it yet." Dinah gave a faint smile. "I suppose I shall have to do something in time. But the notice has got to be sent to the *Morning Post* first, and the wedding presents have got to be sent back." Her voice shook a little. "I shall be kept very busy for the next week or two." She left the two girls to continue their walk saying she had some letters to write, and hurried back to the house. She went up to her room to write them, sitting at the little desk where she had written so many love letters to Clive. Her letter to him was short enough. *"Dear Major Morrell,"* it ran. *"I quite understand that you wish to put an end to our wedding plans, and do so with this letter. D. Bretton."*

The second was to Mrs. Duncan informing her that owing to unforseen circumstances the wedding was not going to take place, and that she must travel to Malta without her. She added her thanks for her and the colonel's kindness and offers of hospitality in Malta and signed herself, "Yours affectionately, Dinah."

Then she wrote out a short notice to be printed in the *Morning Post* stating that the marriage arranged between Major Clive Morrell and Miss Dinah Bretton would not now take place, addressed and sealed all three letters, and putting on her jacket and hat once more went downstairs to walk to the Bretton post office and post them herself.

As she passed the door of the small drawing room her mother called her into the room, where her Great-aunt Alice was seated with Miss Pettit.

"More presents have arrived, Dinah," said Lady Bretton gaily. "A case of china from your Uncle and Aunt Carey—"

"Then I am afraid it must go back." Dinah entered the room and stood there, facing her mother and Mrs. Crichton, the three letters in her hand.

"What do you mean?" The smile went from Helen's face. "Why are you looking so white, Dinah? What has happened?"

"I have heard from Major Morrell," Dinah said steadily, "and because of what he said in his letter I have written to tell him that our wedding plans are cancelled." She took his letter from her jacket pocket and held it out to Helen. "If you will read this letter that I received from him just now, I think you will see that I had no alternative."

Her mother took the letter from her and read it, and then she laughed. "But this is ridiculous!" she cried. "My advice to you, my dear child, is to burn it and say you never received it. You must go out to Malta with Mrs. Duncan as arranged, and he will not dare to make you break it off then. Why, the whole regiment would know about it."

"May I see the letter, Dinah?" asked her great-aunt.

"Of course, and then you may burn it if you wish." Helen handed it on to her and she read it carefully with the aid of the lorgnettes that she always carried in the chatelaine that hung from her substantial waist.

"I see," she said at last. "The young man wishes to break off your engagement, but he knows at the same time that as no gentleman does such a thing, the jilting must come from you, Dinah. It does not occur to him apparently that *you* could incur some very unkind gossip by breaking it off at such short notice. He is a strangely heartless and selfish young man, and in my opinion you are well rid of him, my dear."

"I still say the whole thing is ridiculous," said Lady Bretton angrily. "There's all her trousseau, Aunt. What are we going to do with that, let alone her wedding dress?"

"I shall keep my wedding dress for Julia," said Dinah quietly. "And the rest of my dresses can be altered to fit her and Sophy. The boxes of linen can be sent with the other things to Saltbech, where I am sure Mrs. Jennings will find them a welcome addition to her linen room, because I am afraid Uncle Sep will now have one more in his family at the rectory."

Her voice broke, and she hurried out of the room and walked out of the house and across the empty park to the village, to post her letters.

"Put that letter on the fire, Aunt," said Helen. "I am quite sure there is some mistake. I shall write to Major Morrell myself and tell him so."

"I should not do that, my dear. And I will keep this letter if you do not mind." She tucked it away in the pocket in her underskirt. "It may come in handy as evidence sometime in the future."

"Evidence? What do you mean, Aunt?"

"Evidence that the man she was in love with was not worth a moment's thought," said The Honorable Alice sternly. "*Was* she in love with him, Helen?"

"I suppose so. But you know what girls are, always thinking themselves to be in love with somebody. She got engaged to him just at that time when poor Roger had made a lot of money out of one of his investments—in America, I think it was—but Clive's old uncle did not wish him to marry until he attained his majority, and in any case he thought Dinah was too young. I wish we had insisted that the wedding should take place here at Bretton last summer before he went out to Malta. He got his majority very soon afterwards."

"His love for her does not seem to have lasted very long," said The Honorable Alice. "There is not a word of affection or even of regret in his letter."

"Love?" said Helen and again she laughed. "My dear Aunt Alice, when I was eighteen I was madly in love with one of Sep's Oxford friends, a nice young man, and very good looking, but with no future beyond that of a clergyman in front of him. And then Roger came along, and my Mamma advised me to give up Sep's friend and marry the owner of Bretton Park. A baronet, you know, and this great Place of his. It was quite irresistible."

"So you sent the young man away?" Her aunt seemed a little puzzled and Helen flashed out:

"You are so behind the times, Aunt Alice. Love does not come into many marriages these days, any more than it did when I married Roger. One marries for position and wealth. We live in a very practical world."

"You seem to, my dear." Her aunt said no more until some little while later when Dinah returned from her walk to the village, when she heaved herself out of the chair by the fire in the drawing room and went upstairs to her great-niece's sitting room.

She found her there looking very white and exhausted, staring out at the parkland where the dusk was beginning to gather.

"So you have burned your boats?" she said with surprising gentleness, as she sat down in a chair by the fire.

"Yes." Dinah flung off her little fur hat and jacket, and turned away from the window. She was glad that they were leaving so soon: packing up would take all their energies and all their time and there would be none left over in which to think.

"He is not worth a tear," said her great-aunt. "A man who could write a letter like that—"

"I shall never marry now," said Dinah. "I shall never trust a man again—" And then suddenly she turned her head and saw her aunt hold out her arms to her, and she went to her and knelt beside her and felt herself enfolded in a warm, soundless sympathy and love that her mother had never been ready to give.

In the servants' hall at Bretton a great deal of indignation had been expressed about Major Morrell, as its inmates learned, in the way such things get around in a big household, that it was the gentleman who had made it impossible for Miss Dinah to do anything else but end their engagement.

"If I was her," said Mrs. Foxley, a large lady with a surprisingly light hand for pastry, one of the two cooks who worked under the chef, M. Durand, "I'd sue 'im for breach. That's what I'd do."

"Oh no, Mrs. Foxley." Merrington on his way to the pantry to fetch a bottle of claret for the steward's room, stopped short, shocked. "A lady like Miss Dinah could never do that."

"I don't see why not. Look at all the trooso she's 'ad made. The expense of it. 'E ought to be made to pay for it. In a court of law she could git big damages out of 'im, I shouldn't wonder."

"She's burned all 'is letters," said the housemaid who looked after Dinah's rooms. "They was all done up in blue ribbon—a big bundle of 'em—in that little desk in her sitting room. And she burned 'is photygraph too, in the fireplace."

"That was a silly thing to do," said Mrs. Foxley. "H'evidence, that's what she's destroyed. They must 'ave been worth a lot of money, them letters."

"Not to Miss Dinah, they wouldn't," said Merrington firmly, and went on to fetch the claret, helping himself to a glass of the late Sir Roger's best port on the way to restore his shaken nerves.

The Americans were to arrive in less than a fortnight; and the day after they moved in they were proposing to entertain a party of twenty or more. He wondered if they would appreciate the excellence of Sir Roger's old port.

There was one thing in which he was mistaken, however. One letter remained to be used in months to come as evidence against the major, and that was folded up in the pocket of The Honorable Alice's underskirt.

Chapter Six

The Honorable Alice departed with Miss Pettit and Hannah, and a little while later Septimus arrived to examine the list of belongings that the family wanted to take to Saltbech, and to stay with them for a few days before the pantechnicon arrived for the move.

He did not mention the cancelled wedding to Dinah, except to say that first evening as she kissed him good night, "So I am to have another in my family at Saltbech am I, my love?"

"I'm afraid so, Uncle Sep."

"But as it is to be you, I need not say that you will be as welcome as the flowers in May."

She put a small leather case into his hand. "This is the brooch you gave me, Uncle Sep. I feel that you must take it back."

"Oh no, my dear. It was a gift to my god-daughter and it will remain so. We have a saying in East Anglia, you know: 'Give a gift and take agin, Never goo to God agin.'"

He took the brooch from its case and pinned it into the white collar of her black dress. "There, that's better. That's more like my Dinah." He returned her kiss tenderly, and as he let her go he added, "Tomorrow I shall need your help in the library. There are some volumes there that I think should go to Saltbech. You have the *Encyclopedia Brittanica* and the *National Biography*, neither of which I possess, and which the boys might find useful later on."

"As you please, Uncle Sep." Dinah was relieved that he still said nothing about her wedding and went upstairs to her room.

There she looked at the jade brooch pinned into her collar and decided that she would go on wearing it because it was given to her by her god-father. Then she took out of her jewel-case the small medallion of St. Christopher and thought of the man who had sent it to her and wondered wryly what she should say when she returned it. "It was very kind of you, Dr. Bellingham, but as you know, my wedding plans have been cancelled, and so I am returning your present." No, that would not do. That would give it too much importance. Then how would she put it? It was difficult to think of a phrase that did not sound patronizing or stiff. She put it back in her jewel-case and thought that maybe she would keep it, after all. His words had been that it was to keep her safe on her journey, but maybe she would need the saint to keep her safe on other journeys.

In the top tray of the jewel-case there was a gold bracelet with a bunch of tiny charms on it. She took it out, and on a sudden impulse added St. Christopher to them, and then with a queer sense of comfort she went to bed.

A few days later a lady arrived who had a great deal to say about the cancelled wedding, and it was fortunate that Helen was out paying a round of farewell calls, and Dinah and her sisters, with Miss Stroud's help, were selecting books and pictures from the schoolroom, from the twins' rooms and their own.

Mrs. Duncan was shown into the library by an alarmed

young Wilkins, and Septimus greeted his visitor with some surprise.

"Mr. Crichton?" said Mrs. Duncan, looking in her gray dress and hat and plaid cape like a small battleship moving in to the kill. "I have come for an explanation of Miss Bretton's extraordinary letter." She held out Dinah's letter for him to read, together with the engagement ring wrapped in a scrap of tissue paper. "Has she really broken off her engagement—at the eleventh hour—or is it just a lovers' tiff?"

"From what I hear of the matter, I am afraid she had no alternative."

He cleared a pile of books from a chair for her to sit down, and her wrath subsided a little, though her perplexity remained.

"I simply do not understand how it came about," she said, and then, "unless Miss Bretton had heard about Miss Maitland?"

"Miss Maitland?"

"Yes. Has Major Morrell mentioned her in any of his letters to her?"

"Not as far as I know, but I did not see his last letter to her myself, and I think it has been destroyed. I have heard about it from her sister Julia, and according to her the request to be released from the engagement—carefully wrapped up—came entirely from him. He left the decision to my niece, after telling her that if they continued with their wedding he would be disinherited by his uncle, Lord Morrell."

"May one ask what grounds he gave for saying such a thing?"

"That there was a doubt that my brother-in-law's death was an accident, and that in any case it had left his family practically bankrupt. It seems to me that no gentleman like the major would dare to break his engagement at the eleventh hour, but he practically forced my niece to do it for him."

"That is typical of the man!" She rose to her feet again energetically, her skirts catching a pile of books on a neighboring chair and sending them to the floor. She moved to the window, where she stood for a moment with her back to Septimus, tapping her foot in anger, and then when she had controlled herself sufficiently she turned back to him and said quietly:

"Lord Morrell may be a tightfisted old fellow, as my husband would say, but he is a gentleman and he would never go

53

back on his word. Even if he had disapproved of the wedding under the existing circumstances, he would have held to his promise to increase Clive's income on his marriage, and he would never have threatened to disinherit him. That is absurd. He had met your niece, and heartily approved of her."

She came back to the fire and stood there, holding out her hands to its cheerfully blazing logs, the fierceness in her blue eyes unabated.

"I have been uneasy about Clive Morrell ever since Mr. Stephen Maitland came to Malta for Christmas on his way home from South Africa, bringing his daughter with him."

"Mr. Stephen Maitland, did you say?"

"Yes. Do you know him?"

"I think I may have done years ago. The Stephen Maitland I knew did go out to South Africa."

"Well, he has come home a millionaire, and it soon got round that when his daughter Caroline—a very pretty girl—got married, he would settle half a million on her. You may imagine the effect such a report had on our young officers. They were round her like bees round a honey-pot, and the only one she seemed to favor—possibly because he was engaged to another girl and therefore unobtainable—was Major Morrell. I should imagine that ever since her arrival he has been wondering how he could release himself from his engagement to your niece, and her father's unfortunate accident gave him the opportunity he wanted. I expect he wrote to his uncle asking him to make enquiries about the financial state of the family, or maybe the Brettons' lawyer wrote to him telling him that he could no longer expect a large settlement with his bride, with the result that we know. I do not know Miss Bretton very well, but from what I have seen of her I imagine her to be a proud young lady?"

"It depends upon what you mean by pride," said Septimus. "But if a man told her plainly that he no longer wished to marry her, nothing would induce her to hold him to his promise. You have her ring."

"I have, and you may be sure, Mr. Crichton, that I shall select a very public moment in which to return it to the gentleman. But I think I can see very well what will happen. He will lose no time in demanding sympathy from his new friend, Miss Caroline Maitland, because he has been most cruelly jilted on the eve of his wedding. He is going to make much of that, and I should not be at all surprised if she does not console him sufficiently to become engaged to him before the summer has even begun. He has been talking of resigning his commission for some little while."

She put on her gloves, smoothing the fingers of each hand. "I have a cab waiting to take me back to the station, and I would like to go before I run the risk of meeting any more of your family. I felt that I had to have an explanation from somebody, and I am glad that I found you here alone. My sympathy is entirely with Miss Bretton, and I hope that she will meet another man more worthy of her."

"In time she may," he said, but not as if he thought it likely. He said good-bye to Mrs. Duncan, and she went out to her cab and was driven away.

Septimus debated in his mind as to whether he should tell his niece of the lady's visit and decided against it. Morrell was not a man he cared to talk about, or even to think about, and it was better to let the whole thing die a natural death.

Their next visitor was the harbinger of good news. Emmeline Bromley arrived the next day unheralded, to have luncheon with them all and to tell them the plan she had for Julia and Sophy.

"As we have no family and I am much alone," she said, "Edmund and I would like nothing better than to have your two girls, Julia and Sophy, to make their home with us for the next six years, if you have no objection, Helen. I will give Julia a Coming-out ball and parties and theaters and all sorts of lovely things, and Edmund says he will be very happy to pay for a finishing school in Paris for Sophy. Then next year she can have a Season in London. What do the girls think of the plan? Does it meet with your approval, my lambs?" And she smiled across the table at her two nieces.

They were for a moment speechless with astonishment and then delight coupled with excitement burst bounds and they overwhelmed their aunt with their thanks and delighted acceptance. Only Helen, who thought that her sister-in-law might have offered her a summer in London instead of her half-fledged daughters, remarked rather sourly that Julia would have to be careful how she behaved. "I must warn you, Emmeline, that she says anything and everything that comes into her head," she complained. "It can be very embarrassing at times."

Emmeline laughed and said she would not object to being embarrassed by pretty Julia, and when after luncheon the question of clothes arose, Dinah said quietly that there were trunks of pretty dresses upstairs in her dressing room that could be divided between her sisters.

It was finally arranged that on the day before the family was to leave Bretton Miss Stroud would accompany the girls to their uncle's house in Belgrave Square, and then return to Saltbech to take up her duties again there with the twins.

The last of the wedding presents had been sent back, the last of the cases packed, and the steam engine arrived, drawing the pantechnicon that was to hold their goods. Both were situated in the stableblock, and Octavius and Paul and Paula could not be persuaded to come away from the great monster of an engine and even larger pantechnicon. It took some days to pack up, and the days after it had left would have been an anti-climax had they not been employed in getting Julia and Sophy ready to go to London.

Dinah packed two domed trunks with pretty dresses and lace-trimmed lingerie for her sisters, keeping a small one for her own clothes, in which there was not a single garment that had been included in her trousseau. The box of linen had gone to Saltbech in the pantechnicon.

They went off with Miss Stroud in high spirits, and when they arrived their aunt had a great deal of entertainment in selecting the plainest lingerie and dresses for Sophy's finishing school, and the prettiest dresses and lace-trimmed petticoats for Julia. And after Sophy had been seen off at Victoria Station with the French lady who was taking her and several young ladies to the school in Paris, Emmeline whisked Julia off to her milliner and fitted her out with one of the sailor hats that were popular that year, and several others suitable for garden parties and receptions and At Homes.

In the meantime the family were traveling to Saltbech, Dinah and her mother, the twins, Octavius and Nurse Blackwell in a first-class carriage, and Lovell, guarding her mistress's jewelry in a second-class compartment behind them.

Dinah took Octavius on her lap as he grew sleepy and allowed him to suck his thumb, although he was four years old.

"Do you suppose," he said, looking up at her gravely—he was a solemn little boy—"that we shall find any new flowers at Uncle Sep's?" Octavius had a passion for flowers, and the family said he would be a professor of botany when he grew up.

"Not *new* ones, darling," said Dinah smiling. "We aren't

going to Spain or South Africa or anywhere like that. We shall still be in England."

"But there *may* be different ones, mayn't there?" he asked anxiously, and when she said there might indeed, he settled down comfortably to his thumb and was soon fast asleep.

Septimus had returned to Saltbech to receive the Bretton's pantechnicon when it arrived, the childrens' ponies were installed in the stables, their rabbits had new hutches, and he was there with Digger at the station to welcome the family when they arrived.

With the exception of Dinah and her mother none of them had any idea of what their new home would be like, because for some unknown reason, never explained, they had never visited their uncle there before.

While Digger welcomed the twins as if they had been parted from him for a year, Septimus greeted them all in his usual kind fashion, asking about their journey and telling them that luncheon awaited them at the rectory.

His new family was packed into the station omnibus, which was a new and exciting experience, because the only omnibus they had traveled in before had been the family one at Bretton, which was more like a brake and used for fetching luggage and the servants of Bretton guests from the station. The Saltbech station omnibus had glass windows on each side, a door in the back and two horses to pull it. They scrambled in, accompanied by the excited Digger, while Septimus traveled with his sister in a hired cab.

"Have you no carriage of your own, Septimus?" asked Helen, shocked. "There is always *such* a smell of the stables about these hired cabs."

"I have an open trap," he told her cheerfully. "But I thought you would not care to ride in that. It would blow your hair about. I do most of my parish visiting on foot or on my bicycle."

"The twins have brought their bicycles," said Lady Bretton fretfully. "Roger would never allow Dinah to have one, and I think he was right. I have always regarded bicycling as being undignified and middle-class."

"Then I must buy her a machine so that she can learn to bicycle here," said Septimus with the same maddening cheerfulness. "Because you see, Helen, I am afraid Saltbech is a very middle-class, undignified sort of town."

Helen said nothing. Her thoughts went back to the evening before when she had been sitting with Dinah in the small drawing room and had asked her if she did not feel sad at leaving Bretton.

"Not at all," Dinah had said briskly. "In fact personally I shall be very glad to leave." And she went on to say that at least they would have a roof over their heads, and a very nice one at that. Whereupon her mother had rounded on her and told her that she seemed to forget that, if it had not been for her stupidity, her uncle would at least have had one less mouth to feed.

And then, to her intense surprise and mortification Dinah had risen to her feet, white-faced and with her eyes like stones.

"If you wish to hark back to my broken engagement, Mamma," she had said, "let us speak of it just this once and then no more. My engagement to Major Morrell ended some weeks ago, and as far as I am concerned he no longer exists. He was the figment of my silly schoolgirl imagination and that was all. I shall do my best to be useful to Uncle Sep to pay for my board and lodging, and if you wish to visit any of your friends while we are at Saltbech you will be able to go happily, knowing that I shall be at the rectory to take your place. I am afraid you must make up your mind to have one spinster daughter on your hands from now on, because I have no intention of marrying anybody after my treatment from Major Morrell." And then with a good night kiss she had gone up to bed, remarking that they would have to be up early in the morning.

"I cannot understand Dinah," Helen said plaintively, as the cab approached the rectory. "You would think she would have *some* regrets about leaving our dear Bretton, but when I asked her this morning how she had slept she said she had slept very well, and talked about the journey and whether we should take sponge-cakes and milk for the children as they were having such an early breakfast. My housekeeper had a hamper packed for us naturally, in case we needed refreshment on the way, but I left that to her as I always have done. I am sure I did not sleep a wink after all the tragedy and worry of the last months. Why is Dinah behaving like this, Septimus? So cold, so hard-hearted. I do not think she feels anything at all."

"May it not be possible that she feels too much?" asked her brother. "In which case all I can advise you to do is this: let her alone, Helen, for God's sake and her own."

The omnibus rattled through the streets of the old town,

past the houses with timbered fronts in the High Street, and on through the more countrified road leading to the rectory, where new red-brick villas stood back behind pleasant gardens enclosed in red-brick walls.

The houses were mostly Gothic in style, and were occupied by businessmen, such as lawyers and accountants from Saltbech and retired tradesmen from Easterley ten miles away.

After the houses had disappeared they came to the rectory gates where Septimus's groom, Coppard, was waiting with a handcart for any hand luggage they might be carrying that he could take up to the house.

The small park in front of the rectory was yellow with wild daffodils on that last day of March. They grew up to the very park palings, poking their heads through them as if to have a look at the newcomers, and on that lovely morning it seemed as if the house joined the daffodils to give the family a welcome.

Because it was a welcoming house. Some houses have no friendliness for visitors: there is a blankness in their neatly curtained windows, a coolness inside as you step into a cold, unwelcoming hall. But Saltbech Rectory had long bow windows, rounded and tall, reaching from ground level to the ceilings of the rooms: windows that could be pushed up from the bottom so that anybody in those rooms could step out at will into the pleasant gardens that surrounded the house.

The front door stood open, the porch holding croquet mallets, and yellow, red, blue and black croquet balls, from which most of the paint had disappeared, and at the far end of the settle in the lobby there was a pile of prayer-books, neatly stacked. On a hallstand beyond the settle there was a black clerical overcoat, a couple of stout ash walking sticks, a large umbrella and a shabby clerical hat.

But it was as they went through into the hall itself that Septimus's new family stood and stared about them, scarcely able to believe that they were looking at a hall that seemed larger than the one at Bretton.

"It has been said," their uncle told them smiling, "that a coach and four could be turned in this hall. I have never tried it myself because I do not think the front doorway and the lobby would admit four horses, let alone a coach. But I daresay it is large enough, all the same."

The hall was panelled, and floored with flagstones, and a small flight of stairs led up, with two half-landings, to a gallery that ran round above, doors opening off it to bedrooms and sitting rooms.

Mrs. Jennings, severe in black silk with a neat lace collar and cuffs, was waiting to greet them and to conduct Lady Bretton to the rooms that had been prepared for her and her family. Lovell, thin-lipped and disapproving, followed with her ladyship's jewel-case, while Nurse took Octavius's hand for the little boy's rather weary climb up to the nursery.

When the removal van arrived with their belongings everything had been unpacked and put into the respective rooms, so that the children should be greeted by their treasures when they opened the doors.

Paul's ships were arranged on a table in the window of his room, and in his twin's room next door Paula's dolls were sitting in a row on her bed. In the nurseries on the floor above fires had been lighted, and everything was ready for Nurse Blackwell and her small charge. There was on the same floor a schoolroom for the older children and a fair-sized bedroom, nicely furnished, for Miss Stroud.

Lady Bretton's boudoir at the Place had been reproduced as nearly as possible in the charming room that looked out over the little park: her pink carpet was on the floor, and her pretty chintz curtains were protected from the sun with looped ones of Nottingham lace at the long windows. Her bedroom next door was furnished simply with some new walnut furniture bought in Easterley and a carpet matching the one in her sitting room. A small bedroom next to hers had been set aside for Lovell, who regarded its somewhat plainer furnishing without comment.

Dinah had wished for nothing of hers to be included except a small case of books, and these were accommodated in a shelf above a little writing table in a sitting room of her own. Her bedroom was near those occupied by the twins, and in fact, allowing for the two rooms set aside for Harold and John in the holidays, there were only three guest-rooms remaining unoccupied in the rooms that surrounded the gallery.

Mrs. Jennings had arranged for luncheon to be taken by the whole family together, except for Nurse Blackwell and Octavius, in the big dining room that overlooked the croquet lawn at the back of the house.

"I hope this arrangement will meet with your ladyship's approval today," the housekeeper said anxiously. "If you should wish for any alteration later I will see to it for you. I thought as you had just arrived, you would like to take luncheon with the rector and the family, but it will be no trouble to change it if your ladyship wishes."

"I do not wish to be a trouble to my brother, Mrs. Jennings," Helen said with a sad smile. "I must say that the early start and the train journey has given me a bad headache, and I scarcely feel fit enough to join the family party downstairs. Master Paul and Miss Paula are inclined to be noisy when their governess is not there, but as Miss Stroud is not arriving until later today we must make the best of it. I am like my brother in that way, as you know, Mrs. Jennings. We both like to consider others before ourselves. But when their governess is here I think the schoolroom meals should be served upstairs."

"The rector has engaged another young housemaid, m'lady, to wait on the nursery, so that it will be no trouble if she takes the schoolroom meals up as well. Will that be all, m'lady?"

"Yes, thank you, Mrs. Jennings. Perhaps you will keep luncheon back for half an hour while I have a little rest, and then I will come downstairs."

"Certainly, m'lady." The rector's housekeeper went downstairs to tell Cook that everything must be held back for half an hour, and if the thought crossed her mind that consideration for other people could be interpreted quite differently by the rector and his sister she did not say so.

"She was always spoiled," she told herself ruefully. "And now she is widowed she will put on her parts, aided and abetted by that Lovell."

She did not feel that it was a happy start to the six-year stay of the rector's guests.

Chapter Seven

Luncheon was an unhappy meal, the twins bursting with questions and Dinah doing her best to keep them quiet, warned by her mother's air of martyrdom and the bottle of smelling salts beside her plate. Digger did not help, either.

He lifted his leg against the sideboard and was immediately put outside the long windows, where he sat unwillingly, scratching the glass from time to time to be let in again, until Helen said crossly that if that dog did not behave himself he would have to be put down.

The twins looked at each other in horror and they made up their minds instantly that Digger would never stir from the schoolroom in future, even if he took all the paint off the door.

Afterwards Lady Bretton went upstairs to her sitting room while Lovell unpacked the trunks of clothing that had arrived before them. It was not long before she came to say that there were not nearly enough cupboards or wardrobes in m'lady's bedroom and there did not appear to be a dressing room for them, either.

"We shall have to have more room than *this,* m'lady," she said firmly. "I am sorry to say so, but Mrs. Jennings does not appear to know what a lady requires in the way of wardrobes and cupboards."

"I do not suppose that she does," said Helen faintly from her sofa. "But I cannot be worried by such things now, Lovell. I do not feel at all well. You will have to speak to Mrs. Jennings about it yourself."

So Lovell went off to tell the housekeeper about the lack of room. "We have one hundred pairs of boots and shoes alone to be put away, let alone our dresses, Mrs. Jennings. Her ladyship will not be in mourning forever, and we have a great many toilettes to be accommodated."

Mrs. Jennings, having put up with Lovell's disdain at her table over the mid-day dinner that was the rule of the rectory servants' hall, said rather shortly that she would put one of the remaining spare bedrooms at her disposal for a dressing room.

The twins in the meantime were exploring the gardens with delight, riding their bicycles round the many paths followed by a delighted Digger, while Dinah freed Nurse Blackwell to unpack by taking Octavius off her hands, and conducting him along the footpath across the park to see if he could find any other flowers than the daffodils.

She was coming back with him when a horse and trap entered the drive and as they arrived at the front door the trap stopped there, too, the gentleman handing the reins to his groom before taking off his hat to Miss Bretton.

Then he jumped down, his attention caught and held by her small brother.

"Is this the professor of botany?" he asked, squatting on his heels beside the little boy. "How d'you do, sir? I am your uncle's friend, Bellingham."

"How d'you do Bellenum," said Octavius and immediately held out a small blue flower for him to identify for him. "What is this, please?"

The doctor took it from him and examined it gravely. "I think it is a bugle," he said then. "But your uncle has a large book on his shelves called *Flowers of the Field* by a gentleman with the name of the Reverend C. A. Johns. If you ask your uncle to find the flower for you, I've no doubt at all that he will show you an illustration—a picture—of it. But I am afraid the pictures are not so clear as they should be."

Octavius nodded solemnly. "I will ask him," he said. "Uncle Sep knows everything." He took back the flower. "A bugle," he repeated, and suddenly his grave little face broke into an enchanting smile. "*What* a funny name for a flower!" he said.

Charles rose to his feet and asked Dinah if her uncle was at home.

"I have no idea," she said coldly. "But no doubt Simmons will know."

She left him with Octavius's hand held firmly in hers, and Charles rang the bell, following her in the meantime into the hall and making his way to the great fireplace where logs of wood burned or smouldered all the year through, as if he were better acquainted with the house than the rector's niece, and as much at home there.

Annoyed, Dinah took Octavius up to the nursery promising him that he should ask his uncle about the new flower when he came to say good night to him before going to bed, while Simmons appeared with welcoming smiles for the doctor to tell him that the rector had just gone out.

"Then I will call again on my way back," he said and went back to his trap without another glance at Miss Bretton and her youngest brother.

As soon after he left a cab arrived with Miss Stroud, Dinah's time was fully occupied until teatime.

Lady Bretton said she would have tea brought to her upstairs in her sitting room, and having peeped into the nursery and seen Octavius happily eating his tea with Nurse Blackwell, and then on to the schoolroom where the twins were having theirs with Miss Stroud, who had scarcely had time to draw breath or to remove her hat, Dinah went downstairs to see if her uncle had returned.

She found him in his study, a large book-lined room on the north side of the hall, and he was not alone. Until that moment she had forgotten about Dr. Bellingham, and she bit her lip with vexation at finding him there with Septimus. Their heads were bent over some queer-looking photographs in which they were both so absorbed that they were not aware of her until she spoke.

"I came to see if I could pour out tea for you, Uncle Sep," she said. "But as you are engaged, I will go back to Mamma."

"No, no, my dear, pray don't leave us. I am sure Charles will be glad of some tea before he goes back to his surgery."

The doctor accepted the invitation with deplorable lack of tact. Surely he realized, she thought angrily, that as they had only arrived that morning, her uncle might like to be alone with his family. But it did not seem to occur to him as he followed her and the rector across the hall to a drawing room that had been brightened by one of the Bretton carpets and Lady Bretton's grand piano, its open keyboard facing one of the long windows.

A tea-table had been set out in front of the brightly burning fire, and as Dinah dealt with the silver teapot while Septimus rescued the muffins that had been set on a hob in the hearth to keep warm, the doctor tried to make conversation with the rector's niece.

His attempts failed dismally, every effort being met by a yes or no, and he gave up trying and good-naturedly left her to the teapot while he continued the discussion with her uncle that her entrance into the study had interrupted.

She found herself free to glance at him from time to time, and to observe that he was a good looking man, with a clean-shaven face, a strong jaw, firm mouth and black lashes to his gray eyes. She judged him to be about thirty-five, and she felt a little ashamed of her brusqueness when she remembered the gold medallion that was still on the bangle in her jewel-case and his kindness to little Octavius that afternoon.

Her uncle, always interested in scientific matters, was obviously enthralled by the matter under discussion, and when they had finished tea she left them to themselves.

As they returned to the study to collect the photographs that the doctor had brought with him, Charles remarked that Miss Bretton looked pale and thin.

"And sad," agreed Septimus sorrowfully.

Charles agreed. His interest in Septimus's niece was touched with concern. He had never seen such a change in anyone in such a short time. Her face had lost its color, her eyes their sparkle, and her easy laughter had been replaced by a gravity only broken by an occasional faint smile. In her black dress with her hair drawn back in a knot at the back of her neck nobody could recognize her for the pretty, lively girl of last May. He said he supposed that Sir Roger's death must have been a great shock for his eldest daughter. "And I suppose her wedding has had to be postponed as well?" he added.

Septimus hesitated before saying that it was not so much her father's death as the breaking of her engagement that had affected his niece, and because it still hurt him to see Dinah with that shocked look in her eyes, he told Charles the story of the letter she had received from Malta a week before she was due to set out for her wedding.

"I never saw the letter, mind you," he went on. 'But her sister Julia read it, and even allowing for the passionate resentment of youth I could tell from what she said that the man had acted like a scoundrel. I told you, if you remember, when he was here with her last year that I did not like him. His eyes were too close together."

"I remember," said Charles, with some amusement.

"If I'd been a younger man I'd have gone out to Malta myself and demanded an explanation," said Septimus wrathfully. "And if none had been forthcoming, I swear I would have thrashed him." The rector hit his clenched fist against the palm of his left hand. "To have my Dinah treated like that—and because her father had died leaving them with very slender means. From what his colonel's wife told me, I am pretty sure he had his eye on a rich heiress who was visiting Malta."

Charles Bellingham said nothing. There might have been extenuating circumstances: one could not be certain, and his natural caution had taught him not to believe only one side of a quarrel. Such things as broken engagements were possibly considered scandalous, but he did not think, to give her her due, that Miss Bretton looked as if she had the character of a jilt. A quarrel was far more likely, and that might in the end be resolved.

Upstairs in her mother's room Dinah found herself cross-questioned about her uncle's visitor.

"I do hope we shall not be subjected to a succession of similar friends of your uncle's while we are here," she complained. "It is scarcely the Society to which we are accustomed. What did they talk about?"

"From what I could make of it they were talking about some form of new photography. I forget what they called it, but it seems that if they take a photograph of one's foot or one's hand by this method, the print shows all the bones through the flesh."

"How disgusting!" Her mother shivered.

"The doctor said it could prove very useful when a bone was broken."

"Surely a clever doctor could discover where a bone was broken without any fancy photographs?" said Helen. "I am sure when your brother Harold slipped on the ice the winter before last and broke his arm he knew himself exactly where it was broken, in fact, dear Sir Herbert said he could not have diagnosed it better himself." Sir Herbert Streatham had been the London physician most in favor at Bretton.

"Uncle Sep said he wished they could take a photograph of a man's brain," said Dinah. "But Dr. Bellingham seemed to think it would not be possible."

"A brain." Her mother made a small grimace. "Yes, I suppose poor Septimus would think of that." She changed the subject abruptly. "Do you think we shall ever be able to settle down here in this old rectory with your uncle, Dinah?" she asked. "We shall be terribly cramped."

"We shall become accustomed to it," said Dinah briefly. "And it is a question of necessity, isn't it, Mamma? It is a beautiful old house and Uncle Sep is the kindest creature in the world to take us all in as he has done, and I for one intend to enjoy my years of exile from Bretton. I am sure the others will feel the same. After all, although one does not say so, it was Papa's lack of wisdom that has been the cause of it all, and we cannot be the first, nor shall we be the last, children to suffer through their parents' folly." And she went upstairs to see how the twins and Miss Stroud were faring in the nursery.

Lady Bretton's thoughts went after her with some indignation. She hoped Dinah had not included her in her condemnation of parents: it had been nothing to do with her that Roger had lost so much money.

"Dinah has no heart," thought Helen, her feeling of self-pity growing. "I never thought she could be so insensitive—so unfeeling. No regrets for Bretton, no wretched feeling of inferiority, or of having come down in the world. Clive was perhaps more perceptive than we thought."

She decided to go down to dinner that evening, if only to satisfy herself about the appurtenances of the rector's table. One could not expect rough country servants to have the quiet manners of the Bretton servants, especially when there was no butler there to subdue them, but a glance, a frown at rough movements, and a slight exclamation if dishes were not placed properly on the table could do a great deal, if resorted to at just the right moment.

In the event, the parlormaid Simmons countered the glances with calm indifference, and accepted the frowns and slight exclamations with quiet confidence in herself, but the housemaid who was helping her to hand round the plates was petrified with fright and succeeded in slopping most of Septimus's soup onto the tablecloth in front of him.

As April slipped into May, with every sort of meadow flowers now to tempt little Octavius into the park, it was plain to poor Septimus that his sister was not settling down at the rectory as happily as he had hoped.

The twins were finding new ground to explore every day, and loved going down to the river to watch the boats that came up to unload timber and coal. Being a tidal river at high tide, the Salte was deep enough to take quite a number of small coasting vessels.

Miss Stroud had accepted the situation with her usual cheerfulness and bore with her employer's sharpness, owing to their closer proximity in the smaller space of the rectory, with a patience that Septimus admired. Miss Stroud was not only a clever woman but a wise one.

Nurse Blackwell, however, regretted with Lovell the better accommodation and more servants at the Place, feeling that it had been a slightly lowering experience to have a heavily-breathing little maid staggering up the three flights of stairs with the nursery coals instead of the nursery footman they had left behind.

As for Lovell, although she was invited into the housekeeper's room for her meals, as she should be, she told her mistress more than once that never before had she been expected to share the servants' hall with the lower orders, such as vulgar kitchenmaids and suchlike.

"That Maud," she told her ladyship, "is downright common."

Helen expressed her regret and put up with the martyred air with which Lovell waited on her, hoping that she would not give her notice. It was all very well for Dinah to accept cheerfully the administrations of a housemaid to do her hair and to fasten her dresses, but her hair curled naturally and she had not the same need for an experienced lady's-maid like Lovell, who knew exactly the right heat for the curling tongs before she tried them on her lady's fringe.

"We are not here forever, Lovell," Helen told her maid one day despairingly. "I have not heard from Lady Crowborne yet, but I am sure I shall hear from her very soon. Lord Crowborne is almost certain to be taking his yacht to the South of France again this summer. Let us try to have patience."

"I will do my best, m'lady," said Lovell darkly. "As I'm sure I always have, but there's some things no lady's-maid should be asked to endure, and the manners of that kitchenmaid is one of them. And this is the first time I have ever been asked to stay in a house where there is no butler."

The lack of a butler was the one insurmountable objection as far as Lovell and her mistress were concerned, and as the expected letter from Lady Crowborne did not arrive, Helen felt that her nerves must soon give way under the strain.

One day Septimus was asked to tell Dr. Bellingham to visit her. "I would dearly like to have our own Sir Herbert down from London," said Helen, "but it would be beyond my means these days." She waited for her brother to suggest that she should have Sir Herbert and the expense of his visit would be his concern, but all he said was that Charles Bellingham was extremely clever, and he would send the stable lad down to his surgery with a note asking him to call.

Charles had just finished surgery that morning when he received the note and he left the few stragglers that remained to his partner Mark Annerley, who lived with his young wife in a cottage next door to Charles's house, a cottage that Mark's senior partner said was more like a dolls' house than a dwelling.

Charles came up in his trap to see her ladyship and found her in bed, wearing a pretty lace wrap trimmed with blue ribbons, her hair becomingly dressed, and indeed the lady herself looking extremely attractive.

He took the hand she extended graciously to him, and asked why she had sent for him.

"It is my heart," she told him, fluttering her blue eyes at

him because, general practitioner that he was, he was also a good looking man. "I have such dreadful dizzy spells. I quite alarmed my brother last night at dinner: I was so faint he had to assist me upstairs."

He took her pulse and sounded her heart and found nothing wrong with her. In fact Lady Bretton gave all the signs of being a very healthy woman.

"I do not think you take enough exercise," he told her briefly. "There is a good livery stable in the town and they have some quiet old hacks there. A ride into the country would do you all the good in the world."

She was affronted. "It is years since I have ridden," she told him, her smiles disappearing. "And I certainly would not start again on some wretched hired hack, thank you, Dr. Bellingham. Is that all you can suggest?"

"No. As an alternative I would suggest a glass of port at eleven each morning, followed by a brisk walk until luncheon. There are some nice lanes round Saltbech."

"I detest walking." She turned her head away petulantly. "I daresay you may have heard of our physician, Sir Herbert Streatham?"

"Who has not?" He half smiled.

"He always gave me a splendid tonic at this time of year. He said it was most necessary to one of my physique. I was not strong enough to come through the winter and spring unscathed."

"Then supposing I send you up a tonic?" he suggested. "Shall we see if I can emulate—if not equal—Sir Herbert?"

"No one could equal him," she told him firmly. "But I will try your tonic." As he turned to the door she added, "I expect my brother will settle your account."

He had to bite his tongue at that point, and left the room rather hurriedly. In the hall at the bottom of the stairs he found Dinah waiting for him.

"What did you think of my mother?" she asked anxiously. He would dearly have liked to tell her, but he did not. "She turned very faint last evening."

He did not say that it was probably due to over-eating and no exercise, but he said that he could find nothing wrong and thought she needed a tonic.

"Oh yes," she said and for the first time since she had been in Saltbech the old smile came back and he liked it as much as he had done a year ago. She had a singularly sweet smile.

"The brown tonic: Sir Herbert always used to recommend that."

Brown tonic. Iron. Well that could not hurt the woman if it did not make her any better-tempered. He said he would send it up, and hastened away before the kindness could fade from her eyes.

Dinah went up to her mother and said that she had met the doctor and that he was sending her the tonic.

"Yes, but only because I told him what Sir Herbert used to give me," said Helen scornfully. "If I had not, he would not have known what to do. As ignorant, my dear, as all these country doctors are. He talked of exercise—riding and walking, if you please! Sir Herbert would never have recommended such a thing to anybody with a heart like mine. I cannot imagine how your uncle can make such a friend of the man."

Dinah said nothing and went to her small sitting room. Beneath her window Dimmock the gardener was mowing the croquet lawn in readiness for that afternoon when Septimus, at his wits' end to know how to entertain his sister and make her happier, was having a croquet party. The scent of the freshly-mown grass came up to the open window like a promise of summer, but as she stood there Dinah found herself forced to face some disturbing thoughts.

Was her mother determined to continue to display this peevish discontent for the next six years? And if so, how would they all be able to bear it?

Chapter Eight

The croquet party was not going to be a large one. Septimus thought that Helen would not wish to take part in any other form of entertaining, such as a dinner party, but surely a quiet afternoon at croquet with other ladies who had not the means or opportunity to take houses in London for the season would not come amiss.

Lady Crockett, for instance, had what she referred to as a small house on the outskirts of Saltbech, and never ceased to regret the large country mansion that had been hers and now belonged to her son.

"So hard to be turned out of one's home," she sighed to Helen that afternoon as they sat under the trees that surrounded the croquet lawn, watching The Honorable Bella Crockett and Dinah playing there, partnered by the rector and one of his curates, Mr. Short, a young man with no chin and an irritating desire to please, which was excused on the grounds that he was known to be well-connected. "My sympathies are with you entirely, Lady Bretton. Of course when my husband died and my son came into Claybourne, he asked me to consider it still as my home, but I never liked my daughter-in-law and could not take to some of her friends. So I made the necessary break—not without a great deal of grief, I may tell you."

Lady Bretton did not say that it was her husband's improvidence that had necessitated her own move and agreed, watching Dinah doing her best with the curate's erratic playing.

"Of course there is practically no Society in a town like this," continued Lady Crockett. "If my house had not been owned by the Claybourne estates and offered to me for my lifetime, I would never have come here. You will not believe me, I daresay, but sometimes when I am planning a dinner party I have to include the local doctor—an unmarried man—to make up my numbers. I have always found him to be quiet and unassuming, but some of my friends tell me he is a trouble-maker."

"In what way?"

"I have not enquired too deeply, because one likes to be above petty local quarrels, but Percy Whatley was extremely incensed because he said he thought old working people should have a pension paid by the government when they were too old to work. Percy asked him what workhouses were for. He was rather tiresome about it, I remember."

"I was surprised to find on my arrival," said Helen, "that my brother had made such a friend of him. He is always in and out of the rectory, and at first it worried me a little. But being a clergyman, naturally Septimus has to entertain people that we would never have considered at Bretton."

"I daresay he calls to see him on parochial matters."

"It may be so." Helen then told her in confidence that her

husband had been robbed of a large sum of money, and after he died it had been on the advice of relatives that she had let the Place until Harold came of age. "But one can only hope that everything will be settled long before then."

Lady Crockett said she hoped so, too. "Wise as it may have been to let the Place for a time," she continued, "I am sure it will not be for long, as you have just said. Things have a way of righting themselves in a way one does not expect," she added optimistically.

Helen said she had been glad of an excuse for leaving Bretton for a time, and related in a low voice the scandal of her daughter's broken engagement, and Lady Crockett, who had heard all about it and was avid to hear the story as from the horse's mouth, agreed with her that it had been shocking and quite unnecessary. But had it not been caused by a lovers' tiff, perhaps, and might not it have been better for all concerned if Miss Bretton had gone out to Malta as planned? "Girls are so impulsive and romantic," she added with a tender glance at her own daughter, a heavy, plain young woman with whom it was hard to connect any ideas of romance.

Before she could hear any more about Dinah's broken romance, however, the game had ended and coincided with the arrival of Colonel Lockwill, in command of the regiment now occupying Saltbech Barracks, and his wife, and Lady Crockett deserted her new friend to greet them both tenderly, although she told Helen later after tea, when the colonel had gone and the others were having a last game of croquet before the evening grew too cool, that Colonel Lockwill, poor man, had not had enough means for a Guards regiment, and that was why he had to take a commission in his present regiment instead.

"His wife is an insipid little thing, no help to him at all," she went on as they made their way to the rector's conservatory. "But you must come to a quiet little dinner at my house one day soon, my dear, and I will introduce you to some of my friends. So many of the old families have disappeared, but we have one or two nice new ones that have taken their place. I do not know if you have met the Collingtons? Sir James was Lord Mayor of London at one time—now, was he in carpets or cotton? Carpets I think, because I believe Percy Whatley's grandfather was in cotton. Sir James's wife, Dolly, is one of my greatest friends. She is related to the Aberfelds. The duchess is very fond of her."

Helen said she had met Lady Collington when she was younger, but had not seen anything of her since she married. "I believe she was a friend of Violet Crowborne?"

"One of her greatest friends. What a lovely yacht Lord Crowborne has. I expect you have been included in some of his parties on board in the past?"

Helen said she had, and asked if the Crowbornes were in London, and on being told that they were at their country place before starting out on the *Oleander* for a trip down the Mediterranean in July, she felt happier. Violet would have got her letter and she must reply to it soon. Perhaps she would invite her to join them at Marseilles.

The ladies had by this time arrived at the conservatory, in which there was a particularly fine collection of ferns, Septimus having a love for such plants, and having agreed that they did not care for ferns Lady Crockett went on describing the people to whom she intended to introduce Helen. There were, for instance, the Whatleys. "I am very fond of them both," said Lady Crockett. "Laura was General Datchett's younger daughter."

"I remember her. The general and his wife used to come to the Place for the pheasant shooting, and they usually brought Laura—we called her Lallie—a nice girl, with a wonderful sense of dress, although she was nothing to look at."

"She is still very plain," Lady Crockett assured her. "Sharp featured, you know. Not a type I admire. But she still dresses very well, and she has a wonderfully keen wit. When she describes her husband's relations—when Percy isn't there to hear her—she makes you die with laughter."

"They have a large house at Crossways, I believe?"

"Oh yes, but it is nothing to the Collingtons' West Bresleigh Hall. Sir James did not stop at the family's side of the house when he built it, either. I have been told that the servants' quarters not only have a billiard room but a ball-room as well, and I do not know how many bathrooms. Quite two or three."

"That is hard to believe."

"I know. It is a great mistake to spoil one's servants, and at Bresleigh they are sometimes quite impertinent, but Sir James does not seem to be aware of it."

Septimus here came to tell them that the game was at an end and her ladyship's carriage was at the door, and she thanked him sweetly, saying that they had been admiring his beautiful ferns.

"A really wonderful collection," she told him. "My gardener seems to fill my conservatory with nothing but geraniums and palms, which are so boring."

Soon after the rector's croquet party, they were invited to a small dinner party in Lady Crockett's house, Saltbech Grange, a dinner that turned out to be one of eight courses for ten people.

The drawing room, a double room, was well able to accommodate twice that number with ease, but the dining room was smaller, and it was difficult to seat all the guests comfortably, even with two extra leaves put into the mahogany table.

The Collingtons were there, reminding Dinah of her uncle Thomas Carey and her Aunt Honoria, and the Whatleys, and Captain Rainfold and Captain Greenberg from the barracks, and the numbers were made up once more by Charles Bellingham.

When dinner was announced, Sir James Collington took in Helen, his wife was taken in by Percy Whatley, Laura Whatley was partnered by Captain Greenberg, a heavy-looking young man with a wit to match her own, Lady Crockett had the rector to take her in, and her daughter Captain Rainfold, which left Dinah, to her chagrin, to her uncle's friend Charles Bellingham.

Trying to think of something that might make a topic of conversation with the big silent man beside her, she asked brightly if he had been reading any more interesting items about the new photography.

She was pleased to find that he responded at once, and spent a considerable time in describing the instrument of the photography, variously known as Röntgen radiation or X-radiation.

She was relieved to find herself thus freed from the necessity of doing anything but allow him to run on, which lasted through the soup, fish, and first entrée, while her thoughts followed their own bent. The uniform in which the two officers had appeared reminded her agonizingly of Clive Morrell, and she was recalled with a start when Charles's quiet voice said, "You have not been listening to a word, have you? Your mind was far away."

She tried to smile and told him rather breathlessly that she was afraid that she was not as good a listener as her uncle, and then to make up for her lack of manners, as they waited for the saddle of mutton that was to follow the first entrée she asked him why he had taken a practice in a remote little town like Saltbech. "One would have thought a London practice would have suited you better," she said.

"Now I wonder what makes you think that?" He gave her a somewhat quizzical smile, and she did not answer, wondering indeed why she had said it, unless it was perhaps that even then she was aware of the depth of his understanding and the broadness of his mind. "For one thing," he told her, "I had not the means for a West End practice, and if I had I would not have taken one. I dislike London, and a fashionable practice would not have suited me at all. I am too blunt—I have not the proper bedside manner for such a life."

At that moment, Percy Whatley leant forward to ask Charles where Dr. Bryce had gone.

"Last year about this time, he was buzzing round my ears like a wasp," he went on, not giving Charles time to answer. "Wanted to know what the Easterley Water Company's pipes were like, and then writing to suggest—or rather to demand—that water be laid on to half a dozen villages that had not enough inhabitants between them to warrant a water rate."

"I cannot see why he made such a nuisance of himself," said Laura Whatley lightly. "All the villages he mentioned were near streams, so that the lack of a proper supply was completely unimportant. Did you not tell him so, Percy?"

"I did, my dear."

"I must say when I've been out riding," put in Bella Crockett, "I've seen women walking miles, quite happily, with a wooden yoke across their shoulders carrying large buckets of water. They make nothing of it, do they, Mamma?"

"They have been brought up to it, my dearest," said Lady Crockett. "For a working woman it is nothing at all."

"Dr. Bellingham is looking disapproving," said Laura Whatley laughing. And then as Charles smiled, refusing to be drawn into the discussion, she went on, "Let us change the subject. I would not live in your colonel's house, Captain Rainfold. I went to an At Home his wife gave there last week in that old house of theirs on the quayside, and she said at low tide she had to see that all the front windows were closed. I hope none of your men swim in the harbor?"

The captain laughed. "If they did, they would be confined to barracks for a week and their pay would be confiscated. If they want a swim they can walk to Salte Bay and go in there: it is not more than three miles or so away."

"I hear the regiment has sent its usual challenge to the county for the cricket match at the end of July," Lady Crockett told the rector. "I do hope the weather will be kind this year. July is usually such a rainy month, and everyone seems to choose it for outdoor festivities."

The conversation became general, and as her partner was silent Dinah was trying to find some subject that would interest him when he turned to her abruptly and asked after her little brother, and from then on they talked about the Professor, as Charles called him, and his delight because there was an unlimited supply of wild flowers round Saltbech.

"At Bretton he was not allowed to touch the garden flowers, and in the lawns the wild ones were cut to the bone with frequent mowing. But at the rectory, Dimmock leaves the mowing to the last moment because the daisies and other tiny flowers in the lawns are such a joy to Tavie. He squats down there looking for fresh ones every day and brings them to me to look up for him in the Reverend Johns' book on wild flowers. I am so grateful to you, Dr. Bellingham, for having thought of that book. It is improving my ignorance and his every day."

She talked easily and although he was sure that she had no interest in him as a man, as a dinner acquaintance she behaved with the courtesy of her class. He compared her severe black evening dress, with its billowing sleeves at the shoulders, long white gloves and the small string of amethysts, with her mother's far more elaborate dress on the other side of the table.

Lovell had found a black dress in chiffon over black satin for her mistress that night. The neck of the dress was cut very low, and there were flounced black tulle straps to the shoulders instead of sleeves. Her long black gloves, the hands tucked back into the wrists as she ate her dinner, and the black lace scarf covering her shoulders, with the high jet collar instead of the diamonds that would not have been permissible so soon after her husband's death, all made a concession to that of a widow so recently bereaved, but that was all. The jet collar showed up the whiteness of her skin better than any diamond would have done, and only confirmed what Charles had thought of her at first.

Lady Bretton was a spoiled Society beauty and nothing would change her, and his pity for the rector deepened. His kind heart had led him into a chaotic world, indeed.

The days went by without the expected reply from Lady

Crowborne, and Helen's temper went from bad to worse.

When Septimus mildly suggested that they should return Lady Crockett's dinner party with one at the rectory, he had his head bitten off.

"And how do you propose setting about it, Septimus?" enquired his sister with heavy sarcasm. "I cannot see your cook being able to serve up a six-course dinner, still less one of eight, successfully, and who would wait on our guests? That clumsy little housemaid, I suppose, emptying soup on the tablecloth in front of them."

Her brother apologized, and said that perhaps a tea-party would be better. If the day should be warm, they could have tea brought out to them on the side lawn under the cedar tree.

Helen said she would think about it. She was not so fond of Lady Crockett as she had been. With her carefully touched up chestnut hair, the dusting of rouge on her cheekbones, her thin, claw-like hands loaded with rings, she was always talking about "my little house here in Saltbech," as if it had been a workman's cottage, whereas it was as large again as the rectory.

And then there was her charming little brougham, with the Crockett coat of arms on the doors, and the coachman and footman in the Crockett livery, the high-stepping horse, its coat shining like the skin of a horse chestnut, trotting easily between the shafts.

There were her ladyship's dresses, too, always different, her expensive new hats, her parasols lined with pink chiffon, and her small high-heeled shoes and open-work silk stockings. She made Helen feel like a drab in the black dresses and hats that she hated and was forced to wear in mourning for Roger, from whom she had been separated, though living in the same house, for the past five years.

Helen disliked, too, the soft probing way Lady Crockett had of talking, almost every phrase a hidden innuendo, so that you had to be careful how you answered her.

Her references to Septimus were always prefaced by "the poor dear rector," or "your poor brother, one feels so sorry for him," with her eyes searching Helen's face, and then, if she got no satisfaction from her exploration of Septimus, she would go on to little Octavius.

"I saw him out with his nurse this morning, such a dear little fellow isn't he, my dear?" And then thoughtfully, "I cannot think who he reminds me of, because he is not a bit like the others, is he? He must hark back to some Bretton generations back. It is so odd how likenesses come out in children, isn't it?"

No, Lady Bretton did not find herself nearly so fond of Lady Crockett as she had been at first: she was far too inquisitive, and while skeletons in other peoples' cupboards could be matters for whispered scandal and even laughter, when it came to skeletons in one's own cupboard it was an entirely different matter.

Her dissatisfaction with Lady Crockett sat heavily on her as she went upstairs to her boudoir, where Lovell had some news for her that sent her flying off to the schoolroom, white with fury.

Since their arrival at the rectory the twins had discovered quite a new dimension to their lives. At Bretton the kitchen quarters were separate from the house, and the children had nothing to do with them, and in fact scarcely knew where they were situated, and had they done so they would have been far too frightened of M. Durand the chef to have ventured very far into his domain.

But here everything was different. There was only Mrs. Jennings in charge, and Cook to rule in the kitchen with a little scullery maid Katie to help her, and a boy Tom to run errands and do the lamps and the boots and the knives. Although the rectory was supplied with gas, its lamps were few and far between. The two housemaids were in and out, the parlormaid Simmons occasionally put in her head, and the kitchen itself was an Aladdin's cave to the two ten-year-olds.

The shining dish-covers of varying sizes hanging on the wall by the enormous cooking range, the shelf running round the top of the kitchen walls holding copper jelly moulds in all shapes and sizes, some with patterns on the bottom. (One had a thistle, another a rabbit, a third a fish.) Then there was the vast store cupboard of which Mrs. Jennings had the key: she let them look into it once and their eyes grew round with wonder at the great tins of biscuits, the bins of flour, the sacks of sugar and canisters of tea, mysterious with the queer Chinese characters that decorated them and their gold lettering. Then there was the coffee-grinder, clamped to the vast dresser with a circle of ground coffee surrounding it, and best of all there was the little room where the knife-cleaning machine lived.

They had never seen anything like it before, and they

would dearly have liked to try their hands at it, sticking knives in the slots and then turning the handle, but this Tom would not allow. "You might break the blades," he told them firmly. "And then wouldn't Mrs. Jennings come after me? Not 'arf she wouldn't."

It was unfortunate that Lovell had seen them down there talking to Tom, and she had a great deal to say about it that morning to their mamma, and just as they were settling down to their lessons in the schoolroom Helen burst in upon them.

"Miss Stroud," she cried, "what is this I hear about Paul and Paula being permitted to mix with the servants? It is a thing that never happened at Bretton, and it will not go on happening here. Lovell tells me they are in the kitchen nearly every day, and that they chatter away to the bootboy in the most familiar way. I will not permit such behavior, and I am exceedingly angry that you, as their governess, in whose charge they are, could have ever allowed it."

She then turned on the children, struck dumb with astonishment, and said: "Paul and Paula, listen to me. You will not go into the kitchens again and neither will you speak to the bootboy. If I find from Lovell that you have disobeyed me you will both be packed off to boarding school and Miss Stroud will go." And she whirled about and left the schoolroom to its shattered occupants.

For a moment or two the twins stared at each other in silent horror, while Miss Stroud, who had gone first white and then scarlet, found her handkerchief to wipe her eyes, but not before Paula had seen the tears in them. She jumped up and ran to their governess putting her arms round her.

"Don't cry, Stroudie dear," she said. "It isn't your fault. It is all because of that horrible Lovell. I hate her."

"She's a sneak," said Paul wrathfully. "In her soft slippers always following you so that you never know where she is."

"Why shouldn't we talk to the servants?" demanded Paula. "They're human beans, aren't they Stroudie, just like us?"

"Human beings, dear, not beans," said the governess automatically.

"Tom says human beans," said Paula and Miss Stroud thought that perhaps they were seeing too much of Tom, after all.

In the meantime Helen sought out Dinah, and told her to go and tell her uncle that he was to give orders to Mrs.

Jennings that the children did not go near the kitchen quarters in future.

Dinah said that she would do no such thing. "Uncle Sep has been so kind to us, Mamma," she said, "that if there is anything like that to be said to him, you must do it yourself. Or perhaps you would like to mention it to Mrs. Jennings when she comes to your boudiur to discuss the days' meals?"

And she went out into the park to pick some of the pheasant-eye narciss that had replaced the daffodils there, with Digger hunting for something known only to himself at her heels.

She was returning with a great armful of the scented flowers when she saw her uncle setting out down the drive, and as she drew near him she could see from his worried look that her mother had been speaking her mind.

She went to him quickly. "Uncle Sep," she said. "It's Mamma again, isn't it?"

He nodded. "And what she has been saying to me has some truth in it, I fear, my love," he said wryly. "I was so eager to help you all, to keep the family together, that I did not realise how small the rectory really is. I wish now that I had not interfered, but I could not bear to think of you all being parted so soon after your father's death."

"Uncle Sep, you are a saint on earth." Dinah linked her free hand in his arm, and began to walk with him down to the gate, in companionable silence. Then as they reached the road he said with a sad little smile:

"I have so often noticed in my life that when I try to help most I have not helped at all; in fact, I should have left the matter for wiser people to disentangle. Now it seems I have only made things worse for you all."

"Darling Uncle Sep." Dinah was grieved for him and angry with her mother. "Try not to worry. I am sure we shall all settle down." She kissed him swiftly and went back to the house to arrange a great bowl of her scented flowers on the writing table in his study.

As she arranged them her thoughts went back to Bretton, and how strange it was that only now, when they were at close quarters, could she see her mother clearly, as she had never seen her before.

Only the day before when Helen had been complaining about Saltbech and the rectory, Dinah had asked her if she would have preferred going to her Aunt Honoria and Uncle Thomas Carey with little Octavius.

"I certainly would not have wanted Octavius," her mother had replied impatiently. "That was a very stupid idea. But to be there on my own would have been a very different matter."

It seemed from her mother's tone that little Octavius meant nothing to her at all, and it had shaken Dinah considerably. Octavius, who was their darling and their joy, with his solemn little face and his tuneless humming as he collected his flowers.

By the following morning, however, everything had changed.

The postman brought a letter for Lady Bretton from her friend Violet Crowborne, in which she invited her to join them on their yacht the *Oleander* at Marseilles on the first of July. "We are taking the *Oleander* down the Med as far as Greece, and after visiting some of the islands and Athens we shall make a leisurely way back. I was waiting to write to you until I had heard from somebody else, who would make our numbers right, and now he is coming and says that he is most anxious to meet you again."

The joy with which Lady Bretton received this invitation was momentarily dimmed by pricks of conscience for the way she had been treating her brother, and she sent an urgent note to Dr. Bellingham asking him to call.

He did so and found a very different woman from the petulant lady of leisure who had demanded a tonic for her nerves earlier in the year. There were no signs of nerves about her this morning, and directly he entered her boudoir she greeted him with outstretched hand and a winning smile.

"Dr. Bellingham," she said, "I am so glad you came so promptly. I need your advice. I have been invited by a friend to spend some weeks on her husband's yacht starting from Marseilles on the first of July, and before I accept I feel I ought to ask you if you think I would be wise to do so. You know Septimus so well, and I could not go if I thought it would harm him. But the fact is that my nerves have been getting the better of me lately—I do not think the Saltbech air agrees with me—and I thought they might be improved by a change of air and scenery in the company of old friends."

He did not hesitate. "I am sure your brother will be able to manage without you, Lady Bretton," he said. "Will Miss Bretton accompany you?"

"Oh dear, no. She will stay here."

"Then there is nothing for you to worry about, is there? Miss Bretton will take your place here, and with Mrs. Jennings and her uncle to advise her I am sure everything will go on smoothly in your absence."

"Then you do think I should go?"

"The sooner the better, Lady Bretton. It will do you all the good in the world."

And as she said goodbye to him with a beaming face and he went down the stairs, he reflected that it would do Septimus as much good and more to have her out of his house.

Chapter Nine

Feverish preparations started at once for Lady Bretton's departure, and one morning when Dinah asked if there was anything she could do to help, and was told that Lovell would do all that was necessary, Helen called her back as she reached the boudoir door and said there was just one thing.

"You know that lilac silk dress that was made for you by Worth—the evening dress that Emmeline said was too sophisticated for Julia?"

"I remember it, Mamma."

"I think it would be wise if I were to take it with me, instead of leaving it to go out of fashion in one of your trunks upstairs. I am sure Lovell can soon make it fit me, because you are slightly taller than I am, and lilac suits me, whereas it never suited you."

"I shall never wear it, in any case," Dinah assured her.

"That is what I thought, and it is far too good a dress to moulder away in a box-room."

"You are welcome to it, Mamma; and anything else that may be useful to you. I will go and fetch the dress myself."

"You need not trouble to do that, my dear. Lovell will get it. She knows which trunk it is in."

If Dinah felt surprised at Lovell's powers of perception she did not comment on them. She could not help wondering, however, how many more visits Lovell had already paid to her boxes in the box-room.

The day of departure arrived, and as the cab came to the door to fetch her ladyship and Lovell and the lighter luggage that they were taking with them, Septimus and the rest of the family came out onto the drive to bid her farewell.

Septimus had arranged for one of Cook's couriers to meet the travelers at the terminus to conduct them across London to Victoria Station, and from there across the Channel and for the rest of the journey as far as Marseilles. Berths had been booked on the cross-Channel boat from Dover and in wagons-lits on the other side.

Octavius had been out early gathering flowers from the lawns before Dimmock got on to them with his mower, and he held out a bunch of rather drooping buttercups, clover and pink-tipped daisies to his mother as she said good-bye to them all in the porch.

"Oh, Octavius, I cannot take those." She laughed as he tendered his little farewell bouquet. "They are half dead already, and they will stain my gloves." And then when he wanted to hug her she drew back and shook her head. "No, I cannot have any rough hugs this morning. This hat has been very difficult to arrange and I am not having Lovell's hard work destroyed. You may kiss me if you like." She bent down to him but her cheek was covered with a fine, spotted veil and he drew back, letting the flowers drop to the floor of the porch. "Now don't be naughty, Octavius," said Helen laughing again, however, as she raised herself to say good-bye to the others. "You are becoming a very spoiled little boy at Saltbech. Good-bye dear, and be good while I am away." She blew him a kiss, allowed the twins and Dinah to kiss her through her veil, followed by their uncle, who gripped her hand and told her to enjoy herself.

"I have every intention of doing so," she assured him, her eyes sparkling.

"And where shall I find you, if I want to write to you?"

"Heaven alone knows. But I daresay I shall be able to send you a letter somewhere." And with another laugh and a final wave to them all she stepped into the cab, closely followed by Lovell with the jewel-case, and was driven away to the station.

Nobody had offered to see her off, and Dinah, balancing Octavius on her hip with her arms about him was aware that his face was buried in her shoulder and that it was warm and wet.

"Don't cry, my darling," she whispered.

"Not crying," said Octavius, but he did not lift his head.

"Then help me pick up your lovely flowers and we will put them in a vase in Mamma's room." The little boy nodded, wiped his eyes on his holland pinafore, and once down on his feet again was quick to pick up his flowers, and then taking the hand she held out to him he climbed the stairs to the pretty boudoir that overlooked the park.

A small cut-glass vase was there to receive them, and Dinah filled it with water from the bathroom almost next door. "There," she said as she put the flowers into it, "after a drink of water they will soon pick up. Shall we pick some flowers for her every day until she comes back?"

Octavius's grave eyes met hers and she thought she saw in them a touch of scorn, the scorn of a male for an ignorant woman. "She isn't coming back," he said.

"Why, Octavius, of course she is." Dinah hesitated. "Whatever made you think she wasn't?"

He looked round at the pretty room. "They've put dust covers over the chairs," he said, and trotted off upstairs to Nurse Blackwell.

Dinah stared at the wilting flowers in the cut-glass vase, and then she walked to the window and looked down on the park without really seeing it.

Why did her mother show such little regard for Octavius, she wondered. Looking back she remembered that her father had treated the child with far more indifference than he had shown the others, dismissing his baby love for flowers as unmanly. Perhaps as he was so much younger neither of his parents had really wanted him: seven children, they might have thought, were enough.

Darling Octavius. Somehow she must make it up to him, and in the meantime she tried to be of use to her uncle, offering to take some of his correspondence off his hands. Her handwriting was particularly fine and he was glad to accept her offer, and as she worked with him in his study in the mornings she learned more of his tolerant, gentle character every day.

One morning, soon after Lady Bretton had gone, the twins put their heads round the study door and asked if they might speak to her.

"Uncle Sep isn't here, is he?" asked Paul anxiously.

"No. He went to see old Mrs. Duffy in River Cottages. The Corporation wants to put her into the Easterley workhouse, and he is trying to get her into the All Saints almshouses, but so far they are being hardhearted about it. Dr. Bellingham says they are too busy quarrelling about the new lighting to be installed at the town hall to be bothered with people like Mrs. Duffy."

"Why must she move?" asked Paula.

"Because her son had to leave his post at the Saltbech Customs and take a less well-paid one with the Corporation, and he can no longer afford to give his mother enough to support her and pay her rent. But I daresay she will be very well looked after at the workhouse." Dinah smiled at the twins' solemn faces. "What did you want to speak to me about?"

"About the locked room," said Paula.

"The locked room?" Her eldest sister frowned. "What are you talking about? What locked room?"

"The room at the end of our corridor," said Paul. "The door is locked, and we want to know why."

"To keep out inquisitive children, I should think." Dinah smiled at them. "I don't know why it is locked, I am sure, but perhaps Uncle Sep keeps it as a storeroom for his photographic things. You know how keen he is on photography."

"I don't think it has anything to do with Uncle Sep's photography," said Paul. "His darkroom and camera and stand and everything like that is kept in the cellar. He took us down there one wet afternoon and showed it to us."

"We asked Maud," went on Paula. "She's the nice housemaid with the rosy cheeks—and she laughed and said she didn't know anything about it, and we had better ask Mrs. Jennings."

"And did you ask her?" asked their eldest sister gravely.

"Yes, we did and she wouldn't tell us," said Paula, while Paul went on, continuing the conversation in the way the twins did, as if one mind were speaking with two voices, "She said it was not our business. She was really quite cross about it."

"And she was never cross—even when Lovell was here," added Paula.

"I expect you came upon her at a busy time," said Dinah. "And I do not see why she should not keep some of the rooms locked if she wishes. If they are not required it is better to keep them shut up to save the maids any extra cleaning."

"But the room has got bars on the windows," said Paul. "You can see them from the outside, just where the big old sycamore tree grows. We climbed up into it and we looked in at the windows."

"Then that was very naughty of you," said Dinah severely. "You might have fallen and broken your legs or arms or something."

"It's such an old tree that it is easy to climb," said Paula. "Even you could climb it, Di. Easily. Though I expect your long skirt might get caught and you'd have to be got down with a ladder."

"Thank you, but I've no intention of climbing it or any other trees in Uncle Sep's garden."

"As I said, we looked in at the windows," went on Paula, "and they were dreadfully dirty outside, and with the iron bars half hiding them I couldn't see anything, but Paul crawled along a branch and wiped one of them with his handkerchief and he could see into the room."

"I couldn't see much," went on Paul, "because it was so dark inside. But it's a boy's room, Di. There's a cricket bat in one corner, and his bed is made as if he might be coming back to it today or tomorrow. And there's a beautifully made ship on the table. I wish you'd ask Uncle Sep whose room it is, Di, and when the boy is coming back."

Dinah was silent for a moment while they watched her hopefully, and then she said slowly: "Paul and Paula, I think I may know whose room that was. Aunt Margaret died after she and Uncle Sep had been married for two years, and she left a little boy—his name was Christopher—and I think it must have been his room, because I have been told that he died when he was quite small. But it looks as if poor Uncle Sep has had the room left just as it was to remember him by, and it would be unkind and cruel to ask him anything about it. You must promise me that you never will."

"Of course we won't, Di, now that we know why it is kept locked." Relieved that an explanation had been found for the locked room that had so intrigued them, they scampered off back to the schoolroom without giving it another thought.

Left to herself however, Dinah found that the thought of it came between her and her uncle's correspondence with some persistence. She had heard of the child that had been born to Uncle Sep's young wife, but she had always thought that he had died in infancy. Now it seemed that Christopher had at least grown big enough to be the possessor of a cricket bat and a model ship. Why then had they never met their cousin? And when did he die? And why did nobody ever speak of him?

It was a puzzle that made her vaguely uneasy. Obviously she could not discuss it with her uncle, and it was equally impossible to speak of it with any of the servants—not even with Mrs. Jennings.

But it remained a mystery all the same. A locked room, bars on the windows, a cricket bat and a model ship, and the bed made up as if the boy whose room it was might be coming home at any moment.

These things haunted her for the rest of the morning, and when she had finished with the correspondence she put on her hat, calling to Digger, who was now allowed the freedom of the house, and walked across the fields to the church.

She found her aunt's grave without much difficulty, though the grasses were deep in the churchyard and buttercups and wild parsley were blowing happily over the heads of those who lay there in their last sleep. Margaret Crichton's grave was neatly kept, and some of the red roses from the rectory rose garden had recently been placed in a gray stone vase under the headstone.

The inscription gave the name of the rector's wife, Margaret Anne, who had died in her twenty-third year, and although there had been plenty of room beneath the inscription for the words "and her son, Christopher," they were not there. She looked in vain for another grave, that of the boy, but there was no sign of it, only an empty plot beside that first grave.

What had happened then? Was Christopher still alive, and perhaps an invalid? Consumption, she thought—it was a disease that killed. If he had developed it, perhaps he had been sent away to a private sanatorium not far from Saltbech. She remembered how on the first of every month her uncle would have an early luncheon and go off to catch a train to some small village in the district, in order to see an invalid who used to live in the town.

She had taken it for granted that the invalid was an old parishioner and had thought no more about it, but now other things came back to her. The sadness on her uncle's face on the evenings of those days, for one thing, and she began to wonder if it could be Christopher that he visited and that was why he was so exhausted on his return.

But surely if Christopher had consumption he would not have lived so long? People died of it very rapidly, and there seemed to be no cure for it.

She counted the years from her aunt's death, and discovered that her cousin, if he were still alive, would be a young man by this time.

"He *must* have died," she told herself as she walked back to the rectory. "And it must have been under tragic circumstances, and that is why poor Uncle Sep never talks of it."

She took the path through the fields again, with Digger hunting rabbits all the way, and she came into the hall, dark after the sunlight outside and very quiet.

The grandfather clock at the foot of the stairs showed that it was ten minutes to twelve. In ten minutes' time the house would resound to the twins' voices and their stampede down the stairs from the schoolroom as they raced out for a ride on their ponies before lunch, accompanied by Coppard. And in ten minutes' time little Octavius would come back from his morning's walk with Nurse Blackwell, hungry for his dinner.

But just at that moment, the house was quite silent, the hall shadowed and rather frightening. She felt as if something in the shadows under the stairs was threatening her and full of danger.

She noticed too that Digger had not followed her into the hall but was sitting in the lobby, staring in, his ears pricked as if he could see something that she could not see, and that he did not like it very much.

Then suddenly his head turned and he raced off down the drive, barking a welcome, and she knew that her uncle was back. At the same moment the twins came tearing down the stairs, Octavius came back with Nurse, and the house came to life again, the shadows in the hall dispelled.

She followed Digger down the drive, and her uncle was at the gate, talking to Charles Bellingham. The faces of both men were grave and she tried to lighten them by saying, "Well, did you see Mrs. Duffy off into the workhouse?"

"They took her in last night, my dear," said her uncle gently. "But we went to see her this morning in Easterley."

"They had dressed her up in one of their long white aprons and put one of their white caps on her head." Charles's voice was harsh. "And they had put her poor old hands to work for her keep, hemming sheets as coarse and hard as cardboard."

Dinah looked up at him, puzzled by his anger. "But surely those are the kind of sheets she is accustomed to?" she said. "She is only an old working woman, Dr. Bellingham."

She saw him frown alarmingly, and then he gave her a faint and slightly contemptuous smile. "Of course," he said.

"She is only an old working woman and deserves nothing better. I beg your pardon, Miss Bretton. I am afraid I forgot." He lifted his hat and walked back quickly to the waiting trap.

As they turned to walk up the drive together Dinah slipped her hand into her uncle's arm. "He was angry with me," she said. "Why do I seem to offend that man? I do not mean to annoy him, but I do."

"Charles is sensitive over some things that you would not understand," said her uncle. "I am only thankful that old Duffy is dead, otherwise Mrs. Duffy would have the added grief of being parted from her husband and only allowed to see him for one hour in the week on a Sunday afternoon."

"But—that is cruel!" she cried, dismayed. "They cannot do that to the old and poor—"

"But they *do* do that to the old and the poor, my love," said Septimus, patting the hand in his arm. "And it is such things that put Charles in a rage, nothing else."

He said no more but Dr. Bellingham's words remained with Dinah for most of the day, accusing her of something though she could not think what.

At Bretton she had never come in contact with working people except to say good day to them and ask after their children, but one day she had gone down to the village post office with a special letter for Clive. Instead of waiting for one of the footmen to collect it with others from the family post box, she had gone with it herself, and found the post mistress in tears.

"I beg your pardon, miss," she had said when Dinah asked her what was the matter, "but it's my sister, you see, miss. She's just died, along of her fourth child, and the three that's left will hev to be put in an orphanage, poor mites, and they reckon they'll be separated and it 'ull break their 'earts."

Dinah went back to her mother and asked if something could not be done. "Cannot any of our farmers' wives take them in?" she said. "So that they will not be parted."

"My dear child, it is no business of yours or of mine," said Helen sharply. "What have we an agent for if he does not look into things like that? My housekeepers have always seen that there is a lying-in hamper of sheets and clothes and baby clothes and such like for the women on the estate when it is wanted, and I really think that is all that can be expected of us."

Thinking this over now, Dinah began to realize how far away they had been in reality from the smiling villagers, the bobbing women at the cottage gates, the rosy-cheeked children coming running out of school and stopping short at the side of the road to let Miss Bretton pass. Here in Saltbech things were on a smaller scale, and people mattered more because they were nearer.

The next morning at breakfast, she asked her uncle if she might go and visit Mrs. Duffy at the Easterley workhouse. "I thought I would walk down to her cottage first and pick some of her flowers to take her from her garden," she said. "It might be a comfort to her."

"It might indeed my dear, if your visit were allowed," he said. "But visitors are only allowed for one hour on a Sunday afternoon, and the warden is very strict. And I doubt if she would be allowed to accept them. There would be added trouble of finding a vase for them and keeping them by her bed in the dormitory, unless there is a windowsill handy." He thought for a moment and then he gave an exclamation. "I have it! Lady Collington will take you with her the next time she goes. She is one of the governors of the workhouse and everyone bows down before her. I will write to her today!"

A reply to his letter came at once. Lady Collington would be delighted to take Miss Bretton when she visited the Easterley workhouse on the following Wednesday and would call for her at ten o'clock.

Dinah was ready with a bunch of stocks and mignonette and rose buds picked from Mrs. Duffy's garden when the Collington carriage stopped at the rectory on Wednesday morning, and as she drove off with her ladyship she told her about Mrs. Duffy.

"It seems so dreadful that she should have been so summarily bundled off to the workhouse," she said.

"But, my dear, she could not go on without any support from her son while she waited for the All Saints Charity to act. The workhouse was the only solution, but we will hope it will not be forever." Her face was full of kindness, however, and she was evidently pleased that the rector's niece was interested in an object so near her heart. "I like to visit the workhouse and its inmates as often as I can," she told her young companion. "So many have no relations or friends who are able to see them. The workhouse is three miles from Easterley and eight from Saltbech, and the distances are too great."

The workhouse was a tall, bleak-looking building of yellow brick, with small narrow windows. It was surrounded by a high yellow brick wall, and the ground between house and wall was full of vegetables, cultivated by the ablest of the old men there.

The walls inside were painted brown, the floors right through had brown oilcloth, and there was a strong smell of carbolic—a smell which was to become very familiar to Dinah later on.

The warden's office was almost as cold and inhospitable as the corridor outside. There were only two wooden armchairs with leather seats for visitors, a small rug on the floor, and a swivel chair for the warden in front of a large, roll-top desk.

His welcome to Lady Collington was warm, however, and when she asked if Mrs. Duffy could have the flowers that Dinah had brought from her garden he only took a moment to decide. There was, he thought, a windowsill above Mrs. Duffy's bed, and he would see to it himself that a vase or jar of some sort was provided for the flowers.

Dinah was then taken into the large room where about sixty old women were sitting working under the windows. It had a fusty smell about it as if the old women were not encouraged to take many baths.

The warden conducted Miss Bretton to Mrs. Duffy, and provided a chair for her next to the old woman while he took Lady Collington on her usual tour of the building. She was a lady who liked to look into everything, and no cockroach dared to show its head in the kitchen quarters without being immediately spotted by her ladyship.

Mrs. Duffy was a little, white-haired, bright-eyed old lady, evidently determined to make the best of things now that she had got over the initial shock of the move. On learning that Dinah was the rector's niece, she greeted her with delight and took the flowers from her with tears in her eyes. "That rose, my dear, came from a cutting I took from my mother's garden when I was first wed," she told her. The stocks her son had planted for her, and he had sowed the mignonette because she was so fond of it. She told Dinah that her ladyship was a very kind lady, "And as fur the rector, I reckon he's a saint. I can't say the same fur Dr. Bellingham though, as he swears something frightful when he's put about. 'Doctor,' I says to 'im once, I says, 'You'll niver git to 'eaven if you swears like that.' 'Well, Mrs. Duffy,' 'e says, 'Seeing some of the people what are sure they're goin' there I don't know as I wants to join 'em.' I tells 'im 'e ought to be ashamed talking like that, but he only laffs. Mind you, 'e's a wunnerful kind gentleman, is Dr. Bellingham, fur all 'is swearing."

When Dinah went and promised to come again, the old woman took her hand in both of hers and said "God bless you," and for the first time since she had come to Saltbech Dinah felt that she had met somebody who not only understood her but was a friend.

When she arrived home there was a telegram from her mother saying that she had arrived safely and that the *Oleander* was as beautiful as ever, and a letter from her sister Julia, who said that she had been to a garden party in Putney. *"And who do you think I met there, Dinah, my love? Miss Maitland who is now engaged to be married to Major Morrell, and what is more she was wearing your ring!"*

The telegram and the letter spoke of different worlds. They no longer seemed very real.

All she could think about for the rest of the day was an old bright-eyed woman, and the tenderness with which she had touched the petals of the rose, the stocks and the mignonette.

Chapter Ten

The *Oleander* was a beautiful boat. Painted white, except for her two blue smokestacks, she danced like the lady she was at anchor off Marseilles. Her dinghy was sent to fetch Helen and her maid from the quay, and while her mistress enjoyed the short distance through the calm sea, Lovell turned pea-green and said that she was glad it was no farther.

When they came aboard she scuttled off to the cabin allotted to her down below, while Helen was greeted warmly by Lord and Lady Crowborne, and then by a man who got up lazily from his long deck-chair to take her hand. As she met his appraising eyes she felt slightly breathless.

"This is a surprise," she said.

"Vi did not tell you that I was to be aboard?" he asked

lazily. "She keeps quite a few secrets up those wide sleeves of hers." And his smile was as possessive as it had been five years ago. It was plain that he intended to continue their friendship from where it had left off.

Vi accompanied her to her cabin, a tiny but charming stateroom with an elegant French bed and French furniture and a Chinese carpet covering the floor. It was on the upper deck where all the guests' bedrooms were situated, together with their host and hostess's suite of rooms and the saloon, full of comfortable chairs and with windows looking out over the sea.

Vi asked after the children, and agreed that Dinah had been extremely stupid over her engagement. "Is she as pretty as ever?" she asked.

"She has gone off a lot," said Dinah's Mamma candidly. "So often these dark-haired girls do."

"And pretty Julia?"

Helen spoke of Julia with enthusiasm, and both agreed that Emmeline Bromley was a very good-natured woman, in fact, the pick of the Bretton sisters.

"I am very glad you did not go to Honoria's," said Vi. "She is a most dreadful snob. But I cannot see you settling down in Saltbech. I have never been there but I know exactly what it is like. I dislike those small provincial towns, except at election times, when they can be useful if one's husband stands as a candidate of course." She laughed. "But I cannot imagine you, my dearest Helen, in a rectory, organizing sewing bees and bazaars and all the things that they do in provincial rectories. You would have been bored to tears."

"I have been," agreed Helen, and when the rest of her children were enquired after she said she had brought their photographs and Vi should see them when Lovell had unpacked.

"The stupid woman cannot be seasick on a sea like this," she added.

"If she is, all you have to do is to ring for one of the stewardesses. I shall look forward to seeing those photographs, Helen." At the door she paused, a wicked twinkle in her eye. "Have you brought one of the youngest?" she asked in a whisper.

"Octavius? No, I have not," said Helen firmly.

"Is he like his father?"

"He grows more like him every day."

"It is just as well you did not bring his photograph then."

Vi looked back at her friend, smiling. "You know, with all his faults, Roger behaved very well over that."

"He could not do anything else. He kept mistresses in London for years."

"Most husbands do, but they can be tiresome when the boot is on the other foot."

"Roger was not sufficiently interested to be tiresome about it," said Helen lightly. "He gave the child his name on condition that I did not allow it to happen again."

The two friends looked at each other and laughed, and then a martyred Lovell came to unpack and they parted until dinner, when Helen was introduced to the other guests aboard.

She wore Dinah's lilac-colored dress that night, with the amethysts she had borrowed from Dinah round her neck and in her hair, and as Gerald Wakefield took her down to dinner in the dining saloon below he told her that she was looking more beautiful than ever.

"But then you are one of those women whom the years improve," he added.

"And I notice that your flattery does not get any less, either," she said and they both laughed, and she felt happier than she had done for five years.

Julia was enjoying every moment of her summer in London. From the moment when her aunt took her to her dressmaker to have a white ball-gown made for her Coming-out dance— "young girls," she told her, "must always wear white for their Coming-out dances"—to the evening of the dance itself, held in her uncle's house in Belgrave Square, it was a season of bliss.

Even her social blunders, while covering her with shame, were laughed off by her good-natured aunt.

At times she felt a slight feeling of guilt because the pretty dresses that had been in Dinah's trousseau were so much admired by her aunt and her friends, and she occasionally felt she should not be feeling so happy so soon after her father's death.

But Roger Bretton had never shown any great affection for his children. He had played with them sometimes when they were small, and seen that they were taught to ride when they were older, but he had never shown them any real warmth, perhaps because his was a light nature, not given to any real depth of feeling.

While they had all been slightly afraid of him, they had

more affection for their mother, although she was apt to retire to bed or to her boudoir sofa when anything upset her. They were allowed into the drawing room after tea when they were small, brushed and clean and dressed in party dresses and best suits, but after half an hour or so they were dispatched to the nursery or the schoolroom and seen no more. As they grew older it had been Dinah upon whom they had depended most for confidences and consolation, and then after she became engaged to Clive Morrell and threatened to desert them, they had drawn closer together as a family, while remaining independent of each other.

They had learned to think and act for themselves, and having been left, in the parents' frequent absences, to tutors, schoolmasters and governesses, their behavior was sometimes not quite in line with others of their breed. Julia in particular had been extremely independent and spoke out in a way that while it might amuse her Aunt Emmeline had at times to be curbed.

"Ladies do not argue with their guests," she told her once after a dinner party where the guests had all been rather elderly. "Nor do they say out loud, when an elderly gentleman is expressing his views, that it is a lot of nonsense."

Julia blushed. "But it *was* nonsense," she protested. "He was a silly old man."

"My darling child, a duke, however senile he may be, is *never* a silly old man. When in Society, Julia, you must learn to curb your tongue."

Julia found it very difficult to curb that offending member, and when something annoyed or interested her she found it hard to keep her peace. But nothing hindered her from enjoying the summer: the dinner parties where there were usually some young men to take her in to dinner to make up for all the silly old men, the theater parties, and coming home through lamp-lit streets accompanied by the musical clipclopping of the horses' hoofs, to the supper of sandwiches and wine that had been left out for them on the diningroom table. Then there were the balls and supper parties and garden parties and receptions.

It was one afternoon at the beginning of July when they went to the garden party in Putney, given by a wealthy client of her Uncle Edmund Bromley, who accompanied them. It was a large square house, and it stood back from the road leading to the Common with an imposing, gravelled carriage drive in front of it. Borders on either side of the drive and those under the big ground-floor windows were filled with bedding plants of the kind so beloved by head gardeners throughout Britain at that time. Scarlet geraniums, white daisies and blue lobelia, planted in lines as straight as rows of soldiers in red, white and blue uniforms.

Behind the house was a large lawn, not spacious perhaps according to some standards, but very beautifully kept, and it had a very much smaller fruit and vegetable garden behind it.

On the afternoon of the garden party it was so warm that Julia and her aunt had been glad of the protection of their parasols on the drive through the Fulham streets to Putney, and when they arrived they were greeted by the hot sound of a brassy regimental band playing to the guests assembled on the lawn and in the large marquee where tea and champagne and ices and strawberries and cream were being served.

Her host, Sir Rudolf Stein, was what was known in the City as a financier, and when she asked her uncle what a financier was, he replied in a studied legal fashion that it was assumed that he was somebody who liked money.

"How dull!" said pretty Julia, and her uncle had looked at his wife with lifted eyebrows and they both laughed.

"That is a singularly refreshing view of it," he said. "And not one that is frequently heard these days."

She was introduced to her host and hostess and while her aunt and uncle greeted the friends who happened to be there she was handed over to a young man who appeared to have no ideas beyond Ascot and Goodwood. At last in desperation she asked him if he would mind asking the bandmaster if he could persuade his band to play something else than regimental marches. The young man did not appear to think this an unreasonable request, and went off at once, and while she was waiting for him to come back she noticed a lady beside her take off her left-hand glove and the ring on the third finger shocked her into speech. "Why," she said without thinking, "you are wearing my sister's ring!"

The lady, who was not much older than herself though a great deal more self-possessed, stared at her for an icy moment without speaking, and then pointedly turned her back on her and went on talking to the friends who had her attention.

"Oh dear," thought Julia, utterly snubbed, "I must not *move* from Aunt Emmie's side in future."

She was looking round for her aunt in the crush when her

uncle made his way towards her with another young man and introduced him as "Mr. Jonathan Cottrell."

He was a good looking young man and his eyes were studying her with lively interest: she had her mother's coloring, with fair hair and wide blue eyes, but whereas Helen's were cold Julia's were warm and human. She was dressed in a white silk dress with a pale blue stripe in it, her hat was a wide one of white chiffon with a white rose on the brim, her parasol of white lace lined with pink, and Mr. Cottrell thought she looked rather like an exquisite country flower that had found its way into a hothouse.

As he took off his hat to her and she bowed and said a shy "How d'you do," she wondered if he, too, would only talk about Ascot and Goodwood, and her heart sank. She wondered, too, if he had seen the well-merited snub that she had just received, because after all she had been guilty of two indiscretions at once, the first in speaking to somebody to whom she had not been introduced, and the second in mentioning a lady's jewelry to her face. Behind her back it was permissible to tear it or her dress to shreds, but to comment on either to the wearer was unforgivable.

But instead of talking about Ascot and Goodwood, Mr. Cottrell looked down at the disconsolate and very blue eyes that met his, and asked with some concern if anything was the matter. "You do not look very happy," he said.

"I am not happy," she admitted. "At least, not at the moment. My aunt says that I must think before I speak, and I do try, but when I saw that ring on the lady's finger—so exactly like the one that somebody gave my sister before he went to Malta—I forgot that I had not been introduced, and blurted out that she was wearing my sister's ring. I did not mean it, of course. It was only a joke, because it was so *very* like Dinah's. And she just stared and turned her back on me without a *single* word, and I felt dreadful. Of course, she was perfectly right. I should *never* have spoken to her without having been introduced."

"I saw you speak to her," said her companion pleasantly. "And I witnessed her behavior—which was not very kind. Supposing we find a table in the marquee and eat some strawberries and cream to take the taste out of your mouth?" It was a very pretty mouth.

Julia said she did not think she felt like strawberries and cream just then.

"Then what about a stroll in the rose garden? It is beyond

that high red-brick wall, and we shall not be so deafened by the band if we make our way there."

"Oh dear!" She stopped short. "There was somebody who was going to ask them to play something else besides regimental marches because I asked him to, but I've forgotten his name, and he was very kind and went off at once."

"Blades," he said smiling. "He's an ensign in the regiment so the bandmaster will listen to him. They have stopped playing marches now, I think."

"Yes. They're playing airs from *The Pirates of Penzance*. But Mr. Blades may be looking for me." She hesitated, not wishing to be dragged back to Ascot and Goodwood again. "Do you think I should wait for him—to thank him?"

"Supposing we allow him to find us?" suggested Mr. Cottrell. They went through the red-brick archway into the rose garden, and it was shady and cool and the roses were very beautiful.

"Do you know who she is?" asked Julia, following her own sometimes disconcerting lines of thought.

"The lady with the ring, do you mean?"

"Yes."

"I do. She is a Miss Caroline Maitland."

"Maitland." She knitted her slender brows. "Do you mean the Miss Maitland who is the daughter of the South African millionaire?"

"That is the one. Have you met him?"

"Oh no, but my uncle met him at his club, and everyone is talking about him—because he is so very rich." She paused and under the shade of her hat her blue eyes were suddenly startled and questioning. "But if she is Miss Caroline Maitland she must be the girl who is now engaged to Major Clive Morrell?"

"She is." He watched her expressive face and waited.

"Then in that case it may well have been Dinah's ring that she was wearing," she said with a curl of her lip.

The name of Bretton came back to his mind and he suddenly knew where he had heard it before. "Is your sister the Miss Bretton who broke off her engagement to Major Morrell a week before the wedding?" he asked.

"At his request." He saw her lips close firmly and her blue eyes grow suddenly angry, before she added with a dignified air that made her more charming than ever, "I think if you do not mind we will not discuss the late Major Clive Morrell."

"The late! But he is not dead!"

"He is to my family, Mr. Cottrell. Even my dear Uncle Sep, who is a clergyman and one of the dearest, kindest people on earth, said that he had behaved like a scoundrel, so you see it will be better if we change the conversation. Is that a fruit garden through that other arch?"

"All that is left of it." He accompanied her through the arch to what had been about an acre of fruit garden and was now cut in half, coming up sharp at the bottom with a plain wooden fence.

"Sir Rudolf," he told her smilingly, "had an offer for half his fruit garden because the railway wanted to make a cutting just where it stood. He sold the land to the railway company at an outrageous price, and has been boasting about it ever since."

"A financier," nodded Julia. "Somebody who is very fond of money. Sir Rudolf must have been *very* fond of it to give up his garden to a railway."

They walked up to the wooden fence and looked over it and down at the cutting below and agreed that as a thing of beauty if could not hold a candle to the half of the fruit garden that was gone.

"Sir Rudolf unfortunately is not the only one to attach great importance to money," said Mr. Cottrell as they made their way back to the rose garden. "My cousin, Caroline Maitland, has been a prey for fortune hunters for years—ever since she came out. She will have a great deal of money when she marries."

"Your cousin?"

"Yes. An aunt of mine married Stephen Maitland and went out to South Africa with him, where she died, and he made a fortune out of a gold mine."

"I did not know that anybody made fortunes out of gold mines," said Julia ruefully. "My father lost his fortune over a South African gold mine, because it did not exist."

"Uncle Stephen's exists, I can assure you. He is in England with Caroline for the summer: they have a suite of rooms in a West End hotel."

"I wish Papa's had existed, then we should not have had to burden darling Uncle Sep with all of us in Saltbech."

"Is that where your sister is living now?"

"Yes. There are eight of us altogether, and with Mamma, Uncle Sep wanted us to make it our home until we can return to Bretton, which will not be for six years, when Harold comes of age. Mamma has gone off to stay with some friends on their yacht in the Mediterranean, and I hope her maid, Lovell, will be very seasick, because according to my sister she has been at the bottom of most of the trouble at the rectory. She was upset from the first because Uncle Sep has no butler."

"I daresay lady's-maids do like to have butlers in their servants' halls."

"Oh yes. Lovell is very grand. She says the scullery maid is common."

"I daresay she is, but then so are a number of the workers on my father's estate, and a nicer set of fellows you could not wish to meet."

"Your father's estate?" She sounded apprehensive. "Are you heir to it?"

"No." He laughed, delighted with her youth and naiveté. "I have two brothers, mercifully, who are older than I am. I am only a younger son."

"How much nicer for you!" She put down her parasol as they returned to the shade of the rose garden. "Do you know I think I should like some strawberries, after all?"

They made their way back to the crowded lawn, and in a corner of the big tent they found a table and sat there, companionably eating strawberries and cream and drinking tea rather than champagne.

"What a pity," she said, as she ate her strawberries, "that you did not get engaged to your cousin before she met—that person."

"The late lamented, you mean?" His eyes were laughing into hers but she shook her head.

"I am serious," she said. "Being a younger son you would have been glad of a rich wife."

"But I would not have married Caroline. I know her pretty well, you see, because I was in South Africa for a time making a study of gold-mining, and it did not appeal to me very much so I came home. Caroline is very pretty to look at, but she is very spoiled, and if anyone should cross her, Heaven help him."

"Then I must see what Aunt Emmeline can do for you," she told him comfortingly. "She knows lots of girls, and I am sure she could find one with a fortune who would be suitable for you."

"I am afraid I am rather particular about things like that." He dropped a lump of sugar into the clear golden depths of his teacup and stirred it thoughtfully. "But what about you? Are you looking for a rich husband?"

"Of course." She laughed at him wickedly. "Why do you think Aunt Emmeline is giving me a Season in London, except with the idea of getting me off poor Uncle Sep's hands? But I shall want a *very* rich man, mind you, because I have not a penny."

"You might try your luck with the gentleman over there, then—the one talking to the lady in the red hat—so very warm a color for such a hot day. He is a millionaire twice over, so I have been told."

Julia's eyes followed his to an extremely stout gentleman with a black beard and a cigar, standing in the entrance to the marquee with the lady in the unfortunate hat.

"He's very stout, isn't he?" she said softly. "And very old—"

"He doesn't think so. He is a widower, but he has an eye for pretty girls. He would probably give you a house in Park Lane."

She shook her head.

"And a place in the country as well."

Again came the shake, rather more emphatically this time.

"And a yacht like the one your Mamma is on."

"No, I am afraid not."

"But you cannot afford to be romantic when you are marrying for money," he reminded her.

She put down her cup and he put down his and they laughed, much as the twins Paul and Paula would have laughed over a shared joke. "What a lot of nonsense we are talking!" she said. But it was pleasant nonsense, all the same, and he was sorry when her aunt came and swept her away.

"You seemed to be getting on very well with Mr. Cottrell," Emmeline said as the carriage took them home.

"He is a nice man," said Julia. "In fact I think he is quite the nicest I've met since I've been staying with you, Aunt Emmie. He didn't want to talk about racing all the time."

"For a Cottrell he is certainly the best of the bunch," agreed her uncle, and Julia glanced at him anxiously.

"Should I not have talked to him for so long?" she asked.

"Not at all. You made quite a conquest."

He smiled while her aunt took her hand and squeezed it. "Darling Julie," she said. "You are a pet, and I love you dearly in spite of all my scolding."

Chapter Eleven

The Honorable Jonathan Cottrell walked into the drawing room of his uncle's suite that evening, and found his cousin Caroline Maitland there alone. She was dressed in a singularly beautiful ball-dress, and her head was bent over one of her long white gloves, as she re-buttoned one of the twelve pairs of tiny buttons that had come undone.

"You are going to a ball, I take it?" he said.

"I am."

"And with Major Morrell in attendance?"

"Why not? Is he not my fiancé?"

"Unfortunately, yes."

She looked at him resentfully. "I cannot think why you dislike Clive so much."

"I do not know that I dislike him any more than I like him. But he puzzles me—or shall I say his friends puzzle me? You would think that some of them would say, 'Oh, Clive Morrell—yes, a thundering good chap. I was at school with him.' Or, 'Clive Morrell? One of my oldest friends and one of the best.' But they do nothing of the sort. They shut up like an army of clams, and little Miss Bretton is no exception to the rule. She refused to discuss him and referred to him as 'the late Major Morrell,' because he is dead to her family."

"You mean that insufferable little girl who had the impertinence to speak to me about my ring?"

"Yes. A nice child—very young and very pretty."

"Bretton?" she frowned. "I suppose it was her sister who was engaged to Clive—"

"That is the one."

"And she jilted him at the last moment before the wedding." She was full of indignation. "Clive has told me all about it. It hurt him terribly."

"Mrs. Duncan," he was beginning, when she cut him short.

"Do not speak to me about that insufferable woman. The lies she spread about poor Clive were quite abominable."

"I was going to say," said Jonathan mildly, "Mrs. Duncan was the wife of his colonel when he was in Malta, I think, and this afternoon, after Mr. and Mrs. Bromley had gone, taking their niece with them, I happened to run across the Duncans' son Frank, who has been commissioned in his father's regiment and is joining them in India next month when they move on from Malta. He said his mother was furious about the broken engagement, and had quite a different story to tell. It appears that everything was ready for Miss Bretton to sail with her at the beginning of March when the poor girl had a letter from Clive asking her to break off the engagement as it would come better from her than from him, or some such rubbish. Frank thinks Clive had got himself in a bit of a tangle with another girl out there in Malta, and wanted to free himself from the Bretton family, which certainly had fallen on hard times."

His cousin was silent for a moment and then she said she did not believe a word of it, but she said it uncertainly.

"It is odd, all the same, that Miss Julia Bretton should have recognized your ring," said Jonathan.

"As it happens," Caroline said crushingly, "it cannot be the same ring, because Clive had mine made specially for me from some of his family jewels. He took them to Cartier's to have them re-set, choosing the setting himself."

"I wonder if he said as much to Dinah Bretton?" said Jonathan. "There is always one way in which you could find out, I suppose, and that is by going down to Saltbech to see her yourself and ask her outright if she recognizes her ring. I believe the train journey from London is quite an easy one."

"I would not dream of doing such a thing. Are you coming with us tonight?"

"No thank you. The garden party was sufficient, and I have no small talk left. Also I do not like fashionable crushes."

She had pulled at the glove button so angrily that it came off and she got up. "I must have another pair of gloves," she said, and whisked out of the room to find her maid.

Her father passed her outside and cocked an enquiring eye at his nephew. "What's the matter with Caroline?" he asked.

Jonathan told him about the incident of the ring at the garden party that afternoon, and Stephen Maitland listened in silence. He too had an instinctive distrust of Major Morrell.

"Well, if Caroline will not go down to Saltbech," he said

then, "I think I might go myself and have a chat with Miss Bretton's uncle to set my mind at rest. If anyone knows the truth of the business of the broken engagement, he should. You are not coming with us tonight? Sensible fellow. I am beginning to wonder why I ever decided to spend a summer in London." After a moment he added, "Caroline is being escorted by Clive to the family place on Friday to be looked over, one presumes, by Lord Morrell. I have promised to join them there on Saturday, which will leave me Friday free. I daresay I might make use of it to visit Saltbech. What is the uncle's name? Is he a Bretton, too?"

"No. His name is Septimus Crichton."

"Septimus Crichton, hey? I believe I was at the Varsity with him. He was quite a well known cricketer at one time, and if it's the same fellow he's a nice chap, though I've never met him since I came down. There was some tragedy about his marriage, I believe, the details of which I do not remember. I think his wife died young, or something of the sort. It will be interesting to meet him again."

So it happened that on the following Friday morning, just as Septimus had finished going through his correspondence with Dinah in his study, a visitor was announced, who, from his quiet approach, had evidently walked up from the station.

"Mr. Crichton?" he said, as Septimus got up from his desk to meet him and Dinah whisked out of the room with a bundle of letters to answer. "It is Septimus, isn't it? You will not remember me, though we were both at Clare. Stephen Maitland."

"But of course I remember you!" Septimus shook him warmly by the hand. "My dear fellow, how nice to see you again after all these years. What are you doing now? I have got to go out in half an hour's time, but it is only a short visit in the town and you must come with me. And you will stay to luncheon, of course."

The windows were open onto the garden, and Maitland asked if they could not walk there in the sunshine. "The fact is that London stifles me," he said. "I feel as if I could not breathe. I have always detested crowded rooms and close air."

They walked out together to a seat under the trees and Septimus asked if he were staying in the neighborhood.

"No, I caught an early train and came down especially to see you."

"Indeed?" It seemed early for a social call, but Septimus

waited to hear more and presently Stephen Maitland explained.

"You may or may not have heard that my daughter Caroline is engaged to be married to a chap who has recently resigned his commission in the army—a fellow by the name of Morrell."

He saw the smile fade from the rector's face.

"I believe I did hear that Morrell had got himself engaged to another girl, but I did not pay much attention to it, I am afraid. I hope she will be happy with him."

"I am not so sure that she will, and that is why I am here, Crichton. I am always gathering strange little bits of information about Major Clive Morrell, and I wish I could fit the pieces together. It was the last bit that sent me to you for enlightenment. What was the true story behind the broken engagement between him and your niece?"

"Dinah?" Septimus was silent, clasping his hands between his knees, his eyes on the lawn. "You saw her just now. She deals with my correspondence for me."

"That quiet little creature?" Stephen was surprised. "But she doesn't look as if—" he broke off. "Was there another man?"

"No."

"Then why did she break the engagement at the last moment?"

"She would never have broken it off. I ought not to say this, I suppose, but she was in love with Clive Morrell and due to sail with his colonel's wife, Mrs. Duncan, the following week. Her clothes were all packed, even to her wedding dress. Presents were pouring in, and when I saw her for what I thought would be the last time before she left for Malta for her wedding, she was radiant with happiness in spite of her father's death."

"And yet she broke it off?"

"Entirely at his request. I never saw the letter that he wrote to her, but I understand that she showed it to three others before it was destroyed—one was her sister Julia, who was as furious as any young girl could be at the thought of her sister being treated in such a fashion, the second was her great-aunt, my Aunt Alice Crichton, who said that Dinah was perfectly right to end the engagement, and the third was her mother, Lady Bretton, who, being of a more worldly turn of mind, advised her not to be a fool, but to pretend she had never received the major's letter and to go out and marry him as arranged. Dinah did not need a great deal of advice on the subject. From what I could make out it was plain from his letter that Morrell no longer wanted her, and neither did he want his career possibly ruined by marrying a girl who would bring him no money. So he made the excuse that the stories circulating about her father's death—that it might have been suicide—had so angered his uncle Lord Morrell, on whom his future depended, that he had forbidden him to marry her. Rather than subject him to ruin, Dinah had no alternative. If you wish to speak to her about it yourself you have my permission to do so, but I need hardly say that I would rather you did not. The subject is still too sore a one to be raked up lightly by a stranger."

"I appreciate that. But if I could catch him out in a lie I wonder if—" Stephen Maitland broke off and then said slowly: "Do you know if your niece's engagement ring had any distinguishing mark by which it could be recognized?"

"I do not know, but she would."

"Would she mind very much if I asked her?"

Septimus hesitated, and then he said he would go and fetch her, adding, "But treat her gently, Maitland."

"I will, indeed."

Dinah came out to the two men wondering what they wanted with her and Stephen Maitland said hesitantly, "Miss Bretton, I have something to ask you which may seem unpardonably impertinent, but believe me I do not intend it as an impertinence. I am only thinking of my daughter's happiness."

"Your daughter, Mr. Maitland?"

"Yes. My daughter Caroline who is engaged to be married to Clive Morrell." He saw the light die in her eyes and her face flush faintly, and he hurried on, "There is only one thing I want to know. Can you describe to me the engagement ring that Clive Morrell gave you?"

"Why, yes. There was a large pearl in the center surrounded by an amethyst, a diamond, an opal, a ruby and an emerald, the stones spelling the word 'adore.' "

"I see. And was there any distinguishing mark inside the ring, for instance?"

"There were our initials—C and D— He had them engraved there inside it. Why do you want to know?"

"Because your sister Julia told my daughter that she was wearing your ring."

"Oh Julia!" A smile flickered across Dinah's face. "She is always blurting out things when she should not. Major Morrell had my ring made from his mother's jewels, and I daresay he did the same for Miss Maitland."

"And there is no other mark at all?"

She frowned. "I cannot remember any. Oh yes, there is a tiny crack in the opal, where I caught it one day on one of the stone vases on the terrace outside the north drawing room at Bretton. But you would have to use a magnifying glass to see it, although I was very upset about it at the time." She drew a breath. "Is that all you wanted to know, Mr. Maitland?"

"All, thank you, Miss Bretton, and I apologize for having distressed you."

"You have not distressed me at all," said Dinah, speaking with quiet dignity. "Nothing Major Morrell can do will ever distress me again." She turned from him to her uncle. "That letter of the colonel's from the officers' mess at the barracks, in which he is challenging the county team under your leadership again this year at the end of this month. Shall I say that you will be pleased to accept his challenge?" She was smiling now and Mr. Maitland thought how charming she was, and his anger against Clive Morrell grew.

"Why not?" said Septimus. "Your brothers will be home to swell the county team, and we shall be able to find a full eleven, I am quite sure. Accept the challenge with pleasure, my dear, and say that the match will be held in Folly Fields as usual."

Dinah went off, and Mr. Maitland refused an invitation to stay to luncheon and went back to London on the next train.

He left Saltbech not at all reassured with his daughter's choice of a husband, and the following few days that he spent in Lord Morrell's large country house did nothing to alter his opinion.

The way Clive Morrell fawned on the old man made his blood pressure rise, and he wondered that his lordship could receive it with such evident pleasure. After they got back to their apartment in their London hotel he spoke his mind about it to Caroline, and was laughed at for his pains.

"Naturally Clive must humor the old man," she said carelessly. "Otherwise one of his hard-up cousins will worm his way into the estates and the family fortune. Clive wants to keep it all in the Morrell family." Then, as her father was silent, she continued impatiently: "Why were you so mysterious about your jaunt last Friday? Where did you go? You would not say a word to anybody about it?"

"For a very good reason. I went to Saltbech to see Septimus Crichton."

"And who on earth is Septimus Crichton?"

"He is a parson, and uncle to Sir Roger Bretton's children, to whom he has given a home in his very large rectory."

"Indeed?" She studied him suspiciously. "And why did you go to see him?"

"I wanted to find out the truth about Clive's broken engagement to Miss Bretton, and the truth was largely what I fancied it might be. He wrote to her asking her to break it off, not the other way round. Her uncle says she was devoted to him."

"I do not believe it." Her head went up. "Naturally Miss Bretton would put things in the best possible light where she was concerned, and the worst for Clive. This stupid parson believed every word she said, as he would do."

"I saw Miss Bretton for a few minutes, and she did not strike me as a young woman who cared to speak at all about the matter, in fact she told me that she had not the slightest interest in Clive Morrell, now or in the future. When I told her that her sister had thought she recognized your engagement ring, she simply said it was quite possible that Morrell had had your ring made from his mother's jewels in a similar design. I asked her to describe hers, and the description was exactly like the one you are wearing, and as she did not seem the slightest bit interested, I asked her if there were any distinguishing marks by which she would recognize her ring, and she had to think before she said there were the initials C and D inscribed inside it, and that the opal had a tiny crack in it, only discernible under a magnifying glass."

"Did she say what the initials stood for?" asked Caroline, but the scorn had left her eyes and her face was unusually interested.

"She said that they were their initials and that Clive had them put inside the ring.

Caroline took off her ring and examined the tiny initials inscribed inside, a C and a D. She remembered she had asked what they stood for, and he had replied in his easy way, "Why what could they stand for but 'Caroline' and 'Devotion'?" She said in a strained voice, "Is your magnifying glass on your writing table, Papa?"

He gave it to her and she took the ring to the window and examined it minutely until she discovered the tiny crack in the opal. She returned the glass without a word.

"Well?" he said. "Is it the same ring?"

"It certainly seems as if Miss Julia Bretton was right when she said I was wearing her sister's ring," she conceded.

"What are you going to do? Face him with lying to you? Or are you going to dismiss him?"

"Oh no, nothing like that." She laughed and sat down by the window turning the ring over in her hand. "I have a far better plan."

Clive Morrell had deceived her over this, why should he not have deceived her in other things as well? But this time he had met his match. She was not a Dinah Bretton to creep into a corner to lick her wounds. Her face hardened. It was a beautiful face with its chestnut hair and dark eyes, but there were times when it could be entirely devoid of feeling. She said after a few minutes' thought:

"Next Tuesday is your birthday, Papa. Shall we celebrate it with a trip up the river as far as Hampton Court and back? You could hire a houseboat—one of those lovely boats with geraniums hanging over the rail of the top deck and a saloon large enough to accommodate about twenty people for a champagne lunch. Would it not be enjoyable?"

Her eyes were sparkling now, and there was a look on her face that warned him she was up to mischief.

"I admit that it would be enjoyable," he said. "But why a houseboat? And what are you plotting? Are you going to tip Clive into the river?"

"Oh dear, no. What a shocking thought! As if I would treat my darling Clive so brutally."

"Then what the devil are you up to?"

"You will find out," she said with a wicked little laugh. "And so will my darling Clive."

The houseboat was hired, a lovely boat painted white with a striped red and white awning over the top deck, and red geraniums, as Caroline had requested, hanging over the rails. There was a small orchestra to play the latest dance tunes, and the luncheon in the saloon included salmon and hothouse peaches and ices and champagne. Everyone said how delightful it was to get on to the river for a day, away from the heat and smoke and smells of London streets.

It was certainly a day that some at least would remember. It was as they were returning through Teddington Lock, as they waited to be lowered to the level of the river on the other side, that Miss Maitland complained of the heat and took off

109

her gloves. There was such a clamor going on from the paddles of the boat and from cockneys out for the day in rowing skiffs, their blazers all the colors of the rainbow, and girls in pretty dresses trying to keep them safe from the dripping oars of the young men who were taking them down the river, that nobody heard the small plop of something that fell into the water from the upper deck of the houseboat.

It was not until they arrived home that Miss Maitland discovered that she had lost her engagement ring.

"I know how it happened," she told the dismayed Major Morrell. "It was in Teddington Lock. I was so hot that I pulled off my gloves and the ring must have come off with them and dropped into the river." She shook her head and sighed. "I am afraid it will never be found in all that mud."

"It might be," he said eagerly. "I will go up there tomorrow and have a talk to the lock-keeper—"

"Oh, I wouldn't have you do that for the world," she said smiling. "After all, it was a second-hand ring, wasn't it, Clive?" She saw his disconcerted face and the flush that swept up into it, and went on, "You did say it was your mother's, did you not? So charming. But I would rather have one of my own. So we will go to Bond Street tomorrow morning, darling, and you shall buy me a new one. I think I will have rubies—are not the best called Pigeons' Blood? Such a horrid name for such beautiful stones. And when we have selected the stones, they can advise you what setting to have. A surround of large diamonds, I would say, would look the best. I will come with you darling, tomorrow morning, and we will visit Cartier's together."

A few days later she showed her father the new ring that had been made for her, and he whistled as he saw it.

"Isn't it a beauty?" she said.

"A beauty indeed. And it must have cost Master Clive a great deal of money."

"I did not inquire about that, of course," she said. "And I daresay Clive will get his uncle to pay, in any case."

"And is that your revenge on Clive for his deception? A much more expensive ring?"

"Certainly not." She flashed the jewels in the sunshine from the window and laughed. "This is only the beginning," she said.

Chapter Twelve

Shortly after Lady Bretton's departure the new bicycle, steel-framed, that Septimus had ordered for Dinah, arrived from Coventry, and although Dinah thanked him for it and professed herself as being most grateful for his generous gift, if it had not been for the insistence of the twins it would probably have remained unused in the coach-house where they kept their own bicycles.

But the twins would not be denied. "I'll hold you on," Paul told her while Paula said that if Miss Stroud could ride a second-hand bicycle that she had bought in the bicycle shop in the High Street, surely Dinah could ride her beautiful new one.

"That does not follow at all," said their eldest sister unhappily. "And I would point out that Miss Stroud only had to buy another bicycle because you had been using her old one at Bretton to learn on, and you had damaged both pedals and bent the handlebars beyond repair."

"The one she bought here is much better than the one she had at Bretton," said Paula. "It has a dress guard and both the brakes work—only the front one worked in the old one—and the bell rings, and what is more, it has a lamp so that she can ride it in the dark."

"Miss Stroud never rides her bicycle in the dark," said Dinah. "And I know I shall fall off, which will be undignified to say the least of it. Besides, I might break an arm."

"You will ride just as well as Miss Stroud when you have found your balance," said Paul comfortingly. She found it difficult to do so, much to her disgust and their amusement.

"You mustn't look down at your feet or at the handlebars," Pauls exhorted her as they picked up the bicycle and waited for her to mount it again. "You must look straight ahead."

"So that I can see the next tree I am going to ride into?" she said.

But encouraged by them and by Miss Stroud, and strengthened by her own determination not to be defeated, she practised riding the bicycle until before long there came a day when she was able to venture on a wobbling ride down the drive by herself, and shortly afterwards she ventured upon the road outside the gates, accompanied by Miss Stroud and the twins.

Very soon she began to wonder why she had made such a fuss about learning to ride, as the bicycle became her greatest joy, freeing her from the necessity of borrowing the rector's horse and trap when she wanted to venture beyond Saltbech. One day, she hunted out one of her last summer's white dresses and took it down to Mrs. Bender, the laundry woman who came up every week to fetch the rectory washing, taking it home in her husband's cart, and returning with it as regularly as clockwork the following Friday in the same conveyance.

Dinah had been asked to a tennis party at Lady Crockett's and she was determined to go, although her tennis was not of the best as she had only had a few practice games with her two elder brothers and her sisters at Bretton the year before, and she had to admit that as a player she was not a great deal of good. But she decided that she could no longer wear black dresses, especially for a tennis party, and so she bicycled the four miles to Mrs. Bender's cottage at the mouth of the river, opposite a solitary inn named *The Ship,* where Mr. Bender spent a great deal of his time and most of his wife's hard-earned cash.

The cottage was as lonely as the inn. It stood on a small promontory, its front windows looking out to sea, and behind it on wires strung between strong posts with tall props made of long forked branches, were the billowing sheets and garments that Mrs. Bender washed, ironed and returned so promptly. She asked Dinah into her kitchen, a tiny room warm with the smell of washing, and hot irons and soapsuds, with two china dogs on the chimneypiece and in the center a small china house, with two doorways through which an old lady with a basket on her arm and an old gentleman with a raised umbrella alternately came and went, according to the weather. The old lady was out today, because it was such a fine sunny day, but Dinah could not help wondering why the old gentleman did not stay out permanently with his umbrella up in the steamy atmosphere of the cottage.

She showed Mrs. Bender what she wanted done—a white skirt to be washed and a white blouse with a stiff collar and tiny tucks down the front—fortunately the leg-of-mutton sleeves had been coming in when it was made for her at Bretton—and Mrs. Bender knew exactly what to do, and promised it by the following Friday.

Dinah left the tennis dress with her, and as the breeze was blowing off the sea and the road back across the flat fen countryside had no hills to impede her, she came back faster than when she went, and did not notice the narrowness of the road until a horse and trap suddenly appeared in front of her.

She put on her brakes and jumped off as the horse was pulled up short. The driver of the trap looked down at her with some amusement as he took off his hat: there was no groom with Dr. Bellingham that afternoon.

"You are a long way from home," he told her. "But I must apologize for coming on you so suddenly."

"You should have a bicycle bell," she told him severely. "Or a motor horn, like that on Mr. Whatley's motorcar."

"And set Whitestar bolting?" he asked mildly. "I congratulate you on your bicycling, Miss Bretton. For a novice, you are doing very well."

She thanked him and said she had never dreamed there was so much hazard attached to riding a bicycle. "It was a long time before I dared go out alone on the roads. I couldn't help remembering all the things I could meet there, like farm horses and haycarts and herds of bullocks and flocks of sheep, and other bicycles, and carriages, and errand boys and butchers' carts, and even perhaps Mr. Whatley's motorcar. If I met that, I know I should lose my head and ride straight into it."

"The chauffeur would be very displeased. He would not approve of the paint on his bonnet being scratched."

"The bonnet? Oh, you mean the motorcar's bonnet. What part is that? The front?"

"The front part, yes." While she had been speaking he had been studying the picture she made, standing there with her bicycle on the grass verge and smiling up at him in the way that he was beginning to find so attractive on the rare occasions that they met. Her dark hair was blowing out from under her little sailor hat with its black ribbon, and her white blouse and black skirt outlined her slender figure in the breeze that had brought the color back to her cheeks and the sparkle back to her eyes. Behind her there stretched the green fields of the fens, the road leading back to the two small gray buildings and the sand dunes patched with reeds where the sand ran down to the vast stretch of the blue North Sea, a blue that was deeper and lovelier than the blue of any other sea in the world. "As long as motorcars remain the toys of rich men," he went on somberly, "I suppose life will go on as quietly as it does now. But if the day should ever come when every Tom, Dick and Harry can afford them, as they seem to do with bicycles today, then what on earth will our roads become? Think of the dust and the noisy horns blowing, and at night the smell from the acetylene lamps—too horrible to contemplate. Give me bicycles and traps for my money."

"At least," she said, holding up her gloved hand so that he could see a gold bangle on her wrist with a single gold medallion hanging from it, "I have this to protect me." The look that accompanied the smile was full of mischief, and for the first time she saw him flush and look disconcerted.

"I hoped your uncle would not say where it came from," he said. "The truth is, Miss Bretton, my family was half Catholic and half Protestant, and when my father, who was a Protestant missionary, went to India with my mother and both died there of cholera, I was handed about from relative to relative—to which every one of them would be obliging enough to take me. I was very fond of one Catholic aunt, and she instilled in me a reverence for some of her favorite saints—St. Christopher among them. I took a clock into our local jeweler's early in the year, and found your uncle there choosing a jade brooch for a wedding present for a favorite niece, and I saw a tray of small gold medallions there, one of them of St. Christopher. So I bought it, and I gave it to him telling him to put it in with the brooch to keep his niece safe on the journey. I rather think I outraged his religious feelings, though he was too kind to say so, and I suppose in order to quieten his conscience he said it was from me. I hope it did not offend your susceptibilities in that direction?"

"Not at all. I have grown very fond of it. And there have been times when I have felt inclined to creep into a Roman Catholic church—only there are so few of them and it is hard to find one anywhere—and light a candle to St. Jude—the saint for lost causes."

"Ah yes, a fine fellow, St. Jude. Only don't forget—he likes to be thanked."

He gathered up the reins, and with composure back in his face and distance once more in his manner, he said good-bye and went on, leaving Dinah to mount her bicycle and make her way back to the rectory.

In spite of what she had said about her cycling to Charles, Dinah now rode her bicycle through the town without any difficulty, even on a market day when the streets were filled with cattle, sheep and carts with pigs looking out at her from under stout netting. She contemplated riding it to Saltbech Grange the following week when she went to the Crockett's tennis party, and wished that she could have had some practice at lawn tennis before she went.

Here, however, the rector came to her aid. He would take her down to see Janet Annerley the following morning and ask her to give her some practice.

"She and Mark belong to the Saltbech Lawn Tennis Club," he explained. "And when Mark is free from evening surgery, I have often seen him there. But Janet will probably take you down there in the mornings when not many people will be using the courts."

He took her to call on Mrs. Annerley and she was charmed with the Annerleys' tiny cottage. Janet was a cheerful little creature, with a freckled face and the warm chestnut hair of the Scots, and she was delighted to give Dinah some practice at the club.

"Have you a racquet?" she asked.

"It is rather loose-stringed," said Septimus smiling, "so we are going to buy her a new one." Mrs. Annerley fetched her hat, her tennis shoes, her own racquet and half a dozen tennis balls, and they set out for Twist's in the High Street, that sold everything from garden rollers to cricket bats and tennis racquets and flat-heeled tennis shoes. While Mrs. Annerley selected a racquet light enough for Dinah to handle easily, Dinah bought herself a pair of shoes, and they said good-bye to the rector and made their way to the lawn tennis club in Folly Lane, not far from Folly Fields where the famous cricket match was to be held.

Dinah enjoyed her mornings at tennis enormously and found her heart warming towards the junior partner's wife. On the last morning before the great lawn tennis party at Lady Crockett's, she asked if she would be there.

"Oh my dear, no!" Janet laughed at the idea. "Mark and I are *never* asked to the Grange—not on a social visit. I have been there once on a committee for a church bazaar, and Lady Crockett was in the chair, of course, and after the meeting was over we were refreshed with somewhat tepid tea and stale plum cake. I expect she wanted it finished up!" Her eyes were brimming over with laughter and Dinah laughed, too.

"I thought, as Dr. Bellingham dined there—" she began.

"That we would dine there, too? No, we are on different planes, you see. Mark and I come from very ordinary families, whereas the Bellinghams were well known at one time. That is why Charles is asked there to dinner—when Lady Crockett is short of a man—and I am afraid he goes because those dinner parties amuse him enormously. Charles has a great sense of humor, but perhaps you have not discovered it yet? Of course, Mark and I think he's the greatest person on earth, but we are possibly biased. Good luck to you at the tennis party, and I think you will be quite as good as most of the ladies there!" And so they parted.

Her bicycle raised a certain amount of amusement among Miss Crockett and her friends and she laughed with them.

"I must admit," she told them, "that when I started my first instinct when I wished to stop was to pull on the handlebars as if they were reins."

"And cry Whoa!" suggested Captain Greenberg.

"Exactly. But now I would not be without it for the world. It is excellent exercise, and makes me independent of my uncle's pony and trap."

It was a pleasant afternoon and she enjoyed herself more than she had done since she left Bretton. There were only young people there, and most of them were related to families that she had known at Bretton. She found herself talking and laughing as she had not done for a long time, and encouraging her partners when playing without disgracing them too much by her own play, and when she left it was with the feeling that when the winter came she must persuade her uncle to make a tennis court beyond the croquet lawn.

When she was sitting beside Lady Crockett during a game in which she was not taking part she asked her if Miss Crockett was a member of the Saltbech Lawn Tennis Club.

"Oh yes, naturally we all joined," her ladyship conceded graciously. "Not that Bella would ever think of playing there, of course. It is really only for the townspeople, but one must always do one's best to encourage such activities, mustn't one?"

And so the Saltbech Lawn Tennis Club was dismissed from the conversation.

Her enjoyment of the party made her a great deal happier,

however, and when Dr. Bellingham called the next morning and found that her uncle was out, going off early to see a sick parishioner, Dinah greeted him with the friendliness that she had shown on the fens the week before.

"I do not suppose he will be long," she told him. "Can I give him a message for you?"

"If you will be so kind." He looked relieved. "Will you remind him that my young partner Mark Annerley is a very able cricketer, and if the county eleven should be short of a man he is willing to undertake umpiring or scoring, or anything else for which they may require an extra with a knowledge of the game."

"I will tell my uncle with pleasure." He had walked up to the rectory and she walked back down the drive with him for a little way, wondering if she dare tackle him about the thing that worried her from time to time. Then she said: "Dr. Bellingham, do you know who the relative is that my uncle goes to visit on the first of every month? I have not liked to ask him myself."

"And he has never volunteered any information?"

"No."

He considered the matter for a moment and then he said quietly: "Sometimes it is less hurtful not to be too inquisitive over such things."

"I was not being inquisitive." Her voice was suddenly dignified and aloof. "Do you know where he goes?"

"I do." His eyes met hers directly, slightly reproachful. "But I am sure you do not expect me to tell you, as your uncle has not done so. A medical man is like a father confessor in some ways—secrets that his patients confide in him are never disclosed to others."

"No, I suppose not." But her thoughts were still lingering on the locked room at the rectory and the boy to whom it must have belonged at one time. She said slowly, "I only wondered if those visits had anything to do with my cousin Christopher." Then as he did not answer but glanced at her with sudden interest she explained, "We have always been told that Christopher died when he was a little boy, but since we have been here Paul discovered there was a locked room, and being a curious little wretch, he climbed the old tree outside the barred windows of the room and saw that it was a boy's room. But it wasn't a *little* boy's room, Dr. Bellingham. It was the room of a big boy, a boy who had a cricket bat and was able to build model ships."

117

His face remained impassive; and she wondered what Janet Annerley found so attractive about him. She felt she would have liked to box his ears, but as it seemed their walk to the gates was to be maintained as far as he was concerned in silence, she continued: "I wonder if my cousin did not die as an infant but if he is still alive, because in that case he would be grown up—a little older than I am. So I came to the conclusion that if he is the object of my uncle's monthly visit he might be suffering from some terrible disease, like consumption, impossible to cure."

From the look in his eyes she thought she might have hit on the right solution, but as he neither agreed nor disagreed with her she grew tired of a conversation that threatened to be entirely one-sided and stopped, saying that she thought the practice nets that Septimus had ordered to be ready for her brothers when they came home had arrived and were being unpacked in the stableyard.

"I think I had better go and see that no irreparable damage is being done to them," she said. "He bought them through the *Exchange and Mart* magazine, and they were eight-foot ones and only cost two pounds. The new ones at Twist's cost eight, so they seemed to be a bargain. I can see him having a most enjoyable afternoon erecting them in the paddock, with the aid of Dimmock, Dimmock's boy, and I have no doubt the stable lad and young Tom the bootboy. Uncle Sep is so looking forward to coaching the boys for the great cricket match in Folly Fields."

"I am sure he is. He was a great cricketer in his day." Charles raised his hat and left her, walking on to the gate alone.

His thoughts remained with her as he made his way back to the town: there were times when she was still inclined to keep him at arm's length, and at others, like the time a little while back on the road across the fens, when he had thought the old antagonism between them was dead.

From there his mind went on to the place that Septimus visited without fail on the first of every month, and Dinah Bretton's fancy that he might be seeing a son who was a prey to consumption, and he gave a grim little smile. "I wish to God it was as simple as that," he told himself, and arrived at his surgery to find an urgent call from Bresleigh Hall. The butler had been stung by a hornet, and would Dr. Bellingham kindly come at once?

Normally, he would have sent his partner but as the young

man was out on his rounds he had no alternative but to go himself.

In the meantime, having satisfied herself that the nets and their supports were being unpacked and treated with every possible care, supervised by Dimmock himself, Dinah went back into the house entering by the long windows in her uncle's study. The room was neat, with next Sunday's sermon half written and anchored from any truant breeze by a small ivory paper clip in the shape of a woman's hand.

There was not a great deal of personal atmosphere about the rector's study. True, the smell of tobacco from his pipe still hung about it in spite of the open windows, but the pictures were all steel engravings in maple frames, most of them of cathedrals and some of picturesque ruins. There was only one photograph, standing by the clock on the chimney-piece: a photograph of her Aunt Margaret, pretty and young in a white ball-dress, with a bouquet of stephanotis held lightly in her small gloved hands.

If her son had lived, thought Dinah, walking on slowly into the great hall, and if as she had suspected he had contracted so fatal a disease as consumption; why had not they been told about it? Surely her uncle knew that they would have nothing but pity for their cousin and his father?

There seemed to be no reason for making such a mystery out of it all, until another thought far more awful occurred to her.

Supposing Christopher had done something terrible for which he had been imprisoned? Certainly in that case none of his family would have ever wished to speak of such a scandal as that, even if they knew about it.

She shivered and ran upstairs to take off her hat and tidy herself for lunch, scolding herself for the absurd fancies she had conjured up out of nothing more than a monthly visit of her uncle's to a sick relative in the country. Just as she herself visited old Mrs. Duffy in the Easterley workhouse with Lady Collington.

She determined not to think of it anymore.

Chapter Thirteen

The two elder Collington boys were at Eton with Harold and Johnnie, and the day after they arrived home they drove over in Sir James's shooting brake bringing a younger brother and sister to play with the twins. The two Collingtons had also been enrolled as members of the county cricket team, and they were delighted to start a session of practice at the nets that Septimus had managed to have erected in a mown part of the paddock without a great deal of mishap.

When he could spare the time Septimus did some coaching, which delighted all four boys, and lemonade was brought out in jugs and stood on a rather rickety table borrowed from the harness room.

The twins were quite happy to play with the younger Collingtons at a queer game of croquet that they called "golf croquet," which caused a great deal of argument and balls sent in all directions.

The young people usually stayed to luncheon, and in the afternoon the older boys would either return to the nets or go fishing in the upper reaches of the Salte.

The day of the great cricket match came, and instead of the wet weather gloomily foretold by Dimmock, who was regarded as the weather prophet of the rectory, it dawned without a cloud in the sky, and as the sun rose the day became warmer. Early in the morning tents were erected in Folly Field for refreshments, and chairs had been set up for the ladies who would be there to watch.

The pitch had been rolled and mown and rolled again and nursed tenderly by sundry gardeners sent in by their employers to see that all was ready for the great match which was timed to start at eleven.

Dinah hunted out a white dress with a black belt and a

black hat with a white rose on the brim, and went off with her family feeling as if she were taking a holiday.

Her uncle was already there ahead of them as captain of the County team, and few of his parishioners would have recognized him in his white flannels and ancient panama hat as he stood in the somewhat smaller tent that had been turned into a pavilion for both elevens, greeting old friends as they turned up with younger sons to take their places in the eleven.

Here he was joined by Harold and Johnnie and the young Collingtons and the Bretton boys were introduced to the rest of the eleven all of whom were known to the Collingtons, although the member who had been brought in at the last moment to replace a player who had thought fit to fall from his horse and break his collarbone the day before was not so well known. In fact, it was not until Mark Annerley gave an account of himself on the cricket field that he was welcomed with any enthusiasm.

Dinah would have liked to sit with Janet Annerley, whom she had been forced to desert recently because of Miss Crockett's insistence that she should make up games of tennis at the Grange, but Bella Crockett beckoned to her as soon as she arrived, and she was forced to join her in a shady spot under the trees where a number of young officers who were not playing were gathered with a great deal of laughter, comment and advice to each member of their side as they arrived, immaculate in white flannels, regimental blazers and caps with the regiment's badge.

Miss Stroud found a place beside Mrs. Annerley, however, and was welcomed by her, while the twins went in search of bottles of fizzy lemonade that could be opened by a wooden opener pressed down on the glass ball wedged in the crooked neck of the bottle until it released the drink, which promptly shot out in a way that delighted them.

As for little Octavius, he was perfectly happy finding flowers in the hedges that surrounded the field, accompanied by the little maid Clara, who acted as Nurse's nurserymaid in the afternoons, while Nurse sat under a tree, sipping tea and watching the match in comfort.

The match began with the regiment winning the toss and going in to bat, but the first three batsmen were dismissed speedily, and when Captain Greenberg went in to bat Septimus tossed the ball to Mark Annerley, who promptly got him out for a duck.

The captain was immensely chagrined, and as he walked past Miss Crockett on his way back to the pavilion he said with disgust, "Bowled for a duck by a sawbones! What do you think of that?"

"We think that Dr. Annerley is a very good bowler," said Dinah crisply.

"So I daresay, my dear young lady, is the town blacksmith, but it is no less humiliating to be bowled by him."

And he went to have a drink to settle his ruffled temper.

"Poor Captain Greenberg," said Miss Crockett. "I rather wonder at your uncle for putting Dr. Annerley on so early in the game, but I daresay he thought he would get him out of the way."

If Dinah thought that in so doing her uncle had got Captain Greenberg out of the way she did not say so. Instead she remarked that she thought her uncle knew what he was doing. "He played for the Varsity at one time, though it is a long time ago," she reminded Bella.

"Oh yes, the rector is a wonderful player," agreed Miss Crockett enthusiastically. "Everybody knows that."

It was just before the tea-break when Dr. Bellingham's trap stopped for a moment or two by the field gates, and Charles asked one of the men on duty there how the match was going. It was about level, he was told, but the rector had to go in next.

"Then you ought to see some fun," said Charles, and when he was asked if he could not stay to watch it he shook his head. His eyes had already picked out Dinah surrounded by a group of young men from the barracks, and he had no further interest in the game. He was about to drive on when Captain Speedwell, the regiment's medical officer, spotted him and came to the gate asking if he could have a word with him.

"Of course." Charles jumped down, tied Whitestar's reins to a gatepost, and asked what he could do.

"I'd be glad of some advice." The captain took his arm and led him a little way down the lane out of earshot of the men on the gate. "Dr. Bellingham, how safe is the water in the Salte below the harbor?"

"It depends where it is. If you mean the stretch directly below where the Calder joins it, then I should say it is an open sewer. Why do you ask?"

"Well, although it is out of bounds, I am pretty certain some of the men must have been swimming there at the high tide, and I am rather disturbed about it."

"Is there any need?" asked Charles smiling. "If they have served abroad in India or Shanghai, they will have swum in much dirtier rivers than the Salte. When I was first qualified I decided to take a post as ship's surgeon on a merchant boat, and I assure you I have been in rivers where not only dead dogs and cats but dead bodies floated along without anyone worrying about them." Then as the young doctor beside him still looked worried he asked, "Has anything happened at the barracks?"

The younger man nodded. "Yesterday two of the men came to see me. They had slight fever and complained of headache and slight pains, but nothing else. Oh, and one of them had nose-bleeding. But they only said they had been swimming in the sea the day before, and I put it down to a touch of the sun. It has been extremely hot this week or two."

"It has. Did you send them back on duty?"

"Oh yes. They were not malingering, and in fact they were quite ready to go back. But this morning one of them was back again, and is now in the barracks hospital. His fever has increased to one hundred and three, and he is suffering from diarrhea."

Charles's expression altered at once. "Any sign of a rash on the stomach?"

"None at all. I looked for it at once. I have never seen a case of typhoid, but I made a serious study of it before I entered the army medical corps."

"Very wise. Typhoid takes a long time to develop, and the man may be only suffering from a severe chill caught through bathing in the intense heat. Or, as you suggest, he may have taken a dip in the river and will not admit it. One does not like to jump to conclusions." He smiled reassuringly at the worried young man. "My advice is to watch him pretty carefully, and if the temperature does not go down, and any other symptoms assert themselves, let me know and I will come and see him."

"I expect you have seen several cases of typhoid in your time?" said Captain Speedwell as if Charles were an octogenarian at least.

He saw the doctor's face change, registering some emotion difficult to define. "More than I ever wanted to have seen," he said shortly, and went back to his horse and trap. There he turned for a moment to give some advice. "As a precaution, I should put that fellow in a ward by himself. Allow no visitors, and give him only soft food and boiled water to drink. Oh, and the medical orderly or nurse who looks after him must not attend to any other patient. These are simply matters of common prudence." And with a cheerful wave of his whip, he gathered up Whitestar's reins and was away back to the town.

As he went however his thoughts dwelt on two cases of typhoid he had diagnosed in Burston the day before: they had puzzled him because the patients had both been of good families and in each case the mothers of the girls who had contracted the disease had been careful never to use anything but the Company's water, and the barracks, too, was supplied with the same water.

He remembered the fussy little medical officer of health, Dr. Bryce, and his first meeting with him a year ago, and how anxious he had been to have the water supply from the Easterley Water Company examined. He had had his way, too, but nothing had come of it. Therefore, it would seem that these cases had nothing to do with the water company. He came to the conclusion that the girls in Burston had come in contact with somebody who had the disease, and that possibly the men in the barracks had taken their dip in the Salte in spite of their denials. It was the only explanation he could find for the two separate outbreaks, if the barracks case was indeed the forerunner of an outbreak, which was not nice to contemplate.

In the town square bunting had been put up at the balconies of the Town Hall, and fairy lights in green, yellow, red, white and blue had been strung across the front of the building waiting for the nightlights inside to be lighted at dusk in honor of the cricket ball that was being held that night.

He saw the Town Clerk there, Mr. Johnson, bustling about ordering some Chinese lanterns to be hung on either side of the doorway, with candles in them all ready. There was no breeze in the High Street, so that with any luck they would not catch fire as they had done at almost every cricket ball for years past.

He had just finished surgery when Janet Annerley looked in to tell him the result of the match—the army had been beaten all hands down.

"After tea the rector and my Mark were the last men in and they knocked up a century between them. Wasn't that absolutely stunning?"

"It was indeed." He smiled at her charming little freckled face, as eager as a schoolgirl telling of a school win. "And now

124

I suppose you will be getting yourselves ready for the ball?"

"But you must come, too," she said, and as he shook his head, "Charles you never come to social things, except when Lady Crockett issues a command for you to make up the numbers at her dinner table. This is one of the greatest events of the Saltbech year. And it's no good saying you might be called out: your housekeeper can easily run across to the town hall and get you if necessary. I *insist* that you come with us!" She added as an afterthought, "Miss Bretton will be there."

He did not reply: by his expression it seemed that he had not the least interest in Miss Bretton, and he had no doubt in any case that she would be in Miss Crockett's party.

"I have forgotten how to dance," he said.

"I do not believe that for one moment," she said. "It is no good. I am not letting you off. You will change into tails and a starched shirt and a white tie, and you will come."

"I do not think I possess a starched shirt."

"Then you shall borrow one of Mark's. It will strain a bit across your chest, but as long as the studs do not give way, all will be well."

He laughed and gave up. "Very well," he said. "I know when I am beaten. I will come."

The hall was crowded when they arrived, everybody delighted with the result of the match and a supper had been laid on fit for a king. The town clerk had great ideas of how such functions should be arranged, and not only was there a caterer from London to supply the supper, but there was an awning from the entrance, under the Chinese lanterns, as far as the street, with a carpet laid down across the pavement so that the ladies' dresses might not pick up any dirt. There was also the regiment's band, assisted by an orchestra from Easterley, to play a succession of waltzes, polkas, lancers and two-steps, both band and orchestra under oath to finish the ball in the small hours with a gallop to the tune of "John Peel."

Charles promised himself that he would not stay long: he danced the first dance with his partner's wife, and the second with Mrs. Johnson, and the third with the mayoress of Easterley, who with her husband was honoring the ball as usual, and there he thought his duty ended.

He was looking round to discover how best he could escape without appearing rude, when the rector saw him and called him across to him.

"Just the man I want," he said. "Charles, I have written my name on Dinah's program for the supper dance, but my conscience tells me I should take in the Lady Mayoress instead. Will you please write your initials over mine?"

And before Dinah could do anything more than look taken aback and slightly put out at the same time, her uncle took her little dance program and handed it to Dr. Bellingham.

Charles could not refuse without appearing ungallant. He took the pencil that was attached to the card by a blue silk cord, and wrote his initials over those of Septimus with an amused smile for Miss Bretton's discomfiture, returned the card to her with a bow and a word of thanks, and went off to dance with one of the young ladies of Saltbech who were always delighted to talk to the best looking bachelor in the town.

It was the first dance that Dinah had attended since her father's death, and when she had looked for a ball-dress among those in her wardrobe she had for a moment regretted the lavender silk that her mother had taken from her with her amethysts.

Then the thought came to her that if her mother, a widow of only six months could shed her mourning garments, it was about time that she did so, too. She hunted out a green silk dress that she was fond of—the green almost an aquamarine in color—and she pinned a spray of scarlet poppies to the shoulder, and when Maud, the housemaid that the twins liked so much, had hooked her dress up for her she asked her to clasp a necklace of aquamarines round her throat. The necklace had a diamond clasp, and the earrings that matched it had diamond surrounds.

"Oh Miss Dinah," said Maud as she finished, "Don't you look lovely?"

Charles privately echoed that opinion when the supper dance came and he claimed his partner from under the disapproving nose of Lady Crockett, and as it was a waltz, moved off with her easily onto the crowded floor.

Dinah Bretton was certainly looking enchanting that night, and it was not only the dress and the scarlet poppies and the jewelry that made her so. Her cheeks were pink with enjoyment, and her eyes were sparkling, and he did not think there was another girl in the room who could equal her dancing.

On her side she was surprised by the way in which he danced, suiting his steps to hers and holding her easily, his hand in its white kid glove holding hers lightly. They talked of the match and how delighted everyone was with the result, and she said how proud she had been of her uncle for his batting. "And Dr. Annerley, too," she added quickly. "He made such an admirable partner. Everyone is singing his praises."

He thought he detected in her tone an anxiety to please by praising one whom she did not really wish to know, and he was annoyed with her for her neglect of his partner's wife once she was no more use to her.

He said no more until the dance ended and he took her upstairs into the supper room, finding her a place not far from her uncle.

"What would you like to talk about?" he asked, as salmon and champagne were brought to them by the caterer's waiters. "I promise I will not talk about the new photography. I will leave it to you to find a topic."

"I apologize for that evening," she said. "You must have thought me abominably rude."

"On the contrary, you simply did not pretend to an interest that you did not feel, and it was very honest of you." He was smiling and his eyes held the look of amusement that usually annoyed her, and yet somehow this evening because the ball was such fun and she was enjoying it all so much, she did not find that it annoyed her at all. "The quickest way to avoid listening was to allow me to bore you with an almost entirely one-sided conversation."

"I had a great deal on my mind," she told him seriously. "Dr. Bellingham, is it not splendid that my uncle is really going to take this holiday that Uncle Quin has planned for him for so long? He is to join him next week, and although he said he would not go unless my Great-aunt Alice came to act as chaperone while he was away, I would not let a little thing like that stand in his way. Not that anybody could call Great-aunt A. a little thing," she added with a laugh.

"I hope I shall meet her then, because I have promised your uncle that I will look in at the rectory once a day to see that all is well while he is away."

"Now why did he make you promise such a thing?" Dinah was put out. "He behaves as if I were a child. I am *quite* able to manage the rectory and my brothers and sister while he is away. He is only going for a month, and even if Great-aunt A. does not come there is always Mrs. Jennings."

"Septimus has very oldfashioned ideas of what is or is not

proper for young girls," said Charles and once more his eyes met hers with laughter, and she laughed with him. He thought her laughter the nicest thing he had heard in years.

As they finished supper and moved towards the door Dinah stopped for a moment at the windows that opened onto the balcony overlooking the square. The room was very warm and she stepped through the open windows onto the balcony and Charles followed her.

"You know," she said, looking down at the little square below, "I have never seen a small town square like this all lighted up with fairy lights and Chinese lanterns. It is rather like a stage setting for one of Gilbert and Sullivan's light operas. One expects to see some pirates emerge from that old timbered building opposite."

"Pirates is a good name for the people who work there," he told her gravely. "It is the Rates Office of Saltbech."

She laughed again. "It is delightful," she said. "And with the drinking fountain in the middle, with the statue of the Queen looking down from it. I am sure that was put up to commemorate the Golden Jubilee."

"It was."

"She looks rather a massive old lady, doesn't she? Rather like my Great-aunt A."

"I suppose you have been presented to Her Majesty at a Drawing Room?" he said.

"Not to the Queen. To the Prince and Princess of Wales, which was not quite so dull, I suppose. I wonder when that poor man will come to the throne? Do you think his Mamma will outlive him?"

"I hope not."

They turned back from the lighted square to the supper room, which was empty now except for waiters clearing the tables.

"Those waiters are almost as good as the army ones who waited on us this afternoon," she said lightly as they descended the stairs to the ball-room. "Though not quite so good, I think."

"The army ones?" Suddenly he remembered Speedwell's worry about one of his patients in the army hospital at the barracks.

The men from that barracks had been handing tea and cakes to the ladies that afternoon, and they might have included some of those who had gone bathing with the sick

128

man. They might also have been among those who had been serving drinks to the elevens in the pavilion.

He could not help thinking that Dinah had been one of the ladies who had accepted tea from the uniformed men round Folly Field that afternoon, and that her brothers, Harold Bretton and young Johnnie, had been served with drinks in the pavilion.

"You are looking very grave suddenly," Dinah said with a laughing glance at his face.

"I beg your pardon. My mind had gone back ten years or more to the last time I danced. You will not believe me, I daresay, when I tell you that it is ten years at least since I allowed myself to be persuaded to attend a ball."

Ten years since he had danced with the girl who had been engaged to him at that time, a girl as young and lovely as Dinah, a girl who died a week before their wedding from typhoid.

Chapter Fourteen

The first of August came in hot with a cloudless sky again, and the two elder boys went off for the day to the Collingtons', hiring a couple of hacks from the Saltbech livery stables to get them there.

The twins and Miss Stroud and Dinah went off on their bicycles to Salte Bay, a small fishing village on the coast, where a canvas tent could be hired from the inn there and set up for them on the beach. It was an awkward and risky business, dressing and undressing in that tent. It was round, with a pole in the middle supporting a canvas roof, and a pocket all round the bottom of its canvas wall that had to be filled with shingle before one ventured inside. Tapes secured the one opening to preserve the modesty of those inside, which composed of two at the most.

Below the shingle there was a long stretch of sand however, and the sea was shallow and as clear as crystal, so that the colors of the pebbles at the bottom were as vivid as the tiny crabs that darted across the twins' feet as they went in.

They had brought a picnic lunch with them and bought lemonade from the inn in the village, and started home about three, knowing that the rector would not be waiting for his tea as it was his afternoon for visiting an ailing relative in the country.

Dinah's thoughts were very much with him that day. The twins had accepted the fact that he went off to visit an ailing relative, just as they accepted the fact that it was part of his business to visit parishioners who were sick. But Dinah could see him eating his early lunch alone and then walking off for the train that was to take him heaven knew where, where he would stay until another train brought him back, spent and exhausted at the end of the day.

The railway carriages were like ovens on that hot day, the sun beating down unmercifully on their roofs.

Septimus caught a local train to his destination, a small town only ten miles away from Saltbech, and one to which he could have driven easily in his tub cart. But he preferred to make the journey alone, with not even a groom to accompany him, and he would not even cycle the ten miles in case any of his parishioners saw him and guessed where he was bound. Ever since that awful day when he had to take Christopher to White Lodge Institute at Warren Market, he had never mentioned the boy's name, and only Charles knew for certain where he was and why.

The little local train stopped at every station, taking a long way round to do the ten miles between Warren Market and Saltbech. The journey, Septimus reckoned, must have been enlarged to at least twenty miles to include such a number of villages.

The country in that direction was far more picturesque than the flat fen country round Saltbech, and soon wooded hills rose on either side of the track, broken here and there by a rough common with the yellow gorse in bloom, and they would stop at country stations with apple trees hanging over the platforms, and goats tethered to railings, waiting to be collected, and crates of hens clucking furiously at the arrival of the train.

On the stretches of open country between the stations children hung on gates at level crossings, waving as the train went by, the shadow of the engine's smoke passing over them like a cloud chased away by the sun. At the back of cottages that bordered the railway, sheets were blowing like white sails in the breeze, and towels and pillow cases were thrown over quickset hedges to dry in the sunshine.

Farmhouses too broke the monotony of the journey from time to time, with hens clucking and scratching in the yards and cockerels proclaiming their male superiority, crowing back at some distant cockerel, their tailfeathers scarcely ruffled in the slight breeze of that hot day.

There were the surrounding golden fields from which the grain was being harvested and built into stooks ready to be loaded later into wagons drawn by great farmhorses when it was dry enough and ready. And there were the pigs, large and pink, their flapping ears hiding their small eyes as they ate the roots that had been thrown down for them in the fields, and herds of cattle grazing peacefully, golden Jerseys among them, seeking the shade of clumps of trees, whisking their tails to keep off the flies, or just lying there chewing cud, their placid eyes attracted for a moment's curiosity to the puffs of smoke from passing trains, and then turning back to more familiar things.

Septimus enjoyed the journey, although every moment now was bringing him nearer the end of it and to the visit that he dreaded: every month it was the same, the peace of the countryside and the little train taking him through that peace nearer and nearer to grief and sadness and hope deferred, and yet a hope that he resolutely refused to abandon.

Who knows, he thought. It might be today that he would be told that all was well at last and he was free to take his son home, and as always, when the thought came to him his spirits rose to cheerfulness again.

As he got out of the train and gave up his ticket at the barrier, only two miles remained now of his journey, and he refused the cab that waited for travelers in the stationyard and started out on foot.

The little town was soon left behind, and he was starting out on the country lane that led through hedges white with dust to the great house for which he was bound.

The afternoon became warmer and his black alpaca jacket and panama hat did not seem to make it much cooler. He had his stick with him, a stout ash with a heavy knob to it, and from time to time, as the cottages dropped behind he heard the song of a lark rising from a neighboring field, or the departing "cuk" of a cuckoo as it made ready to fly; and as he cut at the nettles by the roadside with his stick he scared a pair of magpies, their black and white standing out against the green of the fields. In passing a small wood, he heard a woodpecker, and saw the rascal high up, knocking a hole in the trunk of an elm tree.

As he drew nearer his goal, instinctively his walk slackened, he lost his interest in country things, his eyes grew sterner and the momentary hope that had shone in them a little while back died. And when at last he came in sight of a great brick wall with a spiked top, surrounding several acres of beautiful grounds that were not visible from the road, he paused a moment and squared his shoulders as if to gain strength for the ordeal in front of him.

Then he walked more briskly to the porter's lodge beside the tall locked gates: they were solid wooden gates painted green, with more spikes along the tops.

The porter came out in answer to his pull at the bell and touched his hat.

"Arternoon, Mr. Crichton, sir," he said. "Lovely day."

"It is indeed Witney. How are you?"

"Fair to middlin', sir. We'm been quiet lately, though. No excitements."

"That is fortunate. Is Dr. Forsyth at home?"

"He's seldom away, sir."

"No, I suppose not." Septimus waited while a small door in the main gates was unlocked for him and stepped inside.

A gravelled driveway led up through tall trees and shrubs to a large white mansion, resembling in every way an ordinary and very beautiful country house.

The windows of the lower rooms were open on that hot day, and curtains moved inside the rooms as scarcely seen faces took a quick look at Septimus from behind them before twitching them back again.

Beyond the driveway were extensive lawns, where garden chairs and tables had been placed and where a few people were sitting talking cheerfully to some of the inmates of the house, ranging from boys to young men and even to old ones. It was visiting day at the White Lodge Institute, and friends and relatives of patients were welcomed on those days.

On a distant lawn some of the patients who had no visitors that day, or who perhaps never had any visitors at all, were playing a game of cricket, supervised by male attendants who acted as fielders. On the surface it looked very peaceful and English, as a summer afternoon on the grounds of an English country house should be.

It was only when one glanced towards the place where the stable block should have been that one observed a large red-brick building, strongly built, with small windows, all heavily barred.

As usual Septimus was taken to Dr. Forsyth's consulting room, and shook hands with the little quick-eyed man before seating himself opposite him at the writing table.

"How is Christopher?" he asked anxiously, and his heart sank as the doctor pursed his lips and slightly shook his head.

"He has been giving us some trouble lately," he admitted. "But it was not his fault. It was entirely because one of my attendants disobeyed rules. In that block—where Christopher is housed—the attendants are never permitted to go singly, but always in pairs, because it is dangerous to do otherwise. It is well known throughout the institute that those patients are for the most part homicidal cases and will attack on sight. But this man, Ingerman, a big broad-shouldered fellow and ex-prize-fighter, thought he could tackle anyone single-handed, and on the night he went to his room alone Christopher was waiting for him.

"As he entered his room he had him down and by the throat and the breath nearly out of him, before another fellow came running and got him off." He smiled gravely. "It has taught Ingerman a lesson, but it has not done Christopher any good, poor lad. And he had been so much better of late that I had considered putting him back in his old room in this part of the house."

"I am sorry." Septimus's face assumed the lines that Dinah had caught there sometimes at the rectory when he had received letters marked "Strictly Private," letters that he had never given to her to answer for him but had locked away in the little safe in the cupboard beside the fireplace in the study. "My brother Quin wants me to go on a cycling tour with him in Sussex. It is a county neither of us know very well, and we plan to return on the 27th, three weeks in all. But with my sister's family now living with me at the rectory, I wonder if I should risk it. Supposing Christopher should escape from here. He might make his way to Saltbech and attack them in my absence."

"There will be no risk of that. We keep watch here night and day, and the Ingerman incident was a rare one. By all means go on this holiday with your brother. It will do you all

133

the good in the world, and try to put Christopher out of your mind while you are away."

"He is never out of my mind," said Septimus. He added that he had brought with him a tube of red paint that Christopher wanted the last time he was there. "I thought then that he seemed quite interested in painting," he added.

"He is, in fits and starts. In fact, if he had been a normal young man I believe he could have made quite a successful artist. He likes it, too, though if you can persuade him to show you the paintings he has done I think you will agree with me that they are distinctly odd. But clever, mind you. Extraordinarily clever and talented for a man who has never had a lesson in painting."

"I will go and see him now if I may and take this tube of paint to him."

"Do. He is much quieter today and I see no reason why you should not bring him out into the grounds, as long as you keep well within sight. There will be two men following you, of course, just in case you should need help. But it will do the poor lad good to see you, and to hear about your holiday and stroll in the grounds for a little while."

He rang the bell for an attendant, and Septimus was led through the spacious hall with its Turkey rugs to a door that was kept locked. Here the attendant produced a key and unlocked it while another man got up from a stool outside and followed them, and thus guarded, Septimus was taken through the too familiar passages and up the stone stairs to a room on the first floor, where a small shutter was pushed aside from a small grill and the first attendant said, "Mr. Crichton, here is your father come to see you."

"Father!" The young man who had been lying at full length on the narrow bed staring at the ceiling, leapt up and came quickly to the door as it opened and embraced his father. He was a tall young man with broad shoulders and a face that would have been handsome had it not been for the strange look in his eyes, a look that seemed to say he was seeing and hearing things that nobody else could see or hear. His hair was fair, and his beard, though neatly trimmed, was fair and curling, and his father guessed that he was not being shaved because of his record for violence.

The rector gave him the tube of paint he had wanted and asked if he could see some of his paintings, but Christopher did not seem willing at first, and then he said yes, he would show him the last one. "I think," he said, beginning to stammer a little with excitement, "it is good."

He went to the portfolio in the corner of the room and removed a small canvas and set it up on the easal so that the light fell on it.

He had painted it out in the grounds while some of the patients were playing cricket, as they were today. The lawn, the background of trees and their shadows on the lawn, the figures in white flannels, were all exceptionally well done. There was life in the man who was bowling, one could feel the strength of his arm and the effort he was making as he let the ball go, one could feel the readiness of the batsman as he waited for it, and the tenseness in the fielders gathered round the pitch.

There was only one thing that was odd about it: none of the figures had a head.

"It is very well done," he told his son. "You've the making of a good artist, Christopher. But Dr. Forsyth says I may take you out into the grounds for a little while." He linked his arm in his son's as the door was opened again for them. "Come along. Let us go out into the sunshine on this lovely first of August."

They went down the corridors and stairs with one attendant in front to unlock the doors for them and the other behind to lock them up again, and at length they were back in the hall with the Turkey rugs and the open doors onto the sunlit lawn.

The rector took his son across the drive and onto the lawns and found a seat for them under one of the trees, the two attendants busying themselves with getting a little iron table out for tea.

"Father, I have been so miserable," burst out Christopher, when a man in a white jacket had brought a tray out to them with a pot of tea and cups and saucers and sandwiches and cake. "They put me into a straitjacket again, and I had not done anything to deserve it. And I was put into a padded cell. Why do they do these cruel things to me? And why do you let them keep me in this horrible place? And why cannot I come home?"

"My dearest boy, if you look around you I do not think you can call this place horrible," said his father smiling. "And I have promised you, have I not, times without number, that when you are recovered from your illness you will come at

once to Saltbech. I shall fetch you myself in the pony trap."
His hand tightened caressingly on the arm in his.

"Why cannot I come home now?" asked Christopher, a sullen expression coming over his face as he took his arm away. "But you need not tell me. I know why it is. And you need not lie to me about it, because I *know*." He turned on his father angrily, and the two attendants drew a little nearer. "I am well enough to come home now, but you are deliberately keeping me here because my cousins are at the rectory—those wretched Bretton cousins of mine, whom I hate. They have not gone yet, have they?"

"They are still with me," admitted Septimus. "But only because Bretton Place is let for a time. Directly the tenants give up their tenancy they will go back home, thankfully. They do not wish to live forever in Saltbech, Christopher."

"I am not so sure of that," said Christopher, frowning darkly. "How many are there of them at the rectory?"

"There is the eldest girl, Dinah, and there are Harold and Johnnie, the twins Paula and Paul, and the little boy Octavius. The two elder girls are away, one in London and the other in Paris, and your Aunt Helen is staying with friends on their yacht, cruising in the Mediterranean."

"There are a lot of them at the rectory, though," commented Christopher, the frown deepening. "If I could get away from here I would go to Saltbech and I would kill them all, even to the smallest one. I will not allow strange cousins to take possession of my home and my room. What have they done with my ship, *The Northern Star?* Have they destroyed it?"

"My dear boy, they have not touched it and they have not entered your room. The door is locked and your room is as you left it, with *The Northern Star* on the table. Nobody has been into that room since you left, except Mrs. Jennings to dust and air it out, and nobody ever will. It is waiting for you and for you alone, and that is the truth. When have I ever lied to you about anything, and especially a thing like that?"

"I suppose you would not." The frown lifted a little and his father suggested they should walk across to the far lawn, now that they had finished tea, and watch the cricket for a time, but Christopher said the sunlight made his head ache, so they stayed where they were, Christopher lapsing into a sullen silence and not answering anything that was said to him. The only thing that roused him was when his father told him about the cycling tour he was going on with his Uncle

Quin, and that he would be back by the first of September without fail.

"If you do not come back," Christopher said, his eyes fixed malevolently on poor Septimus, "I shall know what to believe."

"And what is that?" asked Septimus trying to speak lightly.

"I shall know then that I am right, and that besides taking my home from me, those Bretton cousins of mine have taken my father as well."

It was no use arguing. He could see that his son was getting excited and he got up and took him back to his room, the attendants relieving him of his charge at the locked door from the hall.

Before he left, he went to see Dr. Forsyth again and the latter asked him if he had seen any of Christopher's paintings.

"Only one," he said with a faint smile.

"The cricketers?"

"Yes."

"I asked him why he had painted them all without heads," said Dr. Forsyth with a twinkle in his eye. "And he said scornfully that you did not need a head to play cricket, only hands and arms and legs and feet. I could not help feeling that there was some sound reasoning there. But I forgot. You were a great cricketer in your time, and no doubt you found your head as necessary as the rest of your anatomy." He took a sheet of paper from his desk. "But you must forget about all this when you start off tomorrow on your holiday. Just give me the name and address of some gentleman in Saltbech whom I can notify quickly if anything should happen to make your return necessary—not that I think it will, but one never knows."

Septimus gave him Charles Bellingham's name and address. "He has promised to look in at the rectory every day to see that all is well there," he said. "He knows all about Christopher, although he has never seen him."

"Then that is the very man." The doctor said good-bye to him, and as Septimus made his way slowly and sadly down the drive past the porter's lodge and came out onto the road back to the railway station his thoughts went to Charles Bellingham and the scientific experiments he was always so interested in studying. "If only," he said to himself, deaf now to the songs of the larks, and blind to the magpies and the woodpecker and the wood pigeons, cooing to each other in the

137

sunshine of the warm evening, "if only Bellingham's new photography could show the damage that has been done to a brain—"

Once in the train, however, his heart lifted a little and the thought of the holiday with Quin became more of a reality.

Dulcie had taken their children to a furnished house in Frinton for August, and Quin, who had no love for sandy beaches and picnics with sand in his tea, was eager for this trip with his brother.

The cycling tour stretched out before Septimus invitingly. It would be good to feel free for three weeks, free from the parish, from his worry over Christopher, and even from the Bretton children, although he loved them as if they were his own.

Chapter Fifteen

The Honorable Alice Crichton had accepted her nephew's invitation to preside at the rectory during his own and his sister's absence by return of post, saying that she would arrive on Tuesday, July 31st, with Pettit and her maid Hannah, in time for dinner, so that he would be free to start off on the following Thursday.

And arrive she did, in time for dinner as she had promised on Tuesday evening, wearing the same black bonnet she had worn for Sir Roger's funeral but with the black bugles and wheat-ears replaced by two rather battered white and mauve roses.

Mrs. Jennings showed her to the large and somewhat cheerless apartment that had been prepared for her, with a four-poster in it and an enormous mahogany wardrobe built in three parts. The two outside parts were hanging cupboards, one containing a bonnet box at the bottom, and between them in the middle compartment there were three large drawers and a cupboard with a mirror in the door and shelves of considerable depth behind it.

Miss Pettit had a smaller room on the same corridor, and Hannah was provided for in the attics above the nurseries.

When Mrs. Jennings offered her Helen's sitting room however Septimus's aunt refused it.

"As I have come here to keep an eye on the family," she told the housekeeper, "I do not wish to be shut away in a room of my own. There are plenty of sitting rooms downstairs, and in his absence I shall probably use the rector's study for purposes of writing letters, and the morning-room to go through the day's menus with you, Mrs. Jennings. I am sure you know by this time what the children like best to eat. I would suggest, too, that the twins and Miss Stroud have their meals with the rest of us in the dining room. There is no point in giving unnecessary work to the small number of servants that there are here. There is the nursery to be waited on as it is."

Her air of authority impressed Mrs. Jennings and made her a great deal happier. In her opinion Miss Dinah was far too young to take the responsibility of her family when the rector was away, Miss Stroud was not the person to do it, and Mrs. Crichton was exactly what they all needed.

The family were already in a state of some excitement in advising their uncle what to take and what to leave behind. Harold's suggestion that he should take a fishing rod was vetoed by Dinah.

"If he is on a cycling tour," she pointed out, "a fishing rod will be of little use."

"But he might find a river where he could fish and it would make a change from cycling," said Harold. "I do think you should take a fishing rod, Uncle Sep."

So the fishing rod was put down on the list and was strapped to the center bar of the machine.

"You must take changes of clothes," said Dinah. "Especially shirts and socks. Think how hot you will become pushing your bicycle up the hills. There are a lot of hills in Sussex. And there are other things that you must not forget to take—such as iodine for cuts and a small bandage or two in case you get badly stung by an insect. Oh, and vinegar for wasp stings and soda for bee stings—or is it the other way about?"

While his aunt listened in silent amusement Septimus pointed out that he only contemplated taking with him a small leather Gladstone bag, strapped on the carrier of his bicycle, and not a large trunk. And the only extra suit he would take was to be one with a waterproof cape, leggings and cap, in case they ran into an unexpected storm. This would be wrapped in a parcel done up in American cloth and would travel under the Gladstone bag.

Like Mrs. Jennings he felt a great deal happier about leaving his family with his aunt there in charge when he finally left the rectory to start on his holiday. The family, with the exception of their great-aunt and Octavius, went in a body to see him off at the railway station. The train was full of excursionists in a holiday mood and he caught some of it as the train drew out of Saltbech and the waving handkerchiefs of Dinah and Paula and the boys were finally left behind. His bicycle and his scanty luggage were safely installed in the guards' van, labelled through to East Grinstead where he was to meet Quin, he had left addresses of various post offices in Sussex where his aunt could write to him to let him know how everything was going on in his absence, and he felt for the first time in years as if a weight had been lifted—if only temporarily—from his shoulders.

The children waved until the train had passed the signal box and the arm had dropped, and then they collected their own bicycles from the station yard, Miss Stroud accompanying them, and went with Dinah to Salte Bay, while the elder boys went off fishing in the upper reaches of the Salte for the morning.

Charles Bellingham had intended to go to the station to see his old friend off on his holiday, when he was stopped by Captain Speedwell from the barracks who asked if he might speak to him for a few minutes.

"Of course." Charles took him into his consulting room. "Are you in trouble again?"

"Yes." The army doctor sat down opposite Charles and told him his news. "We have three cases of confirmed typhoid and six suspects."

"And I have another case at Burston," said Charles frowning. Once again, his patient had come from a clean respectable family, where his orders to boil all drinking water had been obeyed, although that did not preclude one of the older children there taking a drink from the tap water when his mother was not looking. "I do not understand it," he admitted. "Are you sure your men have not been in the river?"

"Absolutely." Captain Speedwell hesitated. "Dr. Bellingham, do you remember that fussy little man we had here about this time last year, inspecting everything and making a general nuisance of himself?"

"The medical officer of health, Dr. Bryce? Yes, he was rather a tiresome fellow. Why have you brought him into it? Is he back again?"

"Good God, no. But he was so insistent about supplies from water companies being tested at least once a year."

"That is so. I seem to remember that he insisted on the Easterley Water Company's supplies being analyzed, much to the fury of its chairman, Mr. Percy Whatley, but in the end he had to admit that it was as pure as most private water supplies are, which everyone felt was a snub for Dr. Bryce and a triumph for Easterley."

"That was a year ago though, and the water may not have been analyzed since."

"Do you think, then, that the supply to the barracks may have something to do with the outbreak?"

"It is difficult to say. We may have a man who is a carrier of the disease, but if so I have yet to put my finger on him. The one I thought might have been responsible has now developed it himself and is extremely ill."

Charles thought it over for a few minutes, and then he got up and went to a cupboard where he kept his records. "I think I have a plan here of the Easterley water supply," he said. "I persuaded one of the clerks there to let me have a copy after Dr. Bryce had departed to examine water supplies elsewhere. Yes, here it is."

He brought out a plan and unrolled it and laid it on his desk so that Captain Speedwell could examine it with him, and he ran his finger down the red lines that indicated the direction in which the pipes ran. "You will see that Saltbech is supplied direct from the Easterley reservoir by a pipeline that follows the main road. It is a fairly straight road and it would have been easy to run the pipes under it. But the supply to Burston, though coming from the same reservoir, follows quite a different direction. When it leaves the reservoir it goes directly along the road to West Bresleigh, the Collingtons' place, where it supplies the Hall and the village, and then continues to the cross-roads. Here it branches to the right—under these fields. Gunter's Farm, they belong to, and a worse farmer than Mr. Gunter it would be hard to find, though I will admit that his land is reputed to be the scrubbiest lot of acres in the county and it is hard for any man to scratch a living from them.

"The pipeline then continues under these fields to Mr. Whatley's place, Crossways Hall, and the village of Crossways, and from there on to Burston, and from Burston it simply follows the Calder as far as the barracks. I suppose the water company found it more economical than carrying the Saltbech supply out to the barracks, though it cannot be more than a couple of miles outside the town."

"I have heard that Whatley is a Yorkshireman, and careful not to spend money where he thinks it may not be needed. You do not suppose that he had cheaper, inferior pipes laid for the benefit of Burston and the barracks?"

"You forget that Sir James Collington's place is included in that source of supply as well as Mr. Whatley's," said Charles.

"That is so."

"I will tell you what I will do," said Charles at length. "I will try and discover if there is any man in Saltbech who was working on the laying of the pipes to Burston and the barracks. It is a pity the rector is away, but I'll speak to Short, one of his curates, and see if he can find out anything about it. I rather think, though, that most of the laborers would have been men employed from Easterley."

"I expect so." The captain sighed. "Well, I am doing all I can. Gallons of carbolic, a whole ward isolated, only liquids and soft food given to the patients, and so on."

"It is all you can do at the moment," agreed Charles. "As a precaution, boil all the drinking water in case that supply should have somehow become contaminated. I do not see how it could, but there are certainly no cases of typhoid so far in the town itself."

And so the two men parted, agreeing to advise each other if the disease spread any more.

On his way out of the town to see some patients at Burston, Charles called up to make the acquaintance of Mrs. Crichton at the rectory. Having arranged the meals with Mrs. Jennings, and agreed that the rector's holiday had been long overdue, The Honorable Alice had taken her knitting into the drawing room so that she could watch Octavius on the lawn outside, busy picking all the daisies he could find before Dimmock came along with his mower. Miss Pettit was with her, reading *The Times,* starting with the Births, Marriages and Deaths, going on to the leaders, then the Court Circular, and ending with the foreign news, as was her custom. Upstairs in the nursery, Nurse Blackwell, assisted by the nurserymaid Clara, was seeing that both day and night nurseries were cleaned properly, that the hearths were washed and scrubbed with Bath stone, and the fires relaid in case a fire was needed if the evening should prove chilly, and in washing Octavius's white socks.

Into this quiet haven Dr. Bellingham erupted with a speed and energy that surprised Mrs. Crichton, although she was not sorry to have the reading of *The Times* interrupted as the third leader was proving rather duller than usual. "You, I take it, are Dr. Bellingham," she said, as he apologized for having walked in on her so unceremoniously.

"I am Charles Bellingham, an old friend of your nephew's," he said. "I am afraid I seldom ring the front door bell or stand on ceremony with Septimus. I presume he has left for his holiday?"

"He went more than an hour ago."

"I am glad to hear that, because I have some news that might have made him hesitate. His conscience is far too active, and there is no reason at all why he should not have gone, but he might have taken a different attitude. Mrs. Crichton, I have been informed by the medical officer at the barracks that there are six confirmed cases of typhoid there, and several more suspected cases, not confirmed as yet. The men will of course be confined to barracks until we can be sure that there are no more cases, and that no infection has been spread from the barracks to the town. But in the meantime, Mrs. Jennings must be so kind as to see that none of her young servants go near the barracks." He smiled faintly. "I know it has a great attraction for young servant-maids."

"I am sure it has. I think you should give your message to Mrs. Jennings yourself, and at once. Pettit, ring the bell, please."

Mrs. Jennings came and received the doctor's order with composure. "I will see that none of them go near the barracks, sir," she said.

"Thank you. Oh, and Mrs. Jennings, I think that the drinking water should be boiled for at least ten minutes from now on."

"But I have never boiled the drinking water, sir." Mrs. Jennings was most indignant. "We do not use that stuff from the taps for drinking. We use the water from our own well in the park, and clearer, cleaner water it would be hard to find anywhere in England."

"Nevertheless, there is always the risk of a dead rat being found in a well," said Charles mildly.

"Not in our well, sir. Never. The lid fits much too tightly."

The housekeeper pursed her lips for battle, and it was Mrs. Crichton who intervened with an authority that could not be disobeyed.

"The doctor is right, Mrs. Jennings," she said firmly. "Please see that all drinking water is boiled for the time he says."

"Very well, madam." But Mrs. Jennings departed in a huff that showed itself in the swish of her skirts and the toss of her head.

As the door closed behind her, Octavius looked up from the lawn and saw Charles in the drawing room and came running to him, a small flower in his hand, clenched among the daisies.

"Good morning, Professor." Charles stepped through the open windows and squatted on his heels as usual beside the little boy. "What have you found this morning?"

"Mornin' Bellenum," said Octavius solemnly, leaning against his knees confidingly. "It's flower I don't know, please. It's like a clover, but it's very tiny and it's yellow."

The doctor examined it. "It's a trefoil, I think," he said. "But if your aunt will excuse us, we will go and look it up in Dr. Johns' book."

They went off together into the study and examined the book together until they found an illustration of the flower, and Octavius went back to the daisies on the lawn satisfied.

"Does he always call you 'Bellingham'?" asked Mrs. Crichton with amusement.

"We are men together," said the doctor smiling, and his eyes dwelt on the small figure outside with momentary tenderness. "He's a fine little fellow."

"You are not married?"

"No, I am not."

"You should be. But there is no need to look alarmed. I have no intention of trying to find you a wife while I am here. I expect the ladies of Saltbech have been doing that for years."

He met her eyes and laughed, and with a request that she would not hesitate to send for him if she should need assistance at any time, he went back to horse and trap and drove off to Burston.

There were no more cases of typhoid at Burston, but the following morning he found a note from the housekeeper at Crossways Hall asking him to be good enough to call that morning to see one of the housemaids there, as she had a high fever.

She had, as it happened, mentioned the fact to Mrs. Whatley when discussing the day's menu with her, and her mistress said with some alarm that she hoped she had not picked up anything from the barracks. "I hear there is an outbreak of typhoid there," she said.

"Oh no, ma'am. She is a very good steady girl, and she always spends her afternoon off once a month in going to see her mother. She comes from a very clean respectable home, and she is not a bit what I call flighty."

"I daresay it is only a chill, then. You say she has a fever?"

"Yes, ma'am. Quite a high fever, I think."

"I am glad you sent for Dr. Bellingham, then, though Dr. Annerley would have done just as well, and he does not charge so much. But if he says she has contracted anything infectious, she will be packed off at once to the fever hospital. Let that be understood."

"Yes, madam." The housekeeper conducted Charles up to the familiar attic floor given over to the women servants, and in a room mercifully so small that there was only space in it for one bed, a girl was lying, and it needed only one look for the doctor to know that she was very gravely ill.

He took her temperature that had run up to one hundred and four, felt her pulse, found the tell-tale rash on her stomach, and asked her how long she had been feeling ill. For some days, she said, but she had done her work as usual. She was not a girl, he thought, to shirk her duties.

When Mrs. Whatley heard that one of her housemaids had typhoid fever, she flew into a temper and said that she must have been visiting the barracks and had lied to Mrs. Dallings about going home.

The housekeeper, however, always ready to stand up for her "good girls" persisted that she always went home on her free afternoon once a month. Her family did not live more than three miles off, at Burston.

On being questioned by Charles before she was wrapped in blankets ready to be taken off to the new fever hospital, the girl said that her father's cottage was owned by Sir James Collington, who had recently had water put in for them from the Easterley Water Company, and that the last time she had gone home it had come out of the pump over the sink quite brown.

"It did not taste very nice," she added faintly. "But it was such a hot day that after walking all the way in the heat I drank some of it, brown as it was."

"Brown, eh?" Charles thought it over after he had seen two young stablemen carry the girl down on her mattress and into the waiting omnibus, warning them to wash their hands and arms in strong carbolic immediately they had got the mattress onto the floor of the omnibus. "Tell the driver to see that the inside of the omnibus is scrubbed out with carbolic directly he gets back," he added.

Mrs. Dalling, conscious of her employer's carefulness, was dismayed to hear that the mattress was not to come back.

"It will only have to be burned with the rest of her bedding," said Charles. "See that is done, please, Mrs. Dalling, and have the room scrubbed from floor to ceiling with strong carbolic before another girl goes into it." And he drove away.

At luncheon, Mrs. Whatley told her husband about the offending housemaid. "Horrid girl," she said. "Bringing a thing like that into the house. I hope none of the other servants have caught it. Mrs. Dalling does not know where she is to find another girl to replace her either—so tiresome, as we have a houseful of guests next week. I am sure she must have been haunting the barracks and picked it up there. There is nothing wrong with the water supply to Burston, any more than anywhere else."

"Burston?" Mr. Whatley put down his knife and fork for a moment. "Is that where this housemaid came from?"

"Most of the servants of the neighborhood come from Burston, my dear. Mrs. Dalling would not know what to do without that dirty little town."

Mr. Whatley did not answer. His thoughts touched for a second on that tiresome little man last year who had wanted to know all about the pipes the water company used. He had sent him to the rightabout pretty quickly, and although there was something that pricked at the back of his mind, he was able to dismiss it as fast as it had come.

His wife was quite right and her housekeeper was wrong. The housemaid had undoubtedly been associating with the men at the barracks.

Maud Dewey's sister Clara, aged sixteen, had been delighted to exchange the place of kitchenmaid at Lady Crockett's for that of nurserymaid at the rectory.

Most of all, she enjoyed taking Octavius for his afternoon walk, thus saving Nurse Blackwell's feet, and very pretty and neat she looked in her starched white dress with its long sleeves and starched cuffs and high collar, and the small black straw hat pinned firmly to her fair hair.

She found Nurse Blackwell almost as strict as Lady Crockett's under-cook had been, and she was dismayed when she was told that in future she must take her charge only into country lanes for his afternoon walk, and that she must not on any account take him into the town or on any road that led to the barracks.

There was a certain young man from the barracks who had recently happened to be on the quayside when she took Octavius there to look at the boats. Octavius loved the quay and all the activity that went on in the little harbor almost as much as he loved gathering wild flowers in the lanes.

Nurse Blackwell did not listen, however, when she said that the dust in the lanes turned the brim of her hat white when she walked in them. "Them water carts never come no nearer than the rectory gates," she told Nurse. "The dust is something shocking and I'm sure Master Tavie gets as choked with it as I do."

"You can take him across the fields, then," said Nurse, unyieldingly, "or down the lane to the churchyard and back. Not many traps and horses go down there because of the ruts."

Clara pouted, but obeyed. As she turned out of the rectory gates and away from the town on the Easterley road, unwashed by rain or the town water carts, the thick dust lay on the hedges on either side like flour spilled from a baker's cart, and the leaves and heads of the flowers growing there were outlined with green as if they had been etched against a gray-white background.

After trudging along for a little while in this fashion they came to a lane on the right, where only a few farmcarts ever made their way, and here the hedges were fresher and greener, and the flowers colored the grass instead of being smothered with dust.

Octavius ran on ahead, gathering flowers, naming each one as he did so and making a kind of song from the names. Ragged robin, crane's bill, scabious, ragwort, yarrow—he knew them all.

At the bottom of the lane there was a ford over a little stream and this influenced Clara in choosing this lane, because just before you came to the stream there was a cluster of cottages known as Deepdene. And in the end one of all, beside the stream itself, was the home of her mother,

Mrs. Dewey. Today a great deal of washing was hanging on the line behind the cottage, and Clara was surprised to see it there.

"I thought you only did your washing Mondays," she said as she stopped beside the hawthorn hedge to the garden, with her mother busy hanging out a sheet with pegs in her mouth. And then before her mother could remove the pegs and reply she went on, "Nurse Blackwell says I'm not to take Master Tavie into the town because of the typhoid at the barracks, so I thought I'd bring 'im long to see Teddie, instead. 'E's always at me to take him to see my little brother Teddie, ever since he knew he was his age and five, like him, next week."

" 'E can't see 'im today," said Mrs. Dewey, the sheet and the pegs disposed of. " 'Twouldn't be fit to take Master Tavie near 'im today. I've got 'im in bed and 'e may be sickening fur something. Measles, or something of that kind."

"What's the matter wiv 'im?" asked Clara while Octavius stood beside her solemnly, staring up at them both, his flowers grasped tightly in his hand.

"I dunno. 'E's a bit feverish and he has this sore throat and this funny sort of rash what's come up all over 'im. I don't s'pose 'tis anything serious, mind," added Mrs. Dewey. " 'E's niver 'ad no measles, so 'tis more'n likely 'tis that."

"Hev you had the doctor to 'im?" asked Clara.

"Lor' bless you, gel, I ain't got no shillings for doctors' visits. And you can tell your sister Maud when you git back as I still hevn't had that last shilling she owes me fur the three pair of black cotton stockings I bought 'er at ninepence a pair in the market three weeks ago." She smiled over the basket of washing at Octavius. "You look 'ot and tired my dear. Let Clara bring you in and set you down in my kitchen and I'll give you a drink of milk when I've hung out this lot. I've got really late wiv me washing this week, what wiv Teddie allus calling me for drinks of water."

"Thank you very much Mrs. Dewey," said Octavius politely. "But I'd much rather have some water, too, if you don't mind."

"Bless the child, 'course he shall hev what he likes." They waited in the little kitchen until she had finished with the washing, and then she fetched a gaily decorated Golden Jubilee mug from the stone sink, rinsed it out under the pump, and filled it from the same source.

"That's Teddie's favorite mug," she said as Octavius drank thirstily. " 'E won't take nothing from anything else but from that mug." She sat and talked to her daughter, giving Octavius a picture book to look at. It was given to Teddie by his schoolteacher, she told him, but he had got tired of it and so she brought it downstairs this morning in case he spilt something on it.

"Teddie loves lookin' at books," said his mother in a worried tone, "but this last day two seems 'e don't take no interest in anything any more." She heard the child call, and taking a small nightshirt that had been airing in front of the fire, she opened the door to a small steep flight of stairs and went up to her invalid, leaving Clara and Octavius to make their way home.

Two days later, Mrs. Dewey came to the rectory in a state of great grief to tell her daughters that their little brother was dead.

Dinah, who had been out to post a letter to Julia, met her as she was coming down the drive from the back of the house, and listened to it all with sympathy.

" 'E was light-'eaded," she told her. "So my John went fur Dr. Bellingham, and right down savage, 'e was. 'I can't perform miracles, woman,' 'e says, and me all frit to death wiv Teddie lying there not knowing me nor John nor nobody. ' 'Is froat is all swolled up and turned septic,' 'e says. 'This is scarlet fever, and you've sent fur me much too late. I can't save 'im now.' I begins to tell 'im we 'adn't the money to pay fur 'im, when 'e rounds on me and shouts, 'Damn you, woman, do you fink I cares 'bout money when a child's life is at stake?' And then he goes on to ask when he'd iver sent in a bill fur all the years 'e come to see my pore old mother, and her suffering as she did. Right down furious 'e was, but late that night 'e come back and tells me an' John to goo to bed, and 'e would sit up wiv Teddie. 'E tried to git 'im to tek a few drops of milk wiv brandy in it, but though my Teddie was clear-'eaded by then, 'e couldn't tek anyfing, and 'e could scarce breave. And at four o'clock in the mornin', just as my John was going to work, 'e comes to tell us that Teddie was gone. 'Just give a little smile and a sigh,' 'e says, ever so kindlike, 'and it was all over.' " She wiped her eyes on her apron. " 'E tried to comfort me by saying as I 'ad others, but they aren't like my Teddie. 'E wur allus be'ind me, see, wiv 'is little cart an' wooden 'oss and whip, an' chatter—'e niver stopped. 'E were such a 'appy little boy was my Teddie."

The rector's niece turned and walked back with her, and as

they reached the cottage door a strong smell of carbolic came out to meet them.

"That's the doctor," Mrs. Dewey told her. "Ivery sheet in the 'ouse was to be soaked in carbolic and 'ot water before I put 'em in the copper, and that's what I done. 'E's been so kind—'e left me two suvrins towards the funeral. I said I was sorry I'd bin sharp wiv 'im like, and 'e says, 'Don't you fret, my dear. It let the grief out of you and did you good.' And then 'e goes back to that big empty 'ouse of 'is all alone."

Dinah walked back slowly through the lanes, thinking of Charles Bellingham, who had such different sides to his nature, and wishing she could get to know him better.

But he always seemed to hold her at arm's length, and she supposed that he always would.

Chapter Sixteen

The rector's aunt received glowing letters from him, posted from various towns and villages in Sussex. They planned a leisurely tour of three weeks, with stops at places of interest for the space of a few days so that they could make excursions from them to ancient buildings that they might otherwise have missed.

Quin's bicycle was a hired one from a cycle shop in East Grinstead, and after the first day it gave trouble from time to time with its brakes.

"It is the back brake that is groggy," Septimus agreed, after examining it with him. "But the front one works splendidly, and as long as we do not run into a herd of cattle or a flock of sheep when going full tilt downhill, you should be returned to your family sound in wind and limb."

After the flat fenland, even Septimus found the Sussex hills too steep for him to ride up them, and as the roads were plentifully strewn with flints he preferred to push his machine, following Quin's example. His brother, being on the stout side, was better on flat roads, but it was evident from the second day that the holiday was doing them both a great deal of good.

Leaving East Grinstead High Street with its fine old timbered sixteenth and seventeenth houses they made their way down to Forest Row, and from there on to the wild and rugged region of Ashdown Forest. Here they crossed wild moorland for three miles, the heather-covered slopes, rugged gorseland and frequent woods of dark firs and young oak trees melting into the blue haze of distance, which was charming because it was so primitive and empty of villages and towns.

The road across the forest and onto Uckfield was not good going: it was made of the ironstone of the district, little heaps of red being left on the highway: the surface was bumpy, but they pushed on and eventually reached Uckfield and the old coaching inn that was to be their first stop.

Here they stayed for a few days before going on, making short excursions into the country round the town, and here Septimus received the only letter he was to have during his holiday from his niece Dinah.

Her great-aunt wrote regularly to report on the family at Saltbech, and if her letters became somewhat confined to the garden and the gardener's refusal to pick certain plums which she thought ripe enough for dessert and he did not, Septimus was more amused than made anxious by her scant references to the children he had left behind.

"I cannot think why I have not heard again from Dinah," he said to his brother when they reached Lewes and found no letter from her waiting for him there. "I left all the post office addresses with Aunt Alice, and Dinah can get them from her. It is unlike her not to write: she is such an excellent correspondent, and promised before I left that she would write frequently."

"She may have posted a letter too late to reach the last post office we called at," said Quin. "Or maybe you will find one from her at the next. There is no need to worry. Your family is in good hands, and you must remember that you are on holiday."

"I would have liked to hear from her all the same," said Septimus frowning. "I know she was a little put out because I left our addresses with Charles as well as with Aunt Alice, but I am sure she would not hold it against me."

"Of course she would not. Dinah is one of the most sensible young women I know," said Quin. "And if we are to reach

Chichester and Arundel before we have to turn back, we should be starting on our way again now, my dear fellow."

But again at the villages and towns where they called for letters at the post offices, there were no letters from Dinah, though again there were short ones from Mrs. Crichton. All was well, she told him, and she hoped he was having good weather. There had been a lot of fogs on the river lately, and the foghorns had been sounding—a most melancholy sound which he was fortunate to have missed.

If he had known the reason for Dinah not writing, there is no doubt that he would have turned home at once, a fact that she and her great-aunt knew only too well.

Septimus had been gone about three days when Nurse Blackwell came to Dinah's room after breakfast with a grave face.

"I don't like to worry Mrs. Crichton, miss," she said. "But Master Tavie is very feverish this morning, and he says his throat hurts. I think Dr. Bellingham should see him when he is on his rounds this morning. If you will write a note to him, I will ask the boy Tom to take it to him at once."

"Of course I will." Dinah went to the night nursery and looked down at her little brother, who was anything but his bright self that morning, and after feeling his hands and finding them to be burning hot, she went downstairs to the morning room where her great-aunt was at breakfast with the rest of the family and told them that Octavius was not well.

"There seems to be signs of a rash appearing, too," she said. "And Nurse thinks I should ask the doctor to call."

"Probably measles," said Mrs. Crichton. "But certainly write the note at once, and in the meantime none of the others had better go near him until we know what it is. We do not want you all down with measles at this time of the holidays."

Dinah wrote her note to Dr. Bellingham, and then sat down to write a letter to her uncle, telling him that they were managing very well, that they had been swimming a great deal, and were all as brown as berries. She weighed the letter in her hand when it was done, wondering if she should wait until the doctor had seen Octavius before she sent it, and decided against it. She did not think that her little brother had anything more serious than measles, and though that could be a nasty disease for a child that age, with Nurse

152

Blackwell to take care of him he would come to no harm. Maybe he had got a chill through getting too hot out in the sunshine, and sometimes he did get nettle rash at this time of the year.

Her great-aunt was busy with Mrs. Jennings when Charles arrived, and Dinah went into the hall to greet him and to thank him for coming so promptly.

"I could not neglect the Professor, could I?" he said, and followed her up the two flights of stairs to the nursery floor, and as they arrived at the door of the day nursery the little maid Clara came out, looking scared and distressed. She said good morning hastily and fled, and Charles went through to the night nursery where Octavius was lying in bed, looking flushed and unhappy.

Charles sat down on a chair beside his small patient and took his hand, feeling for his pulse. "Good morning, Professor," he said smiling. "What have you been doing to make yourself so lazy this morning? You are usually busy in the garden at this time of day."

Octavius tried to smile. "I'm so firsty," he said. "And I'm so hot. And my froat hurts and so does my head and so do my ears."

"Let us see what we can do to make you better then." Charles put down the small hand gently and asked Nurse to fetch a teaspoon. "I'll have a look at your throat first, shall I?" he said.

"Not wiv a spoon!" protested Octavius. "It will make me sick again, and I was very sick in the night, wasn't I, Nurse?"

Charles looked to Nurse Blackwell for confirmation and she nodded.

"He was very sick," she said. "But as he was not feeling well yesterday I put it down to a touch of the sun or too many plums."

"I won't bother him with a spoon, then. Open your mouth as wide as you can, Professor, and then Nurse won't have to fetch the spoon."

Obediently, Octavius opened his mouth and Charles took a quick glance at the white furred tongue, and then gently felt the swollen glands in the neck beneath the ears. As he did so Nurse Blackwell folded down the bedclothes, lifted the little nightshirt, and he saw the rash that had now spread all over the child's body.

"How long has he had this?" he asked Nurse.

153

"Only this morning, sir. He had nothing of it last night. But then it does come on suddenlike, don't it, sir?"

"Yes, it erupts very quickly," he agreed, and he knew that he had to deal with a sensible woman who had seen that rash before. He pulled the clothes back and over the bed; his eyes met Dinah's and she saw in them a gravity that told her that her little brother was very ill indeed.

A large jug of drinking water stood by the bed and as Nurse Blackwell stooped to give Octavius another drink, Charles went out of the room into the day nursery and Dinah followed him.

"It cannot be typhoid?" she asked breathlessly.

"Oh no. Typhoid does not usually attack children as young as Octavius." He added quietly, "He has scarlet fever."

"Scarlet fever?" She was horrified. "But where could he have caught it? He is always playing in the garden when he isn't being taken for walks by Clara in the lanes round here."

"As long as she hasn't taken him somewhere she didn't ought," said Nurse Blackwell ominously, following them into the room.

"The first thing to be done," the doctor told them with a calmness that quietened Dinah's fears, "is to avoid spreading the disease. What about the other members of your family, Miss Bretton? Can they go to Lady Bretton?"

"My mother is still on Lord Crowborne's yacht in the Mediterranean, I am afraid."

"Is she still there? I understood she was only going for a month. But no matter. We must think of something else. May I take it, Nurse, that you have nursed scarlet fever before?"

"Oh yes, sir, several times."

"Good. We shall need a hospital nurse for the nights only then, if you think you will be able to manage nursing Master Octavius during the day?"

"Oh yes, sir. No doubt about that. But the other young gentlemen and Miss Paula should be sent away."

"Let us go down and see my great-aunt," said Dinah. "She will be able to suggest what we can do with them."

Nurse fetched a bowl of water and a strong solution of carbolic in it with which the doctor could wash his hands before going downstairs, where Mrs. Crichton was waiting for them in the morning room.

"Well?" she said, looking from Charles's grave face to Dinah's frightened one. "What is it, Dr. Bellingham?"

He told her and Dinah asked her advice about the others in

154

the family. "They ought to go away," she said. "But where can we send them, Aunt A.?"

Her great-aunt considered. "Let me think which of your Bretton relatives would be likely to have them," she said and began ticking them off on her fingers. "Not the dean. He would not welcome them at the deanery, and neither would his wife. There will be endless committee meetings going on and garden parties, summer balls and dinner parties: no room for a family in quarantine for scarlet fever." She thought it over for a moment and then she said briskly: "The two elder boys can go to their Uncle Horace in Hampshire: it will be getting on for harvest time there now and they will be a help to him, and can shoot as many rabbits as they want. And I am sure Prue will take the twins and Miss Stroud. When should they go, Dr. Bellingham?"

"Today if possible."

"Then they shall. I will telegraph these good people to expect them, and send them all off on an early train this afternoon. Pettit and Hannah will help Miss Stroud and Mrs. Jennings to pack their clothes. They had better take everything they will want. It is a long illness, is it not, Doctor?"

"Six weeks from the onset of the disease."

"Then my niece, Miss Bretton, had better not come in contact with them before they go, as she has been in the child's room."

"It would be wise if she kept away from them. It is very infectious, but not really contagious until the rash starts to peel—then everything in his room must be kept where it is until it can be disinfected or burned."

Dinah asked his advice about her letter to her uncle. "I have written to tell him that all is well here and that I am glad he is enjoying his holiday, but do you think I should destroy the letter and tell him about Tavie? I know it will make him come hurrying home, and he has had so few holidays in his life."

"Say nothing to him yet and let that letter go. There will be time enough to summon him later—if it should be necessary."

"And you will find me a hospital nurse for little Octavius?" said Mrs. Crichton, but here Dinah protested.

"Could not Nurse Blackwell take on the night nursing if I were to be with Tavie in the day?" she asked. "He will hate strange faces round him when he is feeling so ill. If Nurse tells me what must be done I will do it most faithfully."

Nurse Blackwell was summoned and agreed that this was far the best plan as far as the child was concerned. "I will speak to Mrs. Jennings and tell her what we shall need," she added.

It seemed that what was needed most was carbolic acid, and before an hour had passed the smell of it was creeping down through the house from the nurseries, where the night nursery door now had a sheet soaked in it hanging over the doorway.

As he was going Charles suddenly stopped, remembering the little nursery maid he had seen coming out of Octavius's nursery, and he turned to the parlormaid Simmons as she came to open the front door for him. "Have you not got one of the Dewey girls working here?" he asked.

"Two of 'em, sir. One as housemaid, the other is Master Tavie's nurserymaid."

"May I see her, please? The one who works as nurserymaid, I mean."

"I will go and fetch her, sir."

Clara was fetched and burst into tears as she admitted taking Octavius into her mother's cottage when her little brother Teddie was so ill. "But he only hed a drink of water while he was there," she added. "And it come straight from the pump. 'E drank it out of poor Teddie's Golden Jubilee mug, while he was looking at a picture book the schoolteacher had given Teddie and what 'e felt too ill to look at no more, so my mother brought it down from his room 'case 'e spilt anything over it." She broke off, more scared than ever at the expression on Charles's face.

"The book and the mug," he said. "There are the sources of the infection. That settles that problem." He nodded to the unsmiling Simmons, picked up his hat and made for the door beyond which his trap and groom Benson were waiting with a rather restive Whitestar. In the meantime Simmons carried the story of Clara's iniquity to Nurse Blackwell, who rounded on her in the passage outside the nursery door in a fury not lessened by her anxiety over Octavius.

"You wicked girl," she said. "You knew you weren't to go near your mother's cottage when you was out with Master Tavie."

"But I didn't know as Teddie was ill," sobbed Clara. "And I hadn't seen Mother fur a fortnight. I didn't mean no 'arm—"

"Right is right and wrong is wrong," said Nurse Blackwell. "And if Master Tavie dies you'll hev yourself to blame. But don't stand there crying. That's not going to 'elp nobody, least of all Master Tavie. Go downstairs and bring two large pails of water with strong carbolic in 'em. Mrs. Jennings will show you how much to put in. All Master Tavie's things 'as got to go in them buckets before they're washed—nightshirts, sheets and all. Now go, girl, and 'urry up."

Clara wiped her eyes on her apron and ran.

The telegrams to unsuspecting relatives warning them of what was in store for them had already been sent off by young Tom and Miss Stroud, and the rest of the family had been told that they were to leave Saltbech directly after luncheon. Packing was feverish and excited, hampered rather than helped by Miss Pettit who always lost her wits in a crisis. The twins appealed to their great-aunt to allow them to take their bicycles with them, and after some consideration she agreed.

"I know you will be lost without them," she said severely. "Though when I was your age when I wished to visit my friends I either walked or I rode or I went in a carriage. But a *bicycle!* Nowadays, no young person seems able to walk a yard. They will shortly lose the use of their legs. Everything must be done on a bicycle."

Harold and Johnnie had no objection to going to Hampshire. They would write to the head gamekeeper at Bretton, who had charge of their guns, and they would tell him to send them to them. They promised themselves some sport with pigeon shooting and rabbits and, if they had to stay to the first of September, partridge, making their way like animated wine bottles through the stubble of the harvested fields.

After they had gone, waving to Dinah who had her luncheon apart from them in her sitting room, their eldest sister went upstairs to the box-room where her cases of linen were kept and took from one of them some double sheets made of linen, and brought them down to Mrs. Jennings to ask the sewing woman who came in every week to cut each sheet into four for Octavius's bed.

"They will be nice and cool for him, being of linen," she told the housekeeper, and did not add that she would be thankful to destroy the sheets with their beautifully embroidered initials, just as she would be glad to dispose of soft embroidered face towels that would be ideal for bathing the little boy's face and hands.

As far as the sickroom was concerned Nurse Blackwell took charge of everything, and the first morning after the rest of the family had gone, when she went to the night nursery to take over duty from her, Dinah was shown a large white housemaid's apron ready for her to wear.

"Mrs. Jennings has found some extra large ones for you to wear over your dress when you are in Master Tavie's room," she told her. "And she is going to find a large housemaid's cap to wear over your hair. You must touch Master Tavie as little as you can, and when you have to, wash your hands in the bowl of carbolic that I have left ready for you and for the doctor in the day nursery."

Dinah submitted to wearing the vast aprons that were kept for her, hanging up in the day nursery so that she could put them on directly Nurse Blackwell handed her charge over to her care in the mornings. Nurse agreed to taking the duty of sitting up all night with the little boy, leaving a written report for Dinah to give to the doctor when he came. And after the day with Octavius was done, Dinah would hang up the apron and cap in the day nursery and go to her room where she would find a hip bath and cans of hot and cold water waiting for her in front of a fire, in case the evening should have turned chilly. However tired she felt, she would bathe and change into clean clothes and an evening dress and join her great-aunt in the drawing room to discuss the day's news and any letters that might have come for her in the day.

The letters, sweet and sympathetic as they were, from Julia, and Sophy in Paris, and from her Aunt Emmeline and from her brothers and little Paula, had a strangely unreal air about them as if they came from another planet.

Her thoughts were entirely taken up with Octavius, her mind set on the moment every day when Charles Bellingham's visit was due.

The day nursery was kept scrupulously clean, and bowls of disinfectant and clean towels were always ready for him when he came. He smiled the first time he saw Dinah in her vast apron and cap, and told her that she looked like a true hospital nurse, but indeed she looked more like a child playing at being a nurse, although the nursing of her little brother would be no game.

"Wait," she said, "until you have seen what Mrs. Jennings has insisted the sewing woman make for you, and Nurse says I am to see that you put it on before you touch Tavie." She exhibited an even larger and more enveloping apron, with tapes that tied at the back. "Mrs. Jennings has had two or three made so that you will not take the fever on to your other patients. Nurse Blackwell tells me that the doctor to the family where she nursed one of the children with scarlet fever insisted on such precautions."

"It is extremely thoughtful of her," said Charles frowning. "But you may have noticed that when I visit Octavius I do remove my coat first and roll up my shirtsleeves to the elbows. I assure you I do have the safety of my other patients at heart."

"But you must put that apron on, all the same," she told him severely. "Otherwise you will offend not only Nurse but Mrs. Jennings."

"And I would not do that for the world." He gave in meekly, putting on the apron and letting her tie the strings for him at the back. Then he removed his gold cuff-links leaving them beside the bowl of carbolic water, rolled up his sleeves, and read the report that Nurse Blackwell had left for him as to how Octavius had fared in the night.

Attired thus in their aprons they went into the night nursery to visit little Octavius, and she would write down in her turn any directions he had for the day and for Nurse at night. As she watched his care of the little boy and listened to his detailed advice as to warm spongedowns, and ice packs to get the temperature down, and frequent sips of barley water and lemon, obeying his instructions to wash her hands frequently in the bowl of carbolic water in the day nursery whenever she had touched Octavius, she found a new side to the man, a side that perhaps her uncle had found from the beginning of their acquaintance.

Mrs. Jennings made no difficulty about ordering the ice. The fishmonger would send it every day, she said, wrapped in sacking.

One day, encouraged by his acceptance of her as one of the team who were working for Octavius, she asked him how the typhoid cases were progressing, and was told curtly that four men at the barracks were dead, he believed, but he did not know for certain, and dismissed her enquiries at that.

That evening when she spoke of it to her great-aunt in the drawing-room, Mrs. Crichton said that she believed Dr. Bellingham had lost the girl he was going to marry with typhoid some years ago, and it was probable therefore that it was not a subject he cared to discuss.

"How dreadful for him." Dinah was reminded of her own broken romance, severed by the ambition of a worthless man.

How much worse it would have been, she thought, if it had been through the death of a man worthy to be loved.

She felt suddenly ashamed of the hard attitude she had been taking ever since she had that letter from Clive, and the resolve she had made then that she would never think seriously of another man or trust him. Charles Bellingham was a man any girl could trust, even if she could not marry him, and naturally it would not be possible for a Miss Bretton to marry a medical practitioner. He needed somebody like little Janet Annerley, sweet and gentle and sympathetic, and ready to think of her husband before herself at all times. She had been the daughter of a country lawyer, she told Dinah when they were practising tennis at the club in preparation for the Crockett's tennis party. Her conscience smote her a little as she thought of Janet, and how she had neglected her utterly since her usefulness to her was finished.

Not that Janet held it against her. Whenever she had seen her in the town she had smiled and waved a hand, as she struggled back to her doll's house with a basket full of things like groceries and even loaves of bread on her arm. Not for Janet the grandeur of having the grocer come out to her as she sat in a carriage in the High Street to ask her wishes: she liked to have a chat over the counter with the grocer's wife, while as for Adcock the baker, she could never pass his shop without being drawn inside, partly by the delicious smell of newbaked bread, and partly from the joy of a few words with his wife who served at the counter, looking with her beaming face and plump figure with the apron strings tying it round the middle, almost exactly like one of her own cottage loaves.

Chapter Seventeen

"There is no telegram from Mamma," Dinah said, as she opened a letter from Julia some evenings later, posted to her from London but telling her that by the time she received it they would be on their way to Scotland for grouse-shooting, invited by a client of her uncle's who had a castle there as well as a grouse-moor.

"Did you expect your mother to telegraph?" asked the Honorable Alice drily as she perused Julia's ecstatic letter.

Dinah raised her head. "No," she said then. "I do not think that I expected it. But of course," she added quickly, "it must be very difficult to receive telegrams when you are cruising about the Mediterranean on a yacht, and it must be just as difficult to send them."

Her great aunt made no comment, and Dinah went on reading Julia's letter, in which she said that Mr. Jonathan Cottrill was to be one of the house party in Scotland.

"She is always talking about Mr. Cottrill in her letters," her eldest sister said. "It sounds as if this house party is going to be fun for her, bless her heart. She says that Aunt Emmeline had bought some lovely new clothes for her, and an evening dress trimmed with fur, and Uncle Edmund has given her some pearls to wear with it. I think they are spoiling her, don't you, Aunt Alice?"

"Julia is not one to be spoiled," said her great-aunt mildly. "She is a nice, unaffected child. Does she say anything about Tavie?"

"Oh yes. She says how terribly sorry she was to hear about his illness, and she hopes he will soon be better. She also says that Aunt Emmeline knew somebody who had scarlet fever and it affected her eyesight, so that she had to wear spectacles ever after. I cannot imagine our poor darling little Tavie in spectacles, can you, Aunt A.? He would look more like a professor than ever." Her voice shook a little. "I am glad none of them realize how very ill he is."

"The boys sent him a book, did they not?"

"The Gorilla Hunters," said Dinah with a little forced laugh. "They said they thought it would be a bit old for him, so perhaps Paul and Paula would like it when they came back to the rectory. And Aunt Prue sent him *Alice in Wonderland,* but when I tried to read it to him today he did not seem to be listening and kept going off to sleep."

"Does Julia say anything else?" asked her great-aunt, changing the subject abruptly.

"She says one extraordinary thing," said Dinah returning to the letter. "She met Miss Maitland at a dinner party shortly before they were to leave for Scotland, and she gave her a message for me."

"A message for you, my dear?"

"Yes. She said Julia was to tell me not to believe all I heard, that she was to give me her love and say that she had not forgotten me, nor ever would. Isn't that odd?"

"Most strange," agreed her aunt. "I wonder what she meant by it. In her last letter to me Emmeline said that Miss Maitland's wedding date was fixed for October the first, when pheasant-shooting starts, and that as Lord Morrell always has his first large shooting party on that day he was not best pleased."

Dinah smiled. She had no interest in Miss Maitland, or in Major Clive Morrell or in his uncle. The wedding could be when they chose, it was nothing to do with her and had no more power to hurt her.

She was wrong however when she thought that her mother had not received their telegram. It was handed into the yacht a few days before they left Piraeus.

"I hope," said Violet Crowborne anxiously, "it is not bad news?"

Helen opened it and read "OCTAVIUS DANGEROUSLY ILL WITH SCARLET FEVER. COME AT ONCE. YOUR UNCLE ON HOLIDAY. AM HERE AT THE RECTORY IN HIS ABSENCE. A. CRICHTON."

Helen read it twice frowning. It was extremely tiresome that Octavius had scarlet fever, but what good did Aunt Alice think she could do by rushing home to him? And if Septimus had gone away for a holiday the child could not be "dangerously" ill. She sent a reply, "AM GLAD TO HEAR YOU ARE AT THE RECTORY. WILL LEAVE EVERYTHING SAFELY IN YOUR HANDS. LOVE HELEN."

"Is it bad news?" asked Violet.

"Not at all." Helen tore the telegram into tiny pieces and dropped them overboard. "Aunt Alice Crichton is at the rectory while Septimus has gone away for a holiday. I do not know why she wasted sixpence on a telegram when a letter would have done just as well." And she went to ask the steward to see that her reply was sent off before they left.

The Saltbech rectory seemed empty without the children, but every day callers came to ask after the rector's little nephew, whose fifth birthday came and went without comment. His great-aunt sent messages of thanks to the visitors, and if it should be a warm day and she happened to be sitting in the garden, she would ask the callers to join her there for a little while.

She was afraid, she told them, that little Octavius was

gravely ill, but he was in good hands. Dr. Bellingham could not do more than he was doing, and now he was calling two or three times a day. In answer to a question as to whether she had let the rector know, she replied that she had not. He would be so worried if he broke his holiday to come home that he would be up and down the stairs a thousand times a day and in the night as well, wanting to know how the invalid was, and there would be no peace for anyone, including himself.

"It is far better to let him continue his holiday," she said.

Before she took over her duty for the day from Nurse Blackwell, Dinah would go out into the park and pick a small bunch of wild flowers to put in a small vase on the windowsill in the night nursery so that her little brother could see them there by the open window. Nurse was strict about having an open window in Octavius's room: fresh air, she said, was what was needed in a sickroom. The last place she was in before she came to Bretton, when one of the children went down with scarlet fever, Miss Nightingale, who had been a friend of the child's mother, was quoted as saying that open windows were essential for a patient's recovery.

Dinah liked sitting by the open window herself, with the cooing of the ring-doves from the dovecot in the stableyard, and the distant sound of the lawn mower coming in through it, although she began to fear that little Tavie could hear neither, just as he made no comment about the wild flowers she brought fresh every day, and indeed scarcely seemed to see them, only just aware that she was there, too.

"The rash is going, I think," Dinah said one day after the doctor's apron strings had been tied to her satisfaction. "I think it is beginning to peel slightly, so that he must be getting better, mustn't he?" She followed Charles into the room and stood beside him as he stooped over the child.

But it was plain that, in spite of his sister's optimism, Octavius was not so well that day. His temperature had climbed to one hundred and five, the glands beneath his ears were more swollen, and his throat was so inflamed that he could scarcely swallow.

"Yet he must have food," Charles said. "Milk—beef-tea—anything to stop him from growing any weaker. If those glands are not going down by tomorrow I shall have to open them, and he is so weak that I doubt if he will stand it."

"We have tried everything," said Dinah. "And he says he cannot swallow."

The doctor saw the feeding cup of milk on the table beside the bed and took it to the mantleshelf where there was a small flask of brandy that Mrs. Crichton had sent up to the room. He took a teaspoon and put two teaspoonsful into the feeding cup and gave it back to Dinah. "Try and get a little down him, even if it is only a few drops at a time. And keep those cold-packs going on his forehead—his temperature is much too high."

Octavius scarcely seemed to know that the doctor was there that morning: he did not smile when his eyes rested on him, and he shut them almost immediately as if the daylight hurt.

As she followed Charles into the day nursery Dinah began to wonder if the child was going to recover. She stood watching him as he carefully soaped his hands and arms, and as she slipped off his apron and hung it up on its peg behind the door she said quietly, "He *is* going to live, isn't he, Dr. Bellingham?"

He wiped his hands and arms dry before he answered, taking a long time over it, and then he said with a smile she had never seen before, so kind it was and so understanding, "With you and Nurse Blackwell fighting for him day and night, and myself as your aide I believe we *must* defeat this thing between us. But I will not hide from you, Miss Bretton, that now we have our backs to the wall."

And then he shrugged himself into his coat, picked up his hat and went away downstairs.

That night Octavius was delirious, calling for Dinah to pick some honeysuckle that was out of his reach. At midnight, Nurse Blackwell requested that Tom be roused and sent for the doctor.

Charles came at once and sponged down the child's body with tepid water and held cold-packs to his head, staying there all night, moving silently, speaking in whispers to Nurse so that they should not disturb the household, and not allowing Dinah to be roused.

"Better if we face this alone," he said, while little Octavius babbled on about the wild flowers he was picking for his mamma. "She will love them, won't she?" he kept asking. "When she sees that lovely honeysuckle she won't frow it away as she did the others I picked for her, will she? Mamma, I picked it for you"—and so it went on, telling Charles much about the household and the Bretton family. "Dinah not going—Dinah staying here—Dinah with me always—she said so, didn't she?"

164

Poor children of the wealthy, thought Charles. Where did they go for love when they were small? Not to their mothers, often absent, seldom ready to enter into their little pleasures. Not to their fathers, who were out with their friends or in their London clubs, or standing for Parliament or some such nonsense. Their children were small encumbrances that had to have nurses and governesses and tutors and be seen as seldom as possible until they were grown up, when the girls were groomed to be beautiful so that they would make good marriages, and the boys taught *savoir faire* so that they would find themselves partners who would not disgrace the family. Could they not understand, these great ones of the earth, that in avoiding their responsibilities they laid their children open to a host of petty vices that must eventually bring some great families to ruin and disgrace?

By the time the dawn broke, the little boy's throat was slightly less swollen, and Charles felt he might dare to give it another twenty-four hours before operating and subjecting the wasted little frame to an even greater strain, although the temperature was higher. Nurse however managed to get some milk laced with brandy down the child's throat, and Charles told her to keep on with it, and with the sponging, and left in the dawn, with the red light of another day breaking beyond the church spire, its weathercock throwing back the gold as if it were made of that metal.

Dinah had heard him come and the trap drive away, and she had been unable to sleep, unwilling to get up and go to the night nursery in case she should be a hindrance instead of a help, yet longing to know why Charles had been sent for. She heard him go, and getting out of bed saw the back of his tall figure as he walked away down the drive. His hat was off and his face was lifted to the sky and the breaking dawn, and she wondered how many times he had done this—answering night calls, staying with patients until the dawn, and then walking home to a silent house.

To Dinah, time passed from then onwards without her noticing if it were night or the dawn of another anxious day. Keeping the window open she also kept a fire going in the grate of the sickroom, scuttles of coals wrapped in paper being brought up by Clara and left outside the door, so that when Dinah or Nurse made up the fire the wrapped coals would not clatter but could be put onto the fire quietly.

It was the dawn of every day that caused greatest anxiety, but Nurse Blackwell met it calmly, while Dinah still bathed and changed to go down and sit with her great-aunt in the evenings, finding her kindness beyond anything she could have expected. No platitudes, no assurances that there was no need to worry, only a deep understanding of that worry and quiet questions that could be left unanswered.

Letters came, but she left them to her great-aunt to read and to answer for her. She would read them, she said, when Octavius was better. She refused to believe that he would not get better. Some days the fever took over and he would turn and toss and demand drinks of water, and at others he would lie quite still, scarcely breathing, and not hear her when she spoke to him. Many of such times she thought he must be dead. She lived through those days in a constant state of acute anxiety and dread, unable to sleep or rest at night in case Nurse came to tell her to come at once.

And then, one morning when she arrived in the day nursery to find a clean apron and cap waiting for her, Nurse Blackwell told her that she thought Master Tavie was slightly better.

Scarcely able to believe it, Dinah went into her little brother's room and when she asked him if he felt well enough to eat some bread and milk, he smiled for the first time and said, "Yes, I fink I does." She waited with impatience for the doctor to come, because in the end only half a saucerful had been eaten and she wanted reassurance after all this time—so short in actual fact and so endless in fear—and when he came she was waiting for him in Octavius's room.

He came to the bed and looked down at the little boy, and saw that the flush had gone and the eyes were bright.

"Good morning, Professor," he said, and Octavius looked up at him gravely and said in a hoarse little voice, "Mornin', Bellenum."

Across the bed the doctor's eyes met Dinah's and he saw them fill. On a sudden impulse he put out his hand to her, and she put hers into it and felt it gripped for a moment in a strong grasp before he let it go.

"We have won," he said.

After that day time that had seemed so endless began to proceed at its normal level. Meals were sent up and eaten and more was demanded. Custards and jellies and beef-tea and mutton broth gave way to fish and pieces of chicken and the tenderest vegetables from the rectory garden.

Letters that arrived from the outside world were now a

matter of interest, and in a week's time the rector would be home again with his cycling tour behind him.

In the meantime, convalescence had its problems. Dinah had to keep from Octavius his favorite toys, knowing that if he had them or any of his best loved storybooks they would have to be destroyed when the period of infection was ended, causing great grief.

The time came however when the doctor called every fine morning to carry the little boy down into the garden, and there Octavius found joy again in his beloved flowers, walking round the paths gravely, hands behind his back, examining every plant to see what had flowered since he last saw them.

For toys Dinah thought of endless paper games for them to play together on the night nursery floor, and one wet day she remembered a pile of old newspapers that were in the room upstairs where her trunks were stored.

She fetched some down and gave Octavius a blunt-tipped pair of scissors, and together they cut out a Noah's Ark, and all the pairs of animals and birds that should go into it, together with Mr. and Mrs. Noah and their sons.

It kept them occupied all that day, and as the next morning was wet, too, and still more animals were required, she took a paper from the bottom of the pile and saw that it was a very old one, dated ten years previously.

With a stirring of interest she opened it and read some of the news, and then, tucked away in a corner, she saw a small paragraph with the headline: RECTOR'S SON ATTACKS STABLEBOY WITH KNIFE.

She looked at it more closely, and as she read it through a sudden disbelief filled her because the news it contained simply could not be true.

On the Tuesday of the previous week, the paragraph stated, a stableboy working at the Rectory of All Saints in Saltbech was attacked by the rector's son, Master Christopher Crichton, with a tableknife. There appeared to have been no reason for the attack, and the boy was in hospital. The rector, the Reverend Septimus Crichton, had been very upset by the episode, and said that his son, now fourteen years of age, had recently become the subject of ungovernable fits of unreasoning rage, when he would attack anyone without thinking what he was doing. He did not think the stablelad had provoked the attack, and he was finding an establishment where his son could be sent as soon as possible.

Fourteen years of age, and that was ten years ago. Dinah sat on the floor to consider it, trying to view it with compassion and without horror.

Her cousin Christopher must be dead, surely, reasoned one part of her mind, wanting to believe it. But the other half dwelt on the locked room with its barred windows and the cricket bat and the model ship on the table, and her uncle's visits to "a relative" on the first of every month. And she knew that that relative must be her cousin Christopher, now aged twenty-four and still an inmate of the "establishment" where her uncle had placed him ten years before.

Here Octavius demanded more paper for cutting out and she gave him a different paper, putting the old one back under the pile and returning it later to the box-room, but that evening when she sat with her great-aunt as usual in the drawing room she told her of her find.

"Do you not think it is time I knew something about it?" she asked.

The Honorable Alice thought for a long moment, looking into the red ash of the logs in the big fireplace, and then she said with a sigh: "Yes, my dear, I think you should know about it, and then you will see why it is never spoken about in the family or outside it."

Here she was wrong, as it happened, because the whole town knew about the episode, and everyone knew where the rector went on the first of every month. Even the porter who took his ticket would say in a low tone to the stationmaster, "The rector's been visiting that mad son of his agin, poor soul." But to the rector himself not one of his parishioners, or indeed anyone else, ever mentioned Christopher. He did not speak of him, and they respected his wish for silence on the matter and seldom spoke of him even among themselves.

"Your cousin Christopher's brain was damaged at birth," went on Dinah's great-aunt quietly. "From his early childhood he was subject to fits of ungovernable rage, when he would attack anybody or anything. I remember when he was Tavie's age he killed a kitten by strangling it with a bootlace. As he got older, the fits became worse, so that no governess would stay, and even tutors were afraid of him. He hit one poor man with a hammer, and he was unconscious for a week. Then, of course, there came this terrible matter of the stableboy, who only just escaped with

168

his life, and poor Septimus had to find a private establishment where he could be watched day and night and his actions restricted when necessary.

"The brain specialist at the head of the establishment is a very good man, I believe. Oh yes, Christopher is still there. Sometimes, I have heard, he becomes so much better that they think of allowing him home on a visit, and then he will go suddenly wild and attack one of his keepers, and they know it will be no good. I do not think there has been any improvement in the last ten years."

"Poor Christopher—and poor Uncle Sep." Dinah's heart was torn between them.

They talked a little more about the aunt she had never known, who had died when Christopher was a year old and mercifully spared the tragedy that was to strike her husband through him, and then Dinah went up to bed.

And as she went through the great hall, the three globes of its central chandelier throwing deep shadows under the stairs and the gallery, once more she felt that cold shadow touch her, and this time it was as if for one second a madman stood there watching her with a knife in his hand.

The following day the old newspapers were forgotten in a letter that arrived from Septimus. The thing he had feared had happened. Quin's faulty brakes had given way completely when he was going down a steep hill that ended in a small bridge over a stream at the bottom.

The bicycle had struck the bridge, throwing poor Quin over the handlebars into the stream, which was fortunately not very deep. The bicycle was a wreck and Septimus's brother had a broken collarbone besides severe concussion. He had been taken to an inn in a nearby village where the landlady was kind and the beds were clean, and he intended to remain there with Septimus to look after him until the collarbone healed, which the doctor who had been summoned said must be at least three to four weeks.

"Three to four weeks," Dinah repeated with satisfaction when this part of the rector's letter was read out to her. "That is a good thing. Uncle Sep will not be arriving home until Tavie is out of quarantine and the others back home, and everything as he left it. Is it not a splendid thing, Aunt A.?"

Her great-aunt said dryly that it did not seem to be a very

splendid thing for poor Quin to end his holiday in such a way, but that Dinah knew her opinion about bicycles, and if it were to teach him never to ride one again it might not be such a bad thing, after all.

Chapter Eighteen

Only a little while remained before Octavius would be out of quarantine and the family free to return to the rectory, and Charles seemed to be no longer anxious about him, or about the Brettons as a whole. He dropped back into his old habit of calling up at the house every day, as he had promised Septimus he would do, to assure himself that all was well, being content with Mrs. Jennings' reports repeated to him by Simmons.

Dinah felt hurt and neglected, and scolded herself for her lack of reason without success. But they had fought for Octavius's life between them and they had won, and now it seemed that the victory instead of drawing him nearer into the family circle had resulted in him dismissing them from his mind.

He was a doctor, after all, with a large country practice, taking him sometimes miles into the country, and a man who had been up night after night with his patients, as he had been that one night with Tavie, would not feel like wasting time on social calls.

As it happened, there was a cause for his neglect. One morning he was sitting over a late breakfast after a night's session with a very ill old man when Janet Annerley put her head in at the dining-room door.

"I am sorry to interrupt your breakfast, Charles," she said, slipping into a chair on the opposite side of the breakfast table and helping herself to a small piece of toast. "But I met Mr. Short at the Lawn Tennis Club yesterday and he told me you are interested in the Easterley Water Company's supply of water from the reservoir to the barracks, and wanted to find somebody who had helped to lay the pipes. He could not tell me why, and said he was sure all the laborers had been hired from Easterley, which seems sensible. But I happened to go into Adcock the baker's on my way home because I saw some of those lovely little rolls that Mrs. Adcock makes and Mark adores, and I recollected that she had come from Easterley and I asked her if she remembered the water pipes being laid to the barracks, and she said she did remember it because her own brother Isaiah Swingletop, was working for the water company at the time."

"Isaiah Swingletop?"

"Yes. Does it not sound like somebody out of Dickens? Anyway, she said she remembered he had been a bit worried at the time because of something to do with the pipes they were laying, but she could not remember what it was and she did not think anything could have been wrong with them, because Mr. Whatley would never have allowed it."

"The company's engineer certainly would not have permitted it, either," said Charles, pushing the marmalade over to her. "Don't nibble that dry toast. Have some marmalade with it."

"Thank you, but I like dry toast." She went on nibbling.

"Did Mrs. Adcock say where her brother lives now?"

"Oh, in Easterley, though I do not think he works for the water company anymore. He said they were too niggling with their wages."

"Mr. Whatley again," said Charles.

"I daresay. But she said that Mr. Adcock knows all about it, and if you would like to come and see him next Sunday afternoon when I understand he has a rest before starting on the night's baking, he will be pleased to tell you all he knows about it." She finished her nibbling. "What delicious toast your housekeeper makes, Charles. My little maid of all work turns perfectly good slices of bread into blackened cinders of an uneatable hardness." She got up. "I must go back to my dolls' house now, or the butcher's boy will be calling for orders, and my mind will not extend to anything more than mutton chops."

She went off happily, and Charles finished his coffee and decided to drop into the baker's house the following Sunday afternoon.

The shop was on the corner of Ship Lane in the High Street, and when Charles had finished the mid-day dinner that his housekeeper provided for him on Sundays he made his way to Mr. Adcock's house.

Ship Lane was a small narrow street with rows of cottages on either side and fenced gardens bright with late summer flowers. Sunflowers were growing there and hollyhocks, the flowers that remained growing near the top, and stocks, and nasturtiums scrambling over the fences and round the gate-posts.

Mr. Adcock's house was the first on the left and larger than the others, not only because of the bakery to which it was joined, but because Mr. Adcock had rebuilt it to his liking. It was of red brick with a green-painted front door, and a shining brass knocker in the shape of a dolphin, and on either side of the front door tubs with myrtle trees in them.

He found Mr. Adcock in the parlor, sound asleep after a large mid-day meal of roast beef and Yorkshire pudding followed by apple pie and good Cheddar cheese, and he would not have disturbed him had not Mrs. Adcock taken the matter into her own hands and shaken her husband into wakefulness.

"Wake up, Sid," she said. "Here's Dr. Bellingham come for a word with you. About them pipes that was laid to the barracks, the pipes we thought might have something wrong with 'em."

"Nothing wrong with 'em, my girl. Don't you let Mr. Whatley 'ear you say that or 'e'll move 'is custom elsewhere and with good reason. Most careful gentleman is Mr. Whatley, and him chairman of the water company an' all. But set you down, Doctor, and I'll tell you all Isaiah told me, which isn't much, any road."

Charles sat down and waited while Mr. Adcock filled his pipe, and when he had got it going he asked what sort of pipes had been used.

"Why, they be best cast iron, sir. All Easterley Water Company's pipes is cast iron."

"What was thought there might be wrong with them, then?"

"Nothing was wrong with most of 'em, sir. They was mostly new ones when they was laid, but to save buying more than they need they did use up some second-'and ones. They belonged to the water company, mind, being those used for the old fever hospital. That was what my old woman meant just now. 'Why, Isaiah,' she says when her brother tells us about it, 'you niver took water pipes from sich a nasty place

172

as that old fever hospital?' And Isaiah he laughed and says as how they'd niver held nothing but water before and was niver going to hold nothing but water agin."

"I suppose the old ones were in good condition?" said Charles, becoming interested in the way the Easterley Water Company saved money on their pipes.

"There was nothing wrong with the pipes, Isaiah said. It was the jints they hed trouble with, being a bit perished-like, and with moving of 'em they worked a bit loose, so they had a hard time of it making of 'em watertight, but they did it in the end." Then as Charles was silent he went on: "They was only used from West Bresleigh, under two fields of Farmer Gunter's, before going on to Crossways and Burston and the barracks."

"So they had to dig up Gunter's fields, did they? He could not have liked that very much."

Mr. Adcock laughed. "Thet he didn't," he told the doctor. "And the way he ranted and swore, Isaiah said, you'd hev thought as he hed the best bit of land in the country, which the water company was deliberately destroying so as to ruin him. It was a load of nonsense, of course, but Sir James was a bit conscience-struck like, because the man was his tenant, and this last spring he's hed sewage pumped over them fields to give 'em a bit of body to the grass. I don't know what it's done to the grass, mind you, but if you are iver out that way, sir, you'll smell them fields a mile away, and I'm pretty sure it won't do Gunter a penn'orth of good, neither."

He saw Charles's face go suddenly thoughtful and he added hastily: "Not that sewage kin do any 'arm, can it, sir? I've bin told as sewage when used on the land is mostly ammonia and the surface stuff don't do no good, but Gunter swears it's improved 'is grassland, so I s'pose it's a way of manuring land as well as ridding it of cesspools and the like."

Charles agreed, thanked him for his kindness in allowing him to interrupt his Sunday rest and took his leave, and went back to his house to get out the old plan again and study it carefully.

There was no doubt about it, he was forced to conclude in the end, the second-hand pipes had been laid under those fields of Gunter's where sewage had recently been pumped as manure. The sandy ground would be saturated by this time, and if some of it had penetrated any leaky joints of those old pipes there might lay the root of the trouble at the barracks and among his patients in Burston.

173

He determined to call on Sir James Collington and lay the whole matter before him and ask his advice, because he knew if he went to Whatley about it he would be received with incredulity and disbelief. But as it happened, on the following morning, just as he had finished surgery and was in his dispensary making up some medicines, a message came from Crossways Hall requesting him peremptorily to come at once.

"Did the messenger say if it was one of the servants who was ill?" Charles held a glass bottle with its tablespoon measures in raised notches on the sides to the light, measuring drops in carefully, one at a time. If one of the Crossways servants were ill he would send Mark, he thought, because he knew his partner would be more welcome to Mr. Whatley's pocket.

"Please, sir, the man said something about one of the young ladies being taken ill," the little housemaid told him.

Then why the deuce doesn't Whatley send for his fine London physician? thought Charles irritably, finishing with the bottle, corking it with a new cork from a drawer, and fixing a printed label stating how many doses were to be taken in the day. He then wrapped it neatly in a sheet of white paper, taken from another drawer, with dabs of sealing-wax top and bottom to keep the paper in place, wrote the name and address of the patient on it, and left it on the table in the hall with several others that were to be delivered by Gideon, his bootboy-*cum*-messenger lad, later in the day. Then, with the same lack of hurry he went out to the stables where Benson had Whitestar ready harnessed in the trap, and taking the reins drove at a leisurely pace through the town and out over the country roads to Crossways village, taking his time. No doubt the young lady at Crossway Hall had a slight sore throat, and rather than incurring the expense of his London physician for a trifling ailment, Percy Whatley had thought fit to call in a local man who might be expected to deal with sore throats, if with nothing more serious.

But when he arrived at Mr. Whatley's grand mansion it was to find a scene of consternation and fright far exceeding his expectations. Miss Henrietta, the housekeeper told him, in tones of reproof for his tardiness, was in bed with a high fever, and would the doctor follow her upstairs at once please?

She led the way up the wide, carpeted front staircase, with its elaborately carved bannisters and ornate iron lampholders cast like gods and goddesses, holding globes of gas lamps at the half landings. It was evident that his visit to Miss Henrietta was held to be urgent, and he followed the housekeeper's rustling black dress down wide corridors until they arrived at a luxurious bedroom, where a girl of seventeen lay almost unconscious on an elaborate French bed. He went to her quickly and asked her maid, an elderly sensible woman by the name of Annie, about the details of the illness and heard there had been sickness and diarrhea.

He asked her to turn back the bedclothes and lift the girl's nightdress, and across the slender stomach he saw the telltale rings of the rash he had expected, a rash that had probably only just come and would be gone as speedily. He glanced at the marble-topped washstand and saw the cutglass carafe of drinking water, with its cut-glass tumbler catching the sunshine that fell across the room from the windows. He took the patient's temperature and found it to be over one hundred and five, and as she was sufficiently conscious to be able to answer a few questions, he sat down by her bed and asked if she had been drinking water from any of the taps in the house.

"There's nothing but drinking water in every bedroom in the house, sir." Annie was indignant. "It comes direct from the well in the park."

"I did drink some water from a tap once," whispered Henrietta. "It was about a fortnight ago, Annie, after I had come home from Lady Collington's dance. We had anchovies at supper, and I ate rather a lot of them and it made me terribly thirsty. After you had left me to go to bed I emptied my carafe of drinking water, and I woke up in the night still thirsty, so I took the carafe along to the bathroom and filled it from the bath tap. The water was brownish and did not taste very nice, but I was too thirsty to care."

"Thank you," said Charles. "That is all I want to know. Now lie there quietly and we must see what we can do to make you better."

He came downstairs to find Mr. Whatley and his wife in the library, waiting anxiously for his opinion.

"It is a simple case," he said briefly. "Your daughter has typhoid fever, contracted, I am almost certain, from drinking water from one of the taps in this house. I have given directions to her maid, and it would be wise if her mother and brothers and sisters were to keep out of her room."

"I shall certainly not keep out of her room," said Mrs.

Whatley sharply. "I am not afraid of catching typhoid."

"I am sure you are not," he said, liking her for the first time. "But I am equally sure you will not wish to take it to your other young people. It is a deadly disease, extremely contagious and infectious, and it attacks young people of that age more than older ones. But I have no doubt you will be telegraphing for your London physician, and when you do please tell him to bring with him two nurses experienced in nursing such cases."

"But how could she catch it from drinking tap water?" cried Mrs. Whatley. "That reservoir has been analyzed again this year, has it not, Percy?"

Mr. Whatley sat wretchedly silent, and Charles eyed his whitening face with some sympathy as he continued quietly:

"It seems that the water supply to Crossways, Burston and the barracks, may have become contaminated by soil infection from where the water pipes run under two fields rented from Sir James Collington by the farmer, Mr. Gunter. If the pipes were new and fitted properly when they were laid then I am wrong, but if there should have been any faults in the joining of the pipes then the sewage that Sir James is having pumped into those fields on Gunter's farm could have infected the supply beneath them. You will know more than I do about such matters, Mr. Whatley, but it is a suspicious circumstance that it is only below those fields that typhoid has broken out, causing several deaths at Burston and about ten to date at the barracks. I must leave the explanation in your hands, as you will know what pipes were used for the supply that ran under Gunter's fields, and the conditions they were in when they were laid. But I would advise that you approach Sir James at once and request that sewage be no longer used on those fields, so that when it is fit the land can be opened up and the pipes examined. In the meantime, as a precaution, perhaps the water company should cut off supplies of water this side of Gunter's farm."

Mr. Whatley still said nothing, but after Charles had pocketed his half sovereign and left, Mrs. Whatley asked her husband if there had been any truth in what he had said.

Percy Whatley sighed and was unwilling to admit at first that the pipes used had been the old ones from the old fever hospital. "But they were cast iron and in good condition, and they were ours," he added trying to exonerate his actions. "There was some small trouble about the joints leaking, but the engineer told me himself it had been solved. And new pipes are expensive items, Lallie."

"Oh, why will you be so parsimonious, Percy?" she cried. "This time your desire to save money may have cost you your daughter's life."

Percy Whatley set off in his motorcar and called upon Sir James Collington, and the discussion between the two men became heated and slightly acrimonious. Sir James said that all he had done was to try to improve Gunter's fields for the autumn sowing, and if the sewage had affected the water supply beneath those fields, then the Easterley Water Company had better look to its pipes.

From West Bresleigh, Mr. Whatley went on to Easterley, his temper not improved by the motorcar stopping half way and refusing to start again until his chauffeur had nearly broken his arm on the starting handle.

On arriving at the water company's offices, the chairman sent for the engineer and ordered the water supply below the fields to be cut off until further notice.

Water carts would supply Crossways, Burston and the barracks, until all the old pipes from the fever hospital had been replaced by new ones.

The expense would be double that incurred by the laying of new pipes in the first place, but Percy had more than this on his mind. As his motorcar took him home, this time without mishap, he remembered the trouble his engineer had in making the old pipes watertight, and that it was entirely owing to his own insistence that they had been used, which might indeed have lost him a daughter.

He arrived to find their London physician there, with two nurses who had gone at once to Henrietta's room and taken charge. The physician himself had not ventured nearer his patient than her bedroom door, and from there had made his examination with the help of the nurses.

"We called in Dr. Charles Bellingham from Saltbech this morning because she was so ill," Mrs. Whatley explained, her sparkle completely extinguished, as the great man came downstairs.

"You could not do better," he said, adding to her surprise, "Charles Bellingham was one of the foremost of the young physicians of his year, but he refused a West End practice because of some personal tragedy. I forget now what it was. He took a post as ship's surgeon for a year or two, and then came down here to your little town of Saltbech, and nobody has ever heard of him since. But Miss Henrietta will be in very good hands, Mrs. Whatley, and you need not fear to send for Dr. Bellingham if you have cause for alarm. I only hope he will be able to pull the poor young lady through."

Charles was not spared during the next few weeks: he drove back and forth between Saltbech and Crossways Hall until Whitestar knew the road as well as he knew his own stables, and did not have to be told which way to turn at cross roads.

In the meantime, the all important day arrived when Octavius was out of quarantine. He was taken to Dinah's room and given a bath with carbolic in the water, even to his short hair, and then dressed in clean clothes and a new navy-blue sailor suit bought for him especially by his great-aunt. He had grown during his illness and he was far too big now, she said, for velvet suits and lace collars and curls down to his shoulders. While the house smelt of the sulphur candles that had been lighted and burned all day in the rooms upstairs, and decorators moved in to strip the paper from the walls of Tavie's bedroom and repaper and repaint it, the little boy was accommodated with a bed in Nurse Blackwell's room.

During the following week, the rest of the family was to return to the rectory, and on the Saturday before they came the rector was returning, having accompanied his brother home and left him in the safe hands of his valet and Dulcie, who had returned from Frinton leaving the children there with their nurse and governess.

Their friends being now free to visit the rectory, Lady Crockett was the first to call, exclaiming at Dinah's pallor and remarking on how thin she had grown while nursing her little brother, and saying that she wondered Dr. Bellingham had not ordered a hospital nurse as he had for Henrietta Whatley.

"*Two* nurses," she added. "And now that Henrietta is improving, of course everyone says it is entirely due to Dr. Bellingham. His praises are being sung everywhere, my dear Mrs. Crichton, and all because Sir Hartley Brockhurst—the Whatleys' London man—did not want the trouble of attending Henrietta himself. Oh, I know he told the Whatleys that Dr. Bellingham could have been a London physician at one time, and I daresay after this he may consider such a thing now, but the Whatleys are really behaving as if they were royalty and Dr. Bellingham their private medical attendant!"

Certainly the fame of Charles's attendance on the Whatleys and Sir Hartley's opinion of him spread, and the tall house in the High Street had many invitations thrust through its letterbox, inviting him to dinner and to join shooting parties at country houses where he would not have been considered as a guest before. And in spite of what Lady Crockett had to say, even in her house, when he could not find an excuse to refuse her invitations, he was treated as an honored guest and not only as a "nice quiet man and quite unassuming," invited simply to make up the numbers at her dinner table.

Dinah was now free to write to her family, and the first person to receive a letter from her was Julia, whose reply was prompt and full of news.

She was delighted that darling Tavie was quite well again, but she wished she had been at the rectory with Dinah to take turns in nursing him. They were now back in London and they heard that Miss Maitland had insisted that Morrell should buy a house for her in Park Lane, and have it furnished for her from attic to cellar from William Whiteley's, where all the best people went nowadays.

When the abominable Clive had suggested that Caroline might pay for it out of her fortune, she told him that she would not have a penny until her wedding day, when her father would settle half a million on her. Jonathan Cottrell had told Julia that he did not think this was true, although it appeared to be certain that the bride's father would leave for South Africa a week before the wedding, which seemed very odd.

Caroline Maitland had had her wedding present from Lord Morrell—a superb necklace of rubies and diamonds to match her beautiful ring, and many people were giving up the first day's pheasant shooting to come to the wedding, which was to be at St. Margaret's, Westminster.

Having told her sister all this, Julia came then to the most important part of her letter, which was that she was engaged to Jonathan Cottrell. She promised to bring him down to the rectory for Uncle Sep's approval directly he returned from his holiday. "But nobody," she added, "could possibly disapprove of my dearest Jonathan."

Dinah knew a flicker of envy as she read the ecstatic letter from her sister. It reminded her of the time when she had written equally ecstatic letters to her relatives about Clive

179

Morrell. Dear little Julia, she thought. If only this young man were worthy of her, how happy they would be.

She wished that when Charles made his daily call at the rectory he would ask to see her great-aunt if not herself. She could only depend on seeing his back as he drove down the High Street in Saltbech, and of hearing about him from Lady Crockett when she called on her aunt.

"And how is that dear Mamma of yours?" asked her ladyship one day in her sweetest voice as she sat in her carriage in the High Street waiting outside Muddle the grocer's, for Mr. Muddle to come out himself to attend to her. "Is there any news of her return to Saltbech?"

Dinah propped her bicycle against the curb and admitted that she had not heard from Lady Bretton for some time. "But letters take such a long time to reach one from abroad," she added.

"Ah yes, nothing can touch our post office in England," agreed her ladyship. "One can post a letter in Saltbech in the morning knowing that it will be received in the afternoon. I believe it can take a week or more for letters to travel only a few miles on the Continent."

"I am expecting a letter from her any day now," Dinah said. "I think Lord Crowborne was not contemplating more than six weeks or so in the Mediterranean." She added. "Of course she may have broken her journey in Paris on the way home."

This was confirmed by a short letter, posted in Paris a few days earlier, that arrived on the breakfast table the following day. Lady Bretton had accepted the offer of a kind friend who had lent her a beautiful apartment in Paris for the next six months.

"You know, darling," she wrote, *"how much I dislike Saltbech and how bored I am at the rectory. I expect Octavius is well again by now—doctors always make so much of these childish ailments. I shall think of you all at Christmas. Your loving Mamma."*

Dinah showed the letter to her great-aunt without comment, and after reading it Mrs. Crichton observed drily that she hoped her mamma would not be bored in Paris. "But I do not suppose she will be alone there," she added.

"Oh no. She has many friends in Paris," said Dinah, but it did not occur to her what had been in The Honorable Alice's mind until that afternoon, when she was fetched in from the garden to be told that Lovell wished to see her.

Chapter Nineteen

Lovell had been taken up into Dinah's private sitting room, and she was standing at the window looking down at the park with her back to her as Dinah entered the room.

As she turned in answer to Dinah's good afternoon, she could see that she had not altered a scrap. The gray coat and skirt, the black hat skewered onto the gray hair with a long hatpin, the bit of fur round the neck of the severe striped blouse with its high neck, and the gray cotton gloves on the bony hands clasped across her stomach could only belong to Lovell, while her small eyes were harder than ever, and her lips thinner and even more disapproving.

"Well, Miss Bretton," she said as Dinah asked her to sit down, "I expect you know why I am here."

"I am sorry, Lovell, but I am afraid I have no idea." Then as Lovell seated herself on the edge of the hardest chair in the room a sudden thought struck her. "Unless," she said apprehensively, "you have come to tell me that Lady Bretton is ill?"

"Ill? Oh dear, no." Lovell gave a sound that was half snort and half laugh. "I presoom you will 'ave 'eard that 'er ladyship is in Paris?"

"I had a letter from her this morning. A friend has lent her an apartment in Paris for six months, but I am hoping she may be able to come to us for Christmas."

"She won't be here for no Christmas, not when Mr. Gerald Wakefield 'as said she kin live in that fine apartment of his till Sir 'Arold comes of age, if she likes. You won't see your Mamma, Miss Bretton, not fur six years or more, unless she quarrels with Mr. Wakefield, which she is not likely to do. A very wealthy gentleman is Mr. Wakefield."

"I do not understand you." Lovell's tone was so insolent that Dinah's head went up. "If Mr. Wakefield is a friend of

181

my mother's, I do not see that it can be any business of yours."

"Friend, did you say, miss?" Again there came that peculiar sound, half laugh and half snort. "Well, I s'pose you might say as Master Octavius' Papa is only a friend of 'er ladyship."

"Be silent, Lovell!" Dinah was now really angry. "How dare you have the insolence to come here and say such things to me? I am afraid I have no more time to spare for you." She got up and was making for the door when Lovell stopped her.

"Wait a minute, Miss Bretton, if you please." Lovell's thin lips trembled slightly. "I would never have said a word about this—not a word has passed my lips ever since Master Octavius was born, and Sir Roger very kindly acknowledged 'im as his own. But he knew he wasn't his, just as he guessed who the father was. Did you niver wonder why neither Sir Roger nor 'er ladyship ever had the slightest feelings for the poor little boy? But d'reckly I saw Mr. Gerald Wakefield on Lord Crowborne's yacht when we went aboard at Marseilles I knew we was in for trouble.

"Right down nasty 'er ladyship got with me, because I was seasick. I've always been that way, miss. Why even a boat on the Serpentine will turn me up, always has done. But it was that stewardess as well, putting 'er ladyship agin me all the time, and saying as I was oldfashioned and m'lady would do better with a French maid.

"So when we reaches that apartment in Paris—very magnificent, with its French furniture and French servants everywhere, and 'er ladyship says to me that first evening as she wouldn't be wanting me anymore, and gives me twenty pound for old times' sake, and that I was to apply to 'er ladyship if I needed references, I felt as if she 'ad hit me in the face. Me, after twenty years service to be given a pound fur each year of it, and all for the sake of a flighty French maid that was no better than she should be, and well accustomed to sich goings-on as I niver was, nor niver will be agin."

Lovell was so furious that she did not trouble to choose her words, nor did she try to speak in her usual mincing way, but although the woman had always been a troublemaker at Bretton and in the rectory Dinah felt bound to hear the rest of her story. In fact, when she thought of the years of service she had given her mother, she felt a strange kind of pity for her, a pity increased by the depth of hatred and bitterness that she now saw let loose. It must be terrible, she thought, to experience such hatred, letting it eat like a canker into your heart.

"I suppose you have come to fetch the rest of your clothes?" she said. "Have you a cab waiting, or shall the groom drive you to the station in the little cart?"

"No thank you, miss. I told the cabby to wait and it will not take long to put my things into the trunk I left behind."

She left Dinah to her thoughts and went upstairs, and in a very little while Tom carried her tin trunk down the backstairs for her, helped by the housemaid Maud, and it was brought through the hall and out to the waiting cab.

Glad that her aunt was out that afternoon, having tea with Lady Craddock, Dinah said good-bye to her before she left and asked her what she was going to do. "If I can help you in any way, Lovell," she said gently, "you have only to write to me here."

"Thank you, miss. But I'm taking no more places with society ladies. My sister has a boardinghouse in Brighton, and she tells me the house next door is empty, and the rent twenty pound a year. If I take it, her boarders can sleep in some of the rooms when her house is full—she will pay me rent for 'em, of course—and I shall use the ground floor rooms as a dressmaking establishment. I 'ave a plate already made out, S. LOVELL, COURT DRESSMAKER, and my sister says she thinks I shall do very well." For a moment a look of shame almost touched her sallow face as she blurted out, "I'm sorry I let on about 'er ladyship. What she does or doesn't do isn't nothink to do with me, as you said." And she hurried out to the cab.

The housemaid, coming back after helping Tom to get Lovell's trunk onto the cab's roof, stopped a moment beside Dinah, who had come downstairs to see Lovell off, and felt in her apron pocket.

"Clara found something on Master Tavie's floor when the men were in to do the decorating," she said. "She give it to me but I keep forgetting to give it to you. I think the doctor must hev dropped it, don't you, miss?"

It was a gold cuff-link, inscribed on its flat surface with the crest of the head of a boar Dinah took it from her and put it into the pocket of her skirt and said she would give it to the doctor or leave it at his house the next time she went to the High Street. When her aunt returned and they were having dinner together she showed it to her and asked if she had noticed the doctor wearing gold cuff-links.

"I never notice a man's cuff-links, my dear." The Honorable Alice was amused, but she took the cuff-link from the table where her great-niece had put it and examined it through her lorgnettes. "A boar's head," she said then. "Yes, of course. I thought he reminded me of someone I must have met years ago. Evidently he belongs to the Dorset Bellinghams—all of them had very large families and very little money. The girls did peculiar things—I believe one of the younger ones has recently gone to one of these women's colleges at Cambridge—and another became a lady nurse. The boys, too, took up equally strange careers—the merchant service, lawyers' clerks, even schoolmasters—that sort of thing." She smiled and put away her lorgnettes and began eating the apple charlotte that had been provided for their dinner with relish. The Honorable Alice enjoyed her food. "So the old families come down in the world," she commented, "and the new families climb up. I must say that I cannot take to Mr. Percy Whatley, though his wife received me kindly enough this afternoon when I went to enquire after the gel. I am told she is making good progress now, thanks to Dr. Bellingham. Wherever one goes these days one seems to hear of nothing but his praises. Well, at least he comes from a better family than Mr. Whatley, whose father was I think in cotton—or was it in carpets?"

Dinah could not help her. She put the cuff-link back in her pocket, and said that she would give it to the doctor the next time they saw him. "Only we never do see him these days," she added.

Her great-aunt eyed her shrewdly but made no comment, and later in the evening when they were left alone in the drawing-room, Miss Pettit having retired early to take advantage of the bath water being hot, Dinah told her of Lovell's visit that afternoon.

"She gave me the name of the friend who is lending Mamma his apartment in Paris," she added in a low voice. "Aunt A.,—have you ever heard of Mr. Gerald Wakefield?"

"I have," said the Honorable Alice serenely. "He has been one of the guests on Lord Crowborne's yacht this summer, or so I read in the *Court Circular* a little while ago. He is an old friend of your mother's."

"Or is he her lover?" burst out Dinah, tears in her eyes.

She saw that her great-aunt was shocked. "My dear, we do not say things like that, even between ourselves," she rebuked her. "One is discreet, as I am sure Mr. Wakefield and your Mamma are being in Paris."

"But that woman—Lovell—said that Octavius—" Dinah could not continue.

Mrs. Crichton drew herself up, looking rather like a duchess asked to discuss the delinquency of a scullerymaid. "There are some things we shut our ears and eyes to, Dinah," she said severely. "Your Mamma has always been fond of clothes and jewels and admiration. Your father was too slowgoing for her from the beginning of their marriage, but it is only fair to him to say that he behaved extremely well over some aspects it presented." Her mind flickered back to gossip about how Roger had been firmly shut out of his wife's bedroom after the birth of the twins. "It might not be fair to her to say that she only married him for his position, but it could be that it is true. In the meantime, whatever happened in the past, to all our friends and relatives Octavius is a Bretton, and let us say no more about it, please."

Dinah's thoughts were far too confused for her to have said any more even if she had wished to do so, but small incidents crowded back as she sat there by the fire in the drawing-room on that cool September evening. Remarks of friends about Octavius, "He is not a bit like any of you, is he? A changeling child!" And the way her father had tolerated him but never encouraged him to come near him, rather avoiding his touch, while her mother had actively disliked the child, because he had betrayed her.

Everything became clearer and yet more confused, and through it all her thoughts and her aching pity stayed with little Tavie. Darling little oldfashioned Tavie, walking the garden with his hands behind his back, looking for fresh flowers as if he knew that he must learn to walk alone and must look to botany and perhaps later science, for his first and only love.

She shivered suddenly and said she would go upstairs to fetch a scarf. "It has turned chilly," she said, "in spite of the fire."

"Before you go," said her great-aunt, "ring for Simmons. We will have the window shut."

As Dinah went upstairs she paused, aware of something though she did not know what, that was trying to give her a message. Simmons had gone through the hall to the drawing room leaving it very quiet and still, but it seemed for just that moment as Dinah stood there that something was trying to prevent her from going any further, was even trying to warn her of danger. The next moment a cool draught had cut down past her and she ran up to her room, scolding herself for her fancies. It was because she was not really herself again after the long days of nursing little Tavie, and the shock of Lovell's information had upset her. She fetched the scarf, a pretty silk one in deep red, and she heard Simmons closing the drawing room windows. What she did not hear however was Simmons remark to Mrs. Jennings later.

"I was shutting the drawing room windows," she told her, "and just for a moment I thought I saw a man outside. Do you think we ought to get young Tom up to see if there's anyone there?"

"Now don't stand there imagining things," said Mrs. Jennings severely. "I've had enough of young Tom today, saying he nearly broke his back getting Lovell's trunk downstairs. I would dearly have liked to know what was in it to make it so heavy. You get off to bed now, and let me deal with prowlers. The rector will be back tomorrow night, if that will make you sleep safer in your bed."

Simmons went up to her attic room, and Mrs. Jennings was about to pay her evening visit to the drawing room with the ladies' drinks—hot milk with a dash of brandy for The Honorable Alice and only lemonade for Miss Dinah—when she heard a knock at the back door. The other servants were gone up to bed, and there was only herself in the kitchen quarters. It was a strange time for back door callers: at night they usually came to the front door and rang the bell.

She went along the stone passage from the still-room to the back door and asked who was there.

"It's me, Mrs. Jennings, Bob Pickard," said a voice, speaking very low. "Can I have a word with you please, ma'am?"

"Of course. Come in, Bob." She had known Bob all his life, from the time he was born to the time a year or so ago when he had become a policeman in Saltbech. He came in, removing his helmet and, somewhat to her surprise, locking the door behind him.

"Beg pardon for intruding like this, Mrs. Jennings, ma'am, at this time of night," he said. "But seeing as the rector is still away I thought I'd better warn you as his son, Mr. Christopher, has escaped from the institootion. Got away last night, he did, and there's bin no sign of hair nor hide of him ever since. Sergeant Cripps tells me to come and warn you, ma'am, 'case he comes here, but he don't believe he'll do that. Not Mr.

Christopher. He says he allus was a cunning young rascal, and he believes he'll goo different from here, and he won't try to come back to Saltbech. But he thinks as it would be better if you was to make sure as all the bolts was shot in the doors and shutters tonight, 'case he did try to git in. Sergeant Cripps says rector left word with Dr. Bellingham to come every day while he was away, but the doctor called in at the police station day before yesterday and told Sergeant Cripps as he'd be in Lunnon for a couple o' nights, so I don't s'pose he niver got no telegram from the institootion like afore he left."

"No. I know he was going away, but only for two nights he told me. Maybe he'll be back by now. You could call at his house on your way back to the station, Bob, in case he is there and tell him what has happened, and in the meantime I'll see that everything is locked up." Mrs. Jennings remembered uneasily Simmons's story about seeing a man outside the drawing-room windows, and added, "Oh, and Bob, I'd be obliged if you will knock up Dimmock on your way, and tell him to come up and sleep here tonight. It 'ud make me feel a sight safer if there was a man in the house."

"I'll do that gladly, ma'am." Bob left, his bicycle lamp shedding a circle in the yard, but nothing stirred, and Mrs. Jennings shut and locked the door behind him.

She left the drawing room drinks until later and went upstairs to warn Nurse Blackwell, speaking in a whisper and telling her what had happened. "Keep the nursery doors locked, and your own," she said, "in case Simmons really did see that young varmint skulking about outside this evening."

"I'll do more'n that. I'll get dressed agin and set up in the day nursery, case he should come up here and try and attack Master Tavie," said Nurse Blackwell, having heard all about Christopher since she had come to Saltbech.

"Where is Miss Pettit?"

"In the bath." In spite of the gravity of the situation, they could not help exchanging a smile at the thought of Miss Pettit being surprised in such a situation.

"Leave her be, then," said the housekeeper. "She will hev bolted the door any road. I'm going to find Hannah and warn her, and I've sent fur Dimmock to sleep here tonight, and I'll tell the ladies when I take their milk drinks to them and shut and bolt the shutters same time."

She went upstairs to rouse the maids and tell them to lock and bolt their doors and not to come out of their rooms whatever was going on downstairs, and found Hannah before going back to the still-room. Her hand was not quite steady as she held the saucepan over the spirit lamp she used for this purpose, but by this time Hannah had joined her, and although they both agreed that they would be glad to see Dimmock, and that they would have felt a great deal happier had the rector been at home, nevertheless they did not think that Christopher would try to get into the rectory that night.

"He'd have been here before now if he was going to come," said Mrs. Jennings. The milk was just the right heat when Dimmock arrived, and when Mrs. Jennings asked him if he had seen anyone about the drive or the park he said he had not. "But you kin niver tell with these hair lun-atics," he added grimly. "The moon's full tonight—like daylight 'tis now, it's rising over the trees. They're always wuss with a full moon. And what is more," he went on, as if determined to shatter their hopes, "as I come by I looked in my shed and I could see as one of my sharpest pruning knives is gone."

"It looks like he might be here after all," said Hannah, her healthy color fading a little.

"It do look like it, but that's not to say, mind you, as somebody else might not hev been passing and took a fancy to it. I don't trust that new lad the butcher's got to do his rounds coming for orders on a bicycle. Not like the old days when you hed an 'oss to look arter. He could slip off his bicycle in a minute and nobody ud be the wiser. But if when you goes into the drorin' room with them cups of milk, Mrs. Jennings, ma'am, you'd shut the shutters before you tell the ladies what 'as 'appened, so that if he should be about he can't git in that way, tell 'em as I'll set here in the kitchen all night, and mek me way round the rooms ivery little while, to see everything is safe. It 'ull set their minds at rest, poor dears."

Mrs. Jennings said she would see to the drawing room shutters if, in the meantime, he would close and bolt them in the other rooms, and feeling rather more reassured she picked up the tray to carry it across the hall and into the drawing room.

But it seemed that already she was too late. As she reached the hall table, with its array of brass bedroom candlesticks, there came the sudden crash of breaking glass from the direction of the drawing-room, and a wild voice shouting something about Cousin Dinah and how the owner of the voice had got her at last.

Christopher, it seemed, had reached his home with the full moon.

Chapter Twenty

The first of September had come and gone. It had fallen on a Sunday that year, but on August 30th Christopher had received a letter from his father, describing the places he and his uncle had visited, the castles they had looked at, the churches they had seen, and enclosing a small sketch of Battle Abbey, adding that he hoped Christopher would have some more pictures to show him when he came to see him.

Christopher did not believe a word of the letter, nor his father's promise that he would be seeing him again on September 1st, and when he did not come it only confirmed his suspicions.

His father had not gone away on a holiday with Uncle Quin. It had only been an excuse. He was in the hands of those Bretton cousins now, and they would not let him come to see him anymore, Sunday or no Sunday. They had him fast in their clutches, they were there at the rectory, laughing and talking about him, playing cricket with his bat, and taking possession of *The Northern Star*.

Another letter from Septimus telling him of his uncle's accident and that he must delay his visit by some weeks turned his suspicions into certainty.

If he could only get out of this place what would he not do to those Brettons? And he would be justified, because they had stolen his father as well as his home.

But first of all, he had to escape from the men who watched him and locked him up and put him in a straitjacket. He must outwit them in some way, and it needed careful thought.

He became very quiet during the next week or two, and Dr. Forsyth was pleased to find that he was taking his paints and his easel into the garden and painting groups of visitors when they came, sitting at tea under the trees. The table and the trees would be meticulously painted, and the visitors would be recognizable as people, although most of them seemed to have lost an arm, or a head or a foot.

The doctor admired the trees and the tables and the lawn without mentioning the maimed visitors that sat round the tables, and went on to say that he was sorry to hear that his uncle had had an accident. Whereupon Christopher laughed and said that his uncle had not had an accident, in fact he had never gone on a cycling tour with his father.

"It is my cousins, the Brettons," he explained. "They are keeping him prisoner at the rectory, just as I am being kept a prisoner here in your house."

"But you received a letter from your father in which he said the brakes of your uncle's bicycle had given way going down a hill," protested Dr. Forsyth.

"*My* brakes on my bicycle do not give way," said Christopher contemptuously. "I have been riding it round and round the paths here this week and the brakes are as good as they ever were, and the bell rings." He laughed almost sanely. "I led one of your keepers a dance, I can tell you. He likes to keep up with me and I rode so fast he had to run all the way. He was red in the face and quite breathless by the time I had done with him."

"I am very glad that you have begun to ride your bicycle again," said the doctor serenely. "It is very good exercise. I hope the tires are in good condition."

"Oh yes. There is a pump attached to it and I pump them up every day."

It really seemed as if he were going through one of his saner periods, thought the doctor as he strolled on, leaving him to his painting. It was a pity that he still had this obsession about his cousins having stolen his father and his home from him. It seemed impossible to move it from his mind—argument would simply bring on rages that were quite uncontrollable, and reasoning went over his head.

There was one picture in Christopher's portfolio that he would not allow anyone to see. It was tightly fastened between one of a kitten with a string fastened tightly around its throat, and another of the skeleton of a dead bird. The picture between them was of a girl with dark hair, lying on the floor of the rectory study with her throat cut. He did not know what his cousin Dinah looked like; he only knew that her hair was dark, and that was enough. He would know her when he reached the rectory, and he would make sure that he had a knife in his hand.

Two days before Septimus was due to return he had his chance. He had been so quiet and reasonable during the last week that his attendants had taken him down the small staircase that led into the yard by the kitchens, when he wanted to use his bicycle. It was kept in a shed round the corner and it was a shorter way to the garden, and they had helped him bring the bicycle round the narrow paths to the wider walks where he could ride it. When he put it back in its shed, he noticed that it was kept in the same shed that housed some of the bicycles belonging to attendants who came daily to the institute, and he noticed that the door to the shed was not locked.

His future action was clear. He must get the bicycle out and ride it down to the gates, but he must be disguised in some way so that the porter would think he was one of the attendants and not a patient.

That evening when the two attendants came as usual to see that he was in bed, they found him lying on the floor with a gash of scarlet across his throat, staining the underneath of his fair beard.

"I thought he's been too quiet lately!" cried the older man. "He's cut his throat."

"Run for the doctor," said the younger one, kneeling down beside the patient, and as the first one ran, leaving the door open behind him, Christopher's hands came up swiftly like a vise and gripped the other's throat until he lost consciousness. It did not take long.

Christopher then rubbed the oil paint off his throat and beard, hastily removed the man's green jacket and cap with the badges of the institute, and the leather belt that had the keys attached to it, and put them on.

He listened to see that nobody was coming and then went out quickly and locked the door with the key from the man's belt. He had learned over the past weeks that it was the key with the brass handle that fitted his door. Then he ran down the stairs leading to the side door, unlocking it and locking it again behind him, and walked boldly through the yard to the bicycle shed.

He had to pass the kitchen windows, but the scullery boys were making such a noise what with talking and laughing and clattering their pots and pans, that a footstep outside would never have been heard. It took only a moment to find his bicycle and ride it down a path behind the shrubs to the entrance gates.

It was getting dark and the porter recognized his jacket and cap as he unlocked the small door in the gates for him to wheel the bicycle through and out onto the road.

"Warm night, sir," he said.

"A very warm night," agreed Christopher, and once outside and in the road with the gates shut behind him he looked up at the sky and smiled.

The moon was swinging up over the houses of the village ahead and the country lane that led away from it was as bright as day, so that having no lamp on his bicycle made no difference.

But he had to go carefully and the first thing he must do was to find the river. Once when he had been allowed to go for a walk with his father, they had made their way to the river path and he had told him that it was the upper reaches of the Calder. So that he had only to find that path again and follow it downstream, and he would eventually come to the dirty little town of Burston. There was a lane that led off to the right of the river, and you could reach it by a narrow bridge. He remembered that from his rides out into the country round Saltbech when he was a schoolboy.

It took him a little time to find the Calder, but he found it at last and began to cycle down it away from the village. The path was full of bumps and ruts so that he could not go very fast, and the turns and twists in the river did not make it as easy as he had anticipated, and by the time daylight came he had only reached the village before Burston and he was feeling tired and hungry. Also, he had no knife.

There was a baker's shop in the village, and at that hour of the morning there was nobody astir yet except the baker. The smell of hot loaves reached him and increased his feeling of hunger.

The bakery was surrounded by a quickset hedge, and he leant his bicycle against it, taking care to avoid puncturing the tires with the thorns, and felt in his pockets for some money, but in his haste he had left his purse behind.

He went softly round to the back, and luckily the baker had his back to him as he reached for another batch of loaves from the oven, but on the shelf by the door were loaves that had been put out to cool.

It took only a second to remove one of them, slip it into his jacket and button it over it and get back to his bicycle. Long before the baker could discover that he had one less loaf than he had thought on his shelf, Christopher had left the village behind him and was back on the towpath, wider and not so bumpy now, and pedaling away towards the bridge that would lead him across country to Saltbech.

At the first thicket he came to, he laid the bicycle down so that it was hidden from anyone passing, and ate his loaf, tearing it to pieces with his hands and later washing it down with a capful of water from the Calder, a much more innocent stream there than after it had passed through Burston.

He rested for a little, and then he mounted his bicycle again and continued on his way, but a morning mist was coming up from the river and spreading over the fields. As he passed some laborers on their way to harvesting one of them asked him if it was true that a lunatic had escaped from Dr. Forsyth's institution.

"Quite true," said Christopher. "We've been out looking for him all night."

"There's a number of you, it seems," said the man. "Met some just now what said he might be making fur Saltbech. Seems like he's dangerous."

"So he is," agreed Christopher, and with a good day he went on. But now he had been warned. He must avoid the rectory at all events until nightfall, and he knew where he would go. There was an old barn that had been used as a tithe barn in the old days, and he had often hidden up there for hours and never been discovered. The mists helped him, once he was out of sight of the men. The barn was someway off the road, standing behind a little wood on the edge of a field, and fortunately the field had been used to grow mangolds that year instead of corn. The mist had now developed into patches of fog coming in from the sea, but he wheeled his bicycle along the edge of the field until he came to the barn.

It looked rather more derelict than he remembered it, and there was nothing in it but a rotting haywain with a broken shaft, which was directly beneath the large open trap door to the loft above. He climbed up onto it and lifted the heavy bicycle with ease, pushing it up into the loft before following it himself.

There he stayed for the rest of the day, listening in case he could detect any sounds of pursuit, and sleeping for the rest of the time until he woke up to find it almost dark.

He unbuckled the belt so that the keys on it would not jingle and betray him, tossed his cap after it beside his bicycle and swung himself down.

There was a path to Saltbech across the fields, cutting off

Burston completely, and he made nothing of the three miles that led him to the back of the rectory. He walked fast, breaking into a run when it was light enough to see where he was going, and very soon the mist had lifted again and the night promised to be clear, with moonlight again to show him the way.

When he arrived at the rectory he heard the church clock striking ten: it was quite dark now except for the lighted windows and the moon shedding its light on the roof and the stableyard.

He made his way round the house, treading softly, until he reached the drawing room windows where a maidservant was shutting them and bolting them. He found he could see into the room, and that there was a young lady sitting by the fire alone, her head bent over some embroidery. This was his quarry, this must be his cousin Dinah, he thought triumphantly, and then drew back quickly as the maid stopped in her bolting of the windows and peered out almost as if she had caught sight of him.

He made his way back to the stableyard, more cautiously this time, and saw Bob Pickard on his bicycle making his way up the drive. Flattening himself against the wall, he crept round to the back of the house and was in time to see the policeman knock at the back door and be admitted by Mrs. Jennings.

He did not hear what he said but the sight of him was enough. He must find a knife and do what he had come to do without anymore loss of time.

He slipped into one of the coachhouses until the policeman had gone, and after the back door was bolted behind him and the kitchen shutters drawn he came out and made his way to the gardener's shed. The door was unlocked, as always—Dimmock never locked his sheds—and the light from upstairs windows showed him the row of pruning hooks and knives hanging on their rack above the workbench. He felt along the slotted wooden shelf until he found the largest knife, testing it with his finger to see that it had a sharp point, and then he crept back round the house to the drawing room windows.

Here the shutters had not yet been drawn and the curtains were still wide open, and he was able to gaze for some moments into the room. He had expected to see his father there surrounded by his Bretton cousins, but instead he could only see the girl he had seen before, dark-haired, with her

194

eyes on her needlework. He knew at once that this was Dinah Bretton, the eldest of them all. There was no doubt in his mind about that.

He smashed the window with the handle of the knife, and the next moment he was in the room and running at the girl, the knife brandished high.

"Now I've got you!" he shouted, grinning down at her terrified face, and he laughed, a high-pitched laugh with no sanity in it. "My dear cousin, Dinah Bretton, stealing my father and my home from me. I am going to kill you for it—" He lifted the knife, while she stared up at him like a trapped bird unable to move, and then a voice spoke sharply behind him.

"Stop that at once, Christopher!" it said. He turned blindly, his astonishment instinctively making him obey, and he saw a tall old lady who had evidently been sitting in a winged armchair with its back to the windows, so that he had been unable to see her from outside. "I have never met with such behavior before," said The Honorable Alice sternly. "How dare you come breaking into your Papa's drawing room, smashing his windows and threatening your cousin? And you a Crichton! Have you not been taught that a gentleman never shouts at a lady? It is the height of bad manners. Give me that knife at once."

He hesitated, his eyes going from Dinah to his great-aunt and back again.

"At once please, Christopher!" Mrs. Crichton held out her hand for his weapon, and he gave it to her reluctantly and watched as she put it behind the fire. "Now perhaps," she said in a gentler voice, "you will sit down and tell me what this is all about. I have never known a Crichton so far forget himself before, and I have no doubt it is because you are hungry and tired. Dinah, my dear, go and ask Mrs. Jennings to prepare some sandwiches and a pot of tea for your cousin."

Dinah fled, while Christopher sat down in the chair she had vacated and stared helplessly at his great-aunt.

The housekeeper did not seem surprised at the message that Dinah brought her. "Young Bob Pickard was here a few moments ago to tell me as Mr. Christopher had escaped," she said. "And then just as I was bringing your drinks I heard the window go and the shouting. It was a mercy as I didn't let the tray go. But from what I heard it seems it's you he's after, Miss Dinah—mad with jealousy, that's what he is, because you are here and he isn't, poor soul. You go straight upstairs and lock yourself into your room. Dimmock's here and mebbe he'll be strong enough to tackle him if he turns vilent."

But Dinah could not leave the hall while her courageous old aunt was alone in the drawing room with her cousin, and when Dimmock came into the hall she put her finger to her lips and told him to stay out of sight for a while.

She did not know how long she had been there—sometime after Mrs. Jennings had gone through with the sandwiches and tea—when there came the sound of a horse's hoofs in the drive, and she ran softly to the front door to open it before the bell could be pulled, and Charles Bellingham was there.

"Dinah!" He could not choose his words. "What has happened? I had to be in London for a couple of days and have only just got back to find the telegram from Dr. Forsyth. Is Christopher here?"

"Yes. But don't make a sound. He is in the drawing-room with Great-aunt A. having something to eat. You do not know how wonderful she has been." Dinah felt herself shaking, and he put his arm round her and for a moment she turned and clung to him. "Oh Charles!" she whispered. "I was so praying that you would come."

Naturally a woman who had had such a shock as Dinah had experienced that evening did not quite know what she was saying, and when the light of day came she would return to her normal, sensible little self, but just for that moment as he held her there in his arm he could forget the interviews he had had over the past two days.

Then he gently released himself. "Supposing you go up to bed?" he said. "I will attend to Christopher. I expect Mrs. Jennings is getting his room ready?"

"Oh yes. She is making up the bed in his room and Dimmock is here."

"Good. I will just have a word with him then. I'll tell Benson to take the trap round to the back, and Dimmock can let him in. It may need the three of us here in the night ahead. But you go to bed, my dear. You look exhausted."

This Dinah would not do. She went into the study and sat there listening, the gaslight from the hall giving her all the light she needed.

Charles came back to the half open drawing room door.

"Of course it was very wrong of you to hit the poor man and take his clothes," Christopher's great-aunt was saying.

"They had locked me up. He had helped to put me in a

straitjacket in a padded cell," mumbled Christopher through his sandwiches, aware however that the old lady was a Crichton and not a hated Bretton.

"I should expect to be locked up and put in a straitjacket if I went about knocking people down, stealing their clothes and threatening them with knives!" said his great-aunt. "There is nothing extraordinary in that. But you are looking better now, and when you have had a good sleep you will feel better still. I know your room is just as you left it. Nobody else has ever slept in it."

Christopher admitted that he was tired, and as the tea and sandwiches were finished, Charles thought it was time to make himself known and went into the room.

"It is Christopher Crichton, is it not?" he said cheerfully, holding out his hand as the young man sprang to his feet, looking wild and hunted. "My name is Bellingham, Charles Bellingham, and I am an old friend of your father's. We are both interested in the same things and always have been. Your father will be back from his holiday tomorrow, and he will be delighted to find you here to welcome him."

He stayed talking quietly and sensibly, sitting astride a small chair with his arms folded along the back of it, while Mrs. Crichton listened and Christopher stared at him, half suspicious, half trusting, and after a few minutes Mrs. Jennings came to say that Mr. Christopher's room was ready for him.

"I will come with you," Charles said, "and help you into bed. I am sure you are very tired. And then I must be off."

Christopher seemed to be too tired to protest, and almost glad of the doctor's company as he took him up the stairs and along the corridor to the locked room at the end of it.

It was not locked now. The door was wide open and a lighted candle stood on the dressing table, and a paraffin stove stood on the hearth, its red glass panels giving out a cheerful warmth. It seemed to reassure the room's owner that nothing had been changed in ten years and that his ship, *The Northern Star*, still stood on the table where he had left it.

One of the rector's nightshirts had been put out for him to wear, and when he was undressed and into bed Charles put out the lamp and the candle and said good night, softly locking the door behind him.

At the end of the corridor he saw Benson coming to find him and went to meet him, telling him to take a chair from the spare bedroom next to the locked room and settle himself in it for the night.

"The gaslight will be burning all night in this passage," he told him, "and it should throw a faint light into that room through the fanlight. You should be able to see if he is still in bed if you should hear any suspicious noises in the night. But on no account go into the room. He is dangerous. Come for me, instead."

"You are staying in the house then, sir?"

"In the rector's study with the door open, and Dimmock will be with me."

The chair was brought and Charles left Benson there, making his way back to the drawing room where The Honorable Alice was regaling herself with a glass of brandy and hot water, and Dinah was with her, sipping hot water alone and looking deathly white.

Mrs. Crichton immediately offered a glass of brandy to Charles, which he refused saying that he wanted to keep awake. He poured a small glass for Dinah, however, and as she shook her head, saying faintly that it would make her sick, he said briskly, "Nonsense, my dear. Drink it down, and then run up to bed." He held the glass to the girl's lips and she took it from him and gulped it down with a shudder of distaste.

"There," he said, smiling down at her, "that is better, is it not?"

"Much better," she said and then, "thank you, Charles." She kissed her aunt and went up to her room, and when she had gone Charles told Mrs. Crichton of his arrangements for the night.

"If he should break out I think Dimmock and Benson and I can manage Christopher between us," he said. "And there are bars on his windows."

"Yes, they have always been barred," she said sadly.

"May I add," he said gently, "how much I admire you for your courage and presence of mind?"

The Honorable Alice looked faintly surprised. "But he is my husband's flesh and blood and a Crichton," she said, as if that explained it all.

Once or twice in the night Benson thought he heard a movement and climbed on the chair to look through the fanlight, but all he could see was Christopher's back with the bedclothes pulled up, lying quietly on the bed. The near window was open but there were bars outside it, and so Benson sat down again on the chair, and after the second occasion he nodded off to sleep.

Christopher woke at three, just before the dawn broke. There was a fog again from the river, coming in at the open window and the room was cold, and as he lay there, recognizing the room and the objects in it by the light of the gasjet outside the fanlight, the memory of what had happened came back to him.

It was nearly morning and his father would be coming back today. And when he came back he would take him back to the institution. There would be no escape. And once there he would be put into a straitjacket and locked in padded cells. Nobody would listen when he shouted, when he swore, when he wept. And on the first of October his father would come to see him for a little while, and then he would go, and so it would go on for the rest of his life.

He felt deserted by everyone, and most of all by his father. He got out of bed noiselessly and put a chair beneath the fanlight and saw Benson asleep in the chair on the other side of the door. But there was another way of escape, and once away he would never come back, not even to the rectory, because he could not trust anyone anymore.

He took up *The Northern Star* and held it under the fanlight, looking for the little hold he and his father had made so cleverly under the tiny cabin on the deck. But his father had not known that he had taken the cabin off after it had been stuck down, and that underneath it in the hold there was a collection of slim knives and screwdrivers, wrapped in paper so that nobody would know they were there after he had stuck the cabin down again.

He took the cabin off and they were still there. He had used the biggest screwdriver to take the screws out of the windows after they had screwed them down, but with bars outside, they had not thought it mattered and they had not replaced them.

Now it was only the business of removing the screws from the bars outside. He got into his clothes quickly, with the green jacket on top, and put a bolster in the bed, pulling the bedclothes over it so that at first glance it might look as if he were lying there still. Then he started on the bars, very quietly, making no sound, and very soon three of them were undone at the bottom. He was strong enough to lift them one at a time, until there was enough space for him to climb out onto the old sycamore that was pressing its branches against his windows as if it wanted to help.

It was easy to get into the tree and climb down it, he knew

the old footholds on that tree from childhood, and once on the ground he started off across the grass in the direction of the river.

He would go to the quay, where there would be boats lying at anchor, waiting for the tide. He would slip on to one of them and nobody would know he was there until it had sailed.

They would never turn him back. He would not let them. Once out at sea, he would kill the whole crew before he let them put him ashore again.

The fog was thicker than ever when he reached the quay and the sun was like a pale yellow ball floating in a gray shawl that made it almost impossible to see.

There was a ship at anchor there, however, and all aboard was quiet. If he could find the gangway he could stow away in the hold, but the gangway was difficult to find, and when at last his hands gripped two rails that seemed to be the rails of one it was only the space between two ships, anchored side by side, and he went down into the water between them with scarcely a sound.

Chapter Twenty-one

Septimus's homecoming was a sad one, but as The Honorable Alice said, when the inquest and funeral were over and the locked room opened up and its contents dispersed, he would feel a great deal happier. From the time he could walk, Christopher had been a worry and a responsibility with which it had been difficult to cope.

Although the funeral was to be a private one, the church was filled with townspeople, and in respect for their rector during the hour when the short service and interment took place, every shop in the town was closed, and every window had its curtains drawn and its blinds lowered.

It was a sunny morning, and Septimus was touched by the

silent sympathy of his friends: it seemed that everyone but his sister's family had known about poor Christopher, and when Dinah questioned her brothers about it, she was annoyed to find that they, too, had known.

"Papa told me ages ago," Harold told her grandly. "And I told Johnnie. Papa said we were not to say anything about it to you girls because Mamma wanted it kept dark."

Dinah wondered rather bitterly if her mother had thought it might have affected their chances of good marriages.

It was only natural that Charles should be in and out of the rectory fairly often during the next few weeks, and one lovely day in late September, when his aunt and eldest niece were sitting in the garden watching the boys and the twins hitting croquet balls through hoops in a game they called golf croquet, the rector came to join them, looking rather upset.

"Is anything wrong, Septimus?" asked his aunt.

"Not really, although I have just had a shock from some news Charles has told me. He has been offered an important post in Edinburgh, where he was trained and received his doctorate in medicine, and he hopes to leave Saltbech for Scotland at the end of next month."

"But—why?" Dinah felt almost as if someone had given her a blow over the heart. "He has been here so long," she added hastily.

"No doubt he has his reasons," said her uncle, shaking his head. "Charles is a queer chap, and if he does not wish to tell one why he is going then he will not tell. It is a good opportunity for him, of course. It could lead to greater prospects in the future, I suppose."

"Are you thinking of a call to Balmoral and a post as physician to a royal household?" asked his aunt smiling.

"I do not think I would go as far as that," said Septimus. "But whatever his reasons are, I am going to miss him very much. He is a good kind friend, as well as being a first-class medical man." And he went off to see if the Williams' pears were ripe, the croquet players, hearing him, flinging down their mallets to go with him.

In their absence Dinah said she had never thought Dr. Bellingham to be an ambitious man. "I should not have thought anything could have attracted him away from Saltbech," she said.

"Possibly not," said her great-aunt drily. "But I can imagine that something may have driven him away from the town."

"I don't understand?" Dinah's eyes met her great-aunt's questioningly. "Surely everybody likes him here? He is the leading doctor for miles around."

"I was not thinking of his patients," said Mrs. Crichton. She was thinking of a certain night when the doctor had held a glass of brandy to Miss Bretton's lips and her grateful look at him as she had said, "Thank you, Charles." Christian names were all very well, but things had gone far enough, and she thought the moment might have come to put her foot down.

"I think, my dear," she said gently, "that Dr. Bellingham is head over heels in love with you, and he knows as well as anybody else that it is quite out of the question for a country doctor to entertain any ideas of marriage with a Bretton. You will not be here forever: the time will come, perhaps sooner than you think, when you will be back at Bretton again, and rather than be tortured by meeting you here at the rectory or at dinner parties in the county, or even seeing you riding about on that ridiculous bicycle of yours, he has made up his mind to break with Saltbech. In which decision—if I am right, and I am pretty sure that I am—he is showing great good sense."

Dinah was silent for a long moment, and then she said slowly, not looking at her aunt, "But if I were to be in love with him, too, what then? Why should I not marry him?"

"My dear, pray do not let us suppose any such thing." Mrs. Crichton treated the suggestion lightly with a laugh. *"You* could not marry Charles Bellingham—you, a Bretton! You would very soon discover how very little you had in common: you would lose your friends and your position in Society, and you would be forced to entertain people like the Annerleys, very decent, respectable people no doubt, but utterly middle-class."

"Yet you, a lord's daughter, married a curate."

"That was quite different. The Crichtons are as old a family as mine were, and my father-in-law was at Eton with my father and belonged to the same clubs. In other words, they spoke the same language. Mr. Crichton settled twenty thousand pounds on your great-uncle when we married, and my father gave us the best living of several that were in his gift. Your great-uncle became Dean of Ridlington Cathedral, and would have become a bishop had he lived."

Dinah thought it over, and then she said in a strained

voice, "So you would have me lock myself in my room—as poor Christopher was locked in his?"

"Yes, my dear, I would. You know your room and everything that is in it, but outside you will not be so sure and only unhappiness could follow. I have seen it happen, and I have always been sorry for the man or woman who has married outside his or her class." She added with a thump of her hand on the wooden arm of her garden chair, "I dislike the middle and professional classes! They either have an assurance that borders on impertinence, or they are not satisfied until they have been knighted for being a lord mayor."

Dinah did not reply. The shadows were lengthening over the grass, and the croquet mallets were left lying in the dappled shade of the trees as her brothers and Paula had left them.

She wondered if her great-aunt were right. Charles might come of a better family than Percy Whatley, who was forgiven much because of his fortune, but he would never make a great deal of money because he was too generous and too unselfish. She wondered, too, if the self-assurance that her great-aunt resented was because professional men usually knew a great deal more than Mr. Percy Whatley and his kind.

She looked at the battered croquet balls and thought: "That's what I am like—a croquet ball, knocked every way by people who think they are only doing it out of kindness."

She went indoors to change her dress for a dinner party at the Collingtons'. She did not think that Charles would be there, but she was mistaken. He was not only there but he took in the eldest Miss Collington, a pretty girl with a roguish eye and a continual flow of lighthearted conversation. She did her best to flirt with the grave Dr. Bellingham, and to Dinah, sitting opposite, it seemed that he responded, until during an interval in the courses his eyes met hers across the table with a look that it was impossible to misunderstand.

But when, after dinner there was music in the drawing room, he did not come near her, and it proved to be a most unsatisfactory evening.

The next morning, however, her uncle called her into his study and said that Charles had just left, and that he had told him that he thought Miss Bretton was looking pale and peaky after nursing Tavie for so long, and that Tavie himself was far too thin. He suggested that she and Tavie with Nurse

Blackwell go for a month to stay at the seaside, preferably Sheringham, as soon as rooms could be found for them there.

"But the others—they have not been back long, Uncle Sep."

"Miss Stroud will take care of Paula, and when I was away Quin thought it was time Paul joined his boy, Henry, at his boarding school before they both go on to Eton. They are of the same age and he thinks they will get on together famously. So I have been in correspondence with the headmaster of The Elms School, and he has agreed to take Paul as soon as his schoolclothes can be got together. Aunt Alice has said she will superintend all that."

Was there anything, thought Dinah, that her great-aunt was not prepared to superintend?

Certainly the two elder boys had not left for Eton more than a day or two before Paul and his new clothes—all marked by Miss Stroud and Mrs. Jennings—had also departed, leaving a Paula who was only comforted by the thought that Digger had been left solely in her charge. Dinah hoped that rooms would not be found at Sheringham, but here she was disappointed. In no time at all, she was bustled off with Nurse Blackwell and Tavie to some rooms in a small house in Sheringham, and after a day or two she knew that Charles as well as her uncle had been right.

The shock of her cousin's sudden attack, on top of the weeks of anxious nursing of her little brother, had taken their toll, and the complete change and the benefit of being away from Saltbech began to make her feel better already.

A day or so after Dinah had gone, Julia brought Mr. Cottrell to Saltbech to meet her uncle and great-aunt, and was relieved that Dinah was not there.

"Because," she told them over luncheon, "everyone in London is laughing at Major Morrell. Jono will tell you what has happened, because being Caroline Maitland's cousin he knows more about it than I do."

"I always thought Caroline was up to something," Jonathan said with a smiling glance at his pretty fiancée. "But of course, Morrell did not know her at all. He only thought that she was headstrong and spoiled, and was ready to put up with her whims for the sake of her fortune. He bought her a new engagement ring—she lost the first one by dropping it over the side of a houseboat into the Thames, I saw her do it!—and the new ring cost him a great deal of money, which naturally he had to borrow from old Lord Morrell, who did not like it at all. Neither did he like buying the house in Park Lane that Caroline said she wanted, or the furnishing of it. There was some consolation in the thought that my Uncle Stephen was to pay for the wedding reception and the wedding at St. Margaret's and so on, and then just one week before the wedding Morrell came flying round to see me in a hansom cab, white to the lips. "Mr. Cottrell," he said, "do you know that your uncle and your cousin Caroline sailed from Southampton for South Africa last night?" "Yes," I said, "I did know it," and I gave him the letter that Caroline had left with me for him. I knew what was in it because she showed me what she had written before she left. She had apologized for breaking their engagement at the last moment, but she had changed her mind and was going back to South Africa with her father. She was afraid he would have to see to the returning of the wedding presents, as she would be out of the country, but perhaps his next bride would take to the house in Park Lane and all its furniture, which she personally thought quite hideous. She was keeping the ring he had given her as it was far too beautiful to part with, and the ruby necklace dear Lord Morrell had given her went with it so well. And she signed herself, 'Yours sincerely, C. Maitland.'"

"That is what Caroline meant that day when she told me to send her love to Dinah and say that she was not to believe all she heard," said Julia laughing.

"Do you mean to tell me, Julia," said Mrs. Crichton in a voice heavy with disapproval, "that Miss Maitland put Major Morrell to all that trouble and expense for nothing?"

"Not for nothing, Great-aunt A.," said Julia with a demure little smile. "She did it to pay him out for his outrageous behavior to our beloved Di. You saw his letter to her yourself, so you know what it was like."

The Honorable Alice continued to look disapproving for another minute, but she could not deny that she had seen Morrell's letter, although she said nothing about it being at that moment in her little writing-desk upstairs. And then she, too, laughed, and taking up her glass of wine drank a health to Mr. Maitland and his daughter.

Later on in the drawing room, before the rector and Jonathan joined them she asked her great-niece who were to be her bridesmaids when she married, which was to be just before Christmas.

"I understand Dinah has already had her wedding dress packed up and sent to you, my dear," she said. "And of course you will have to be married by your uncle the dean, while I understand Harold is determined to give you away. But I would not suggest Dinah as a bridesmaid."

"Oh, don't you think so, Aunt A.?" Julia was disappointed.

"It would be the height of bad taste, my dear. But fortunately you have several cousins of Paula's age and a trifle older, both at the deanery and the Traceys. I would suggest selecting some of the better looking gels from those two families—the deanery ones are *very* plain—but your Aunt Emmeline will select styles of dresses and hats that will show them in a good light, I have no doubt." She did not mention the unlikely prospect of Helen leaving Paris to receive the guests to her daughter's wedding with Edmund and Emmeline Bromley in their house in Belgrave Square.

"I hope you like Jonathan, Great-aunt A.?"

"Very much." The Honorable Alice strongly approved of Mr. Cottrell though he was only a younger son, because she knew his family and that his father would settle a good income on him when he married. When the two men joined them, she said she would like to take a turn in the garden with Mr. Cottrell while Julie had a talk with her uncle. Miss Pettit was sent to fetch the garden hat that hung beside the rector's on the stand in the lobby—a rather battered, wide-brimmed black straw, with a faded purple ribbon round the crown, which was skewered onto the gray bun on top of Mrs. Crichton's head with a long hatpin with a gold horse's head on it, and with one of the Berlin wool shawls wrapped round her shoulders she took the young man's arm and walked with him through the falling leaves, where Dimmock's michaelmas daisies still bloomed among the late dahlias in the borders.

As they walked, she told him that his father's lawyer would be hearing from hers during the next few days about the drawing up of Julia's marriage settlement.

"I cannot have a Bretton going to her husband penniless," she said. "And I have no children to inherit whatever I may have to leave." She was, in fact, a very wealthy woman.

Her thoughts went back to Clive Morrell several times during the evening, after the young people had left, and when she went up to bed she searched among the letters in her small traveling writing-desk until she found one dated the previous February and bearing a Maltese stamp.

As she read it through again it seemed to her that although

the man who had written it might have been suitably punished by Miss Maitland, there was another, higher price that he must be made to pay if what he had said about his uncle was not true.

The Honorable Alice had met Lord Morrell once or twice, and like Mrs. Duncan she did not think that the action attributed to him was in the character of the man. She wished that she could show him the letter and ask him if he had been prepared to disown Clive had he married Dinah, and that chance came rather sooner than she could have foreseen.

Lady Crockett came to call on the rector's aunt, whom she regarded with some awe while referring to her among her friend as "that old gorgon at the rectory."

The "gorgon" was at home and received her graciously in the drawing-room while Simmons served them with tea, small cakes and sandwiches, and after she had left them alone with Miss Pettit to take her place and wait on the ladies, Lady Crockett said what a pity it was that Miss Bretton would not be at home for Lady Collington's ball.

"It is to be quite a grand affair," she said. "Orchestras from London, and caterers too, champagne flowing. You know the sort of thing, I am sure."

Mrs. Crichton, with a slightly grim smile, admitted that she had been to a few balls in her time. She asked how many guests were to be there.

"At least three or four hundred I believe," said Lady Crockett. "It is for the coming-of-age of the eldest boy, Bernard, and it coincides with their first shoot of the season. I believe Lord Morrell is coming. He could not very well hold his own shooting party because of the scandal of his nephew's broken engagement. For the second time, too!" Her eyes became suddenly sharp and probing. "I suppose Miss Bretton gave no reason for breaking *her* engagement to Clive Morrell?"

"Your supposition is correct," said the Honorable Alice imperturbably.

"One begins to think there must be something wrong with the man," said Lady Crockett, not put off in the least.

"Perhaps one does," said her hostess equably, and began to talk of her ladyship's garden. "I hear your dahlias have been exceptionally fine this year," she said and kept the conversation to horticulture until her visitor left.

The invitation to the rector and his aunt was propped up behind one of the brass candlesticks in his study, and that evening The Honorable Alice startled her nephew by saying that she thought she would accept for them both. "It will do us both good, besides being a compliment to Lady Collington and young Bernard," she said. "Lady Collington is an exceptionally nice woman."

When Lady Crockett learned that Mrs. Crichton was going to the Collington's ball she was very much amused. "I cannot imagine the gorgon at a ball at her age," she told her friends. "I wonder what she will wear. One of the Berlin wool shawls her wretched little companion is always knitting for her, perhaps." She and her friends had a great deal of amusement about Mrs. Crichton's probable appearance at the ball.

When the night came, however, even the rector was taken aback by his aunt's appearance. She wore a dress of black velvet, cut low over her imposing bosom, and round her neck there was a collar composed of five rows of superb diamonds. Diamonds, too, sparkled in her ears, in a large brooch in her corsage, and from a magnificent tiara that sat firmly over the bun of gray hair on top of her head.

"Well, Septimus," she said, as the rector helped her into the ermine cape that she proposed to wear in the carriage. "Am I grand enough for Lady Collington's friends?"

"Aunt Alice," said Septimus, awed, "you look wonderful."

She smoothed her white kid elbow-length gloves, a diamond bracelet clasped over one, and a gold one set with rubies over the other, and then she took up her ostrich feather fan and was ready to go.

Her appearance created quite a sensation, and Lord Morrell who was about to make his way to the card room was stopped in his tracks by The Honorable Alice.

"We have met before I think, Lord Morrell," she said, smiling in a somewhat ogreish fashion. "Some years ago, at Marlborough House."

"Of course." He took her hand and bowed, and looked round for a means of escape, but having secured her prey, she was not one to let go.

She put her hand in his arm and accompanied him across the room to a small anteroom where a few of the guests were sitting talking. Here she advanced to a small sofa, and he was forced to go with her and to sit down beside her.

"We came within an ace of being related to each other a little while ago," she told him conversationally, waving her feather fan, her beady eyes regarding him through its feathers like the eyes of a bird of prey.

"Indeed?"

"My great-niece, Miss Dinah Bretton, was at one time engaged to be married to your nephew, Major Clive Morrell, until he asked her to break it off."

"He asked her—" His lordship's face grew suddenly dark. Had this wretched woman hunted him out in order to throw doubts on his heir's integrity?

"Yes. Poor Dinah, she had all her wedding things packed, even to her wedding-dress, because she was to travel out under the chaperonage of Mrs. Duncan, the wife of Major Morrell's commanding officer, to Malta, where she was to be married from their house. And then this letter came, putting an end to the whole thing. My poor little great-niece was at first brokenhearted, but mercifully she has recovered now. And since we have heard that Miss Maitland has also broken her engagement with your nephew, one cannot help wondering if there was some tangle about *her* inheritance, and once more your lordship had intervened to stop the marriage."

"*I* intervened?" Lord Morrell went slowly purple. "I fail to understand you, madam. I have had nothing to do with my nephew's engagements. Both young ladies were entirely of his choosing, and he only brought them to me for my blessing. That is the truth, whatever evil-minded gossip may say to the contrary."

"And yet in his letter to my niece he distinctly said that if he married her—now that her father was dead and the family in financial straits—it would be against your wishes, and that you would not only cut off his income but you would not acknowledge him as your heir."

"I do not believe a word of it. I should very much like to see that letter myself, madam."

"I thought you would, which is why I brought it with me tonight." A pocket in her underskirt was dived into, and a letter was brought out and put into his hand. "It was given to me to read on the day my niece received it, towards the end of last February. She told me to read it and then to burn it, but I kept it, forseeing an occasion such as this when it might be useful. I will leave it with you, Lord Morrell, so that you may ask your nephew if it is his letter and in his handwriting, and then if he admits it you have my permission to burn it. It is not pleasant for a family such as yours to have letters of this nature in the family archives."

She got up and left him, diamonds flashing, her velvet-clad

back as flat as a soldier's, and she went back into the ball-room to find Septimus looking for her.

"I wondered where you had got to," he said.

"I was paying a long overdue score," she said. "And now I intend to enjoy myself. Will you be so good as to attract that waiter's eye, my dear? I see he has a tray of champagne and I would like one of those glasses to celebrate."

"To celebrate what, Aunt Alice?"

"A victory over a very unpleasant young man," she said.

A week or so later a story was going round London clubs that Clive Morrell had sold his house and its contents in Park Lane, and had left England for Australia. There was also another story to the effect that Lord Morrell had altered his will, instructing his lawyers at his death to sell his estate and to divide the money obtained from such a sale together with his personal fortune between four very distant and impoverished cousins.

Chapter Twenty-two

It was on the second morning of her stay in Sheringham that Dinah learned from her landlady that it had been Dr. Bellingham who had arranged for her rooms to be rented by the rector.

"I don't usually let rooms after September, miss," Mrs. Hawkins said. "But then, you see, I was maid to Dr. Bellingham's Mamma for years before they went off to India. Mr. Bellingham went to be a missionary there, and they hadn't a penny between them before they left, so I don't know what it was like out in them places, I'm sure. I had to be nurse, cook, housemaid, scullerymaid, everything to everybody in the little vicarage where they lived when they were here in England—some said the vicar hadn't no more than ninety pound a year. When the bills come in, Mrs. Bellingham and me would spread them out on the kitchen table with the housekeeping money for the month, and we would decide how much we could pay off each, like five shilling off the milk, three and sixpence off the butcher, and another five shilling off the grocer. Sometimes, she would sit back and laugh and ask how much that left for my wages, and of course there wasn't any left at all. But at Easter the gentry was kind and generous over the offertory, and that would tide us over for a time. But she was so delicate: Mr. Charles was the only child that lived, all the rest died almost soon as they was born."

Dinah encouraged her to talk about Charles and how he was passed from one relative to another after his parents died in India.

"When he happened to be near me I'd go and see him on my days off," Mrs. Hawkins said one day. "I had to get another place, you see, after his parents left England. And when I did see him, wasn't he pleased? 'It's little Mother Maggie,' he'd say, and he always had a kiss for me. Poor boy, all his relations was as poor as his father had been, and didn't welcome another mouth to feed. One uncle was in the merchant navy, and died of fever in the east somewheres, and there was his Aunt Betty what was a lady nurse in a hospital, and his Aunt Annie who went for a schoolteacher, and one of his uncles, Mr. Herbert Bellingham, was a schoolmaster."

A schoolmaster, thought Dinah with an inward smile. Almost the lowest form of employment that an educated person could take in Aunt A.'s opinion. Yet, every evening as she ate her solitary dinner, she was eager to hear more.

She learned how Charles had stayed with an aunt who had become a Catholic, and gave up her life to working for the poor in London's East End, and how, seeing her there and the people she tried to help, he had developed a wish to become a doctor.

It was through this aunt that he realized his ambition, because, poor as she was, among her friends was a well-to-do lady who had offered to pay for his schooling and his training in Edinburgh, and he had rewarded her brilliantly.

That month of October in Sheringham was almost like summer. When Dinah hired a cab to take them for a drive inland, the trees, slow in turning, still had brilliant colors of yellow, gold and scarlet, while in other places it looked as if summer had never gone. Never had the country looked more beautiful, Dinah thought, and never had the days seemed to pass so happily, now that the burden and worry of her family in Saltbech was left behind.

All morning she would sit with Nurse Blackwell and Octavius on the beach, Nurse busy with her knitting, Dinah writing a lazy letter or two, and Octavius gravely digging castles in the sand.

Castles, thought Dinah, watching him carefully raising a fortress of sand that would be washed away with the incoming tide: that was what one's life was like. A series of castles, a new one being built—if one had the determination—every time the old one was washed away.

She thought of her great-aunt's philosophy and wondered what it was worth: one only had one life. Was it better to live on the surface as her mother did, like a butterfly hovering over ever brighter flowers until killed off by the frost, or was it better to live like little Janet Annerley and Mark? Life meant a great deal to those two, every moment of every day packed with incident, with the comings and goings of a provincial town, and their contentment shone in their eyes and in their faces. Was it because their lives were bound up in the wants and illness of other people that they were never bored, she wondered. There was no time to shut themselves in locked rooms.

There were so many things to admire in most walks of life, she thought, sitting there with her letters unwritten and her eyes on the absorbed back of Tavie. The spirit and courage of people like Aunt A., for example, who would never fail to meet emergencies with sound common sense, because if she did not she would feel that she had failed her family. And then there were professional people with their determination to get on, to become landed gentry like Percy Whatley's grandfather, or just to do the best they could for those who depended on them for their lives, like Charles. And there were the working-men and women at Bretton, whom her father had treated as if they were of his family, because he knew all about their families and the way they lived. He joined in their sports, their cricket matches on Bretton Green, and depended on them to act as beaters when his friends came down in the autumn with their guns.

Servants, too, not the grand ones like Lovell and Nurse Blackwell, but those employed in smaller places like the rectory: how kind and good-natured they were, however late they were required to sit up, however early they had to be astir in the mornings.

The waves came rolling up along the beach, receding with a long drawn out hiss from protesting pebbles beyond the stretch of sand where Tavie built his castles and his forts, and her thoughts gradually became more coherent. She saw her great-aunt's philosophy in its proper perspective, as she saw many other things, like the opening of a locked room and what it would mean for its tenant: fresh air, perhaps, and a sense of freedom.

On the last day of their stay, as she sat there under a groyne wrapped in a tweed cape because there was a cold east wind blowing above it, while Nurse Blackwell took Tavie along the front to see a fishingboat that had just come in with its net full of a silvery catch, there was a footstep on the shingle behind her and Charles was there, dropping down beside her in the shelter of the groyne.

"You are looking as you did that day I saw you when you had been visiting your laundrywoman," he told her with satisfaction. "Your eyes have got back their sparkle and your face its color." He had not forgotten how very pretty she had looked that day, and it was as if she had been away from him since then, traveling in a far country, and had just come back.

"I am quite well again, thanks to you, Charles," she said sedately. "And I have had a most entertaining time while I have been here, listening to stories of your past."

"Maggie is an old gossip." He frowned, taking up a couple of stones and rolling them from one hand to the other. "I'd forgotten how talkative she is. I am afraid I only thought of your health—and Tavie's."

"I know," she said, and then, "Why are you going to Edinburgh, Charles?"

He wished she would not keep calling him Charles: it made him feel lightheaded, as if at any moment he might blurt out something he would regret.

"If you really wish to know," he said, his attention on the stones in his hands, "it was to get away from—somebody."

"From me?" she asked.

"Well—yes," he admitted, frowning.

"Aunt A. said she thought it might be that," she said calmly. "And she thought it was very wise of you. Aunt A always applauds good sense in the professional classes."

Privately, he damned her great-aunt. He said without looking at her: "I cannot go on in Saltbech for six years with you at the rectory because I am in love with you. It boils down to that." And then, gripping the stones so hard that his knuckles turned white, "Damn it, Dinah, you know I cannot

213

ask you to marry me. You'd be cut off from your family for the rest of your life. They simply would not approve of it, nor of me, and their opinion would be the same as that of The Honorable Alice, that a Bretton could not marry an ordinary professional man."

"But you do not want to marry my great-aunt, nor my family," she pointed out, happiness lying under the quietly spoken words like the hidden depths under a calm and sparkling sea. "Naturally my Mamma will be outraged, because she is living in Paris with the gentleman who owns her apartment. Very discreetly, you understand. Mamma is very discreet about these matters. She was very discreet about Octavius, and so was Papa. So that if Mamma should write to protest I would simply telegraph back, asking which was blacker, the kettle or the pot, and I do not think I should ever hear from her again." She paused. "When do you start for Edinburgh?"

"In the New Year." He was bewildered by her change of mood, trying to follow her line of thought.

"That will give me a nice long time in which to get ready," she said. "Though you will have to take me as I am, because I've no money to spend on clothes, and I am sure Aunt A. won't give me a penny."

"Look," he said, dropping the stones and taking her hands in his. "Shall we leave your great-aunt out of this for a moment? The only question I want answered is, do you love me enough to marry me?"

"I think I knew I loved you at the moment when you looked at me over Tavie's bed and told me that we had won the fight for his life," she said. "But lately, since the Collingtons and the Whatleys and their friends have taken you up, I've been afraid one of their girls would tempt you to take advantage of their father's wealth. With a rich wife behind you, Charles, goodness alone knows where you could finish. Probably in Windsor, or at Osborne, with an appointment to the Royal Household."

"If you don't stop being so irritating," he said, "I shall shake you. Dinah, will you consider for a moment what it would be like to be married to me—losing perhaps all your friends and leading a completely different life to the one you have always been used to?"

"But if I lose my friends when I marry you," she said, her eyes sparkling, but her voice not quite steady, "will any of them be worth keeping? And if I lead a different life, with you there to share it how can I fail to find it interesting, even exciting, and because I love you so much will it not be a more complete life than I have ever known before? My darling Charles, I must mention Aunt A. once more, and then I have done with her forever. She wants me to shut myself away from you in a locked room—as poor Christopher was locked away. Only with me, that room will never be unlocked again, and it is one I know by heart and do not like very much." She thought of her mother in Paris with her rich lover, of her Bretton aunts, of little Julia, whose engagement to Jonathan Cottrell had been so much approved because he was a younger son in an old and wealthy family.

"Do you not see," she said gently, "that on the day I marry you I shall be freed from my locked room forever, and if the key is to be turned against me, so that I cannot return, I shall not care a straw, because I shall have you beside me, my dearest, wonderful Charles."

The wind was blowing cold above the groyne, but on the beach below it, sitting in its shelter on the clean-washed pebbles, with his arm about her, they discussed their future plans.

Dinah thought her great-aunt would stay on at the rectory for as long as the children were to be away from Bretton.

"As for Tavie," she added, "I can see words of notice trembling on Nurse Blackwell's lips, and good as she was when he was so ill, I think he has outgrown nurses now. I believe Miss Stroud will be delighted to have him in the schoolroom, and maybe the little room next to her bedroom might be turned into a bedroom for him, instead of the night nursery. He is very clever. Do you know I have been teaching him to read, starting when he was convalescent and going on with it here, and he can read almost anything now."

At that moment Octavius appeared, flying over the beach to them, looking much more grown up with his cropped fair hair under his flat sailor's cap with the letters VICTORY picked out in gold on its navy-blue ribbon, and his reefer jacket with the brass buttons and the long navy-blue serge trousers.

"How d'you do, Bellenum?" he said when he arrived. "I did not know you were coming to Sheringham."

"Neither did I," said Dinah. "And you must not call him Bellingham, Tavie, but Charles, because he's going to be your brother."

Tavie stared at Charles incredulously. "Aren't you a bit old to be my brother?" he asked.

"Well, does brother-in-law sound better?" asked Charles.

"Much better," agreed Tavie. He went on eagerly, dismissing Charles himself as unimportant. "There aren't many flowers here, Bell—I mean, Charles—but there are hundreds of lovely shells—all colors—pink and gray and blue and green—almost as beautiful as flowers, really."

Charles agreed that seashells came in many forms, and his future brother-in-law said he would show him his collection after tea.

That evening after he had gone, a hint of what was in store for Dinah when her engagement was announced at the rectory came from Nurse Blackwell, when she told her the news.

"Well, I suppose you know your own mind best, Miss Dinah," she said, her mouth going down in disapproving lines. "But I do not think Mrs. Crichton will be best pleased." It was evident that she felt some slight degradation herself in it, just as she had felt their stay in rooms in a small house that could almost be called a cottage had been a distinct come-down. In all the families she had been with, she told Maggie Hawkins, she had never been asked to go into furnished rooms. A house had always been taken for the summer months at Eastbourne or Bournemouth or some similar resort, and she had moved into it with her charges, the nursery and schoolroom servants, several housemaids, one of the under-cooks and a groom who had been there to look after the horse and private carriage that had been sent with them. Hiring cabs had never been considered.

Naturally, in other quarters the engagement was not approved either, Mrs. Crichton telling Septimus that she had feared it all along, ever since Octavius was so ill and the doctor had come sometimes twice a day. "They saw far too much of each other," she said. "In my opinion Helen should come home and put a stop to it."

"I cannot see her doing anything so foolish," said Septimus with spirit, in which he was proved right because Helen ignored her eldest daughter's engagement completely. "And personally, I am delighted."

During the weeks that followed, after Nurse Blackwell had departed to a much grander situation where once more she had footmen to wait on the nursery, as she had had at Bretton, it reassured Dinah a great deal to see how warm was Miss Stroud's welcome to Tavie in the schoolroom, and how gradually he began to transfer his requests for information from Charles to his Uncle Septimus.

She would come on them in the rector's study, sitting side by side at the center table covered with its green serge cloth, the Reverend Johns's book on wild flowers or a book on seashells open between them, the prematurely white head of her uncle and the fair one of Tavie bent over the pages, both too absorbed in what they were studying to do more than look up and smile at her entrance.

Septimus told her that directly Tavie was old enough he intended to teach him Latin and Greek, and he thought it was time he began to learn to ride. He could start on Paula's pony, while she was transferred to Paul's larger one, and when the boys came home for Christmas holidays, he would see that there would be horses enough in the stables for them all to ride.

The rectory had become home to them all now, and especially for Tavie, and as Dinah saw the way he turned to Septimus and the response of her uncle to the little boy, it seemed to her that while Octavius had at last found the father he had never known, Septimus, too, had discovered a son in place of the one he had lost. She wondered if Tavie would ever return to Bretton when the time came, or if he would not regard Saltbech as his permanent home.

Gradually, on closer acquaintance, The Honorable Alice conceded that Dinah's future husband showed a surprising amount of knowledge and common sense, and even that he was quite a nice looking man with an air of breeding. And one day when she felt "not quite the thing" she was greatly encouraged by his sympathetic way of avoiding any opinion that such feelings could be due to approaching old age.

From then onwards, he was given his name "Charles" instead of the formal "Dr. Bellingham," and when Honoria came to luncheon and dared to criticize him in her hearing, she was told sharply that Charles was one of the Dorsetshire Bellinghams, and it was a very fortunate thing for them all to have a clever physician in the family.

Julia's wedding before Christmas was a very sumptuous affair, with bridesmaids galore and a reception for five hundred guests. Her mother had not been there, and Dinah found a certain coolness between her and her Aunt Honoria and the dean and his wife, but it did not concern her in the least. Julia's happiness was all that mattered, and Julia was radiant.

When she had left her uncle's house in Belgrave Square Sophy came home from Paris to take her place, complaining bitterly that her Mamma had not been to see her once during the whole time she had been there, and she spent Christmas with the Bromleys in London. Julia was taken by her husband to his father's place in Shropshire and could almost think herself at Bretton again. There was a Boxing Day meet in the Hall grounds, with footmen taking round the stirrup cup as they had done at Bretton, and she felt very much at home there, and was made a fuss of and shown off as Jonathan's pretty bride.

While in Saltbech Rectory the Christmas tree in the hall was rather larger than usual that Christmas, and presents were heaped around the table at its base, Tom standing ready to extinguish any of the candles that threatened to set fire to the branches.

Logs blazed in the great hearth, and there was warmth and gaiety in the hall as the family gathered there with the servants on Christmas afternoon, to receive their presents at the hands of Octavius, after a mid-day dinner of turkey and Christmas pudding celebrated with champagne in the dining room and the best port in the servants' hall.

It was the happiest Christmas Septimus had spent in years, and as he smiled benignly on the folk assembled there in his great hall, on his Aunt Alice and Miss Pettit, and Hannah, on his schoolboy nephews, and the twins' faces bright with laughter, on Miss Stroud, a much happier lady than when she first came to Saltbech, on Dinah with her eyes reflecting nothing but happiness as she stood beside Charles with her hand in his, watching Octavius's grave face as he carefully handed out the presents, on Mrs. Jennings and the maids and the groom Coppard, and Dimmock and Mrs. Dimmock, and young Tom, his hair neatly plastered for the occasion, he felt that he had been led into pleasant places at last, and that God was in his Heaven and all was well with his world.

In spite of their determination to have a quiet wedding in the New Year, Dinah and Charles found themselves completely routed by The Honorable Alice. No Bretton, she told Dinah severely, was going to have a hole-and-corner wedding if she had her way. And have her way she did.

Invitations were sent out, a reception for about fifty to a hundred guests planned for the great hall at the rectory, and for days beforehand the still-room was locked with Mrs.

Jennings and Simmons inside, while Hannah retired to the old day nursery where the sewing machine was heard clacking away as she worked on what was to be Dinah's wedding-dress. The dress having been planned by her great-aunt, Dinah wondered with some trepidation what it would be like, but as that door, too, was locked on Hannah's activities she could not see it for herself.

The wedding day dawned with sunshine and a sparkling frost, and after breakfast had been brought to her in bed by her great-aunt's orders, Hannah came into Dinah's room with the dress—a white satin with a Limerick lace veil.

"The mistress says you are to wear this, Miss Dinah," said Hannah as she laid the dress out on a chair, the veil over another. "It was cut from her own wedding-dress, and I borrowed one of your dresses so as to make it stylish and I think it should fit. And the veil is the one she wore, too."

And as she stared at the beautiful dress and veil, her great-aunt sailed in, already dressed for the wedding in purple velvet, with a purple toque looking rather like a rajah's turban on her head.

"I brought you this," she said, putting a leather case into her hand. "My pearl necklace. It will look very well if you ever have to accompany Charles to Balmoral."

"Oh Aunt A! Darling Aunt A!" Half laughing, half crying, Dinah reached up to receive a hug and a kiss, and then Hannah helped her to dress, and when she was ready she found Harold alone waiting in the hall to take her to the church in the smart little carriage that their great-aunt had recently had brought to Saltbech from her own home.

In the meantime in the house in the High Street that now held only Mark Annerley's brass plate on its railings, Charles shrugged himself into a new frock coat, made sure that his partner and best man had the ring safely in his waistcoat pocket, and swore because he could not get his tie right.

"That damned old woman at the rectory," he said. "I said that Dinah and I wanted a quiet wedding, but oh no, Dinah is a Bretton and she must have a wedding suitable for her family, with all the town looking on, damn them."

"Will you stop swearing for a moment and look out of the window?" said Mark mildly.

Charles looked and blanched a little. "Good God," he said, "they are lining the whole street!"

"And that is not because you are marrying a Bretton," said Mark. "It is because most of those people out there are your

219

patients. My dear fellow, has it occurred to you that to Saltbech Dinah is only the rector's niece, but the man she is marrying is *their doctor?* Look at that old lady at the window opposite. Do you recognize her?"

Charles looked. "Mrs. Duffy!" he exclaimed. "They'll kill her, bringing her all the way from Easterley to sit at an open window on a day like this. Run down, Mark, and tell them to shut that window at once."

"Mrs. Duffy is a very strong old party," said Mark. "You need not reduce that tie to a rag, Charles. It was all right the first time you tied it."

Charles left the tie and went back to studying the street. He could see Mrs. Dewey and her husband, and the Adcocks and their daughter, and quite a lot of men from the barracks mingling with the crowd.

"I detest being a peep-show," he said and then more anxiously, "Have the bridesmaids received their presents?"

"Mrs. Crichton is giving them to them at the church door." There were to be six little girls, including Paula. "Mrs. C. said that the gold bangles with each child's initial in pearls were in excellent taste," Mark went on, and then, "I'm going to miss you a lot, Charles. For weeks now your patients have been telling me that they were sure I would do my best, but, begging my pardon, it would not be the same as having Dr. Bellingham. To which I heartily agreed. I know now exactly what Elisha felt when the mantle of Elijah fell upon him."

"Rubbish. You are a damned good doctor, and you know it. And when you and Janet have moved in here and your assistant—what is his name? Ah yes, Pringle—is in your dolls' house, everything will go on as it did before. Pringle is a personal friend, is he not?"

"Oh yes. Gerry's a good fellow. We were at St. George's together."

"There you are then."

If Charles found it embarrassing to face the crowds in the streets, however, he felt it even more so to find a packed church waiting for him. The Collingtons, the Whatleys, Lady Craddock and Bella, and many other friends from Easterley and the county, with Colonel and Mrs. Lockwill, and patients from Burston, from Crossways and from West Bresleigh, all were there in strength, and if for once the Brettons were thin on the ground nobody noticed or cared.

Six little girls in velvet dresses the color of holly berries, carrying small posies of red and white hothouse roses, and wearing lace caps and their bangles, stood in the porch waiting for the bride, and Charles made a dash through them with Mark at his heels.

"If this is The Honorable Alice's idea of a quiet wedding," he whispered fiercely to his best man as they found their places reserved for them in front of the congregation, "I'd like to know what the devil her idea of a big one is."

"Remember where you are, for pity's sake, Charles!" said Mark, and then the choir trooped into the chancel, the organ began a voluntary, and Septimus stepped out to face the bridegroom and the best man at the chancel steps. And as Charles turned his head and saw Dinah coming towards him on Harold's arm in her beautiful dress, followed by her small band of bridesmaids, and he went to meet her, he forgot everything else.

The wedding breakfast at the rectory has been spread out on long trestle tables, covered with snowy damask cloths, the length of the great hall, trails of ivy and sprigs of myrtle surrounding an enormous wedding cake, made by the rectory cook and iced by Mrs. Jennings herself, and there was champagne with which their friends and relations could drink to Dinah's happiness and luck to Charles in his new appointment. And then it was all over and Dinah went upstairs to change, while Charles went to Septimus's dressing room.

It was while Mark was making sure that Charles had all tickets and reservations in his waistcoat pocket and knew all the arrangements he had made for him, including the journey to Scotland, breaking it for a night at a hotel in York, that Benson asked to have a word with him.

Mark came back looking slightly apprehensive.

"What has happened?" asked Charles, picking up the fur-lined coat that had been Septimus's present to him.

"It's them young devils, sir," said Benson. "Young Sir 'Arold and Mr. Johnnie and them young Collingtons and Whatleys—nearly a dozen of 'em, all told. They're out there in the drive waiting till you and your lady comes out and git into the kerridge-like, and then they're going to un'arness the 'osses and take the shafts themselves and race with you to the station."

"And tip us out on the way and probably break their limbs into the bargain." Charles thought a moment. "Have you got the trap in the yard, Benson?"

"With Whitestar, sir, in case you wanted me."

"God bless you for that. Mark, see that the luggage is put on the carriage outside the front door, and you Benson, go back to the yard and wait for me. I'll not be a moment."

He raced along the gallery to Dinah's room and found her ready, the sable wrap that her father had given her fastened snugly round her shoulders over her cloth coat. He told her what he planned to do. "Are you ready, sweetheart?" he asked.

She clipped the gold chain that held her muff round her neck and held out her hand. "Quite ready, Charles," she said.

They ran together to the back staircase and down it and along the deserted kitchen passages out to the yard. Here Charles lifted Dinah up into the trap beside the driver's seat, wrapping his rug round her, and then swinging himself up beside her. Then he took the reins from Benson, and with the groom up behind them, he drove out of the yard and along the stable entrance to where it joined the drive.

Here he lifted his hat to wave to the crowd of disappointed boys and the friends who had gathered behind them: Dinah waved her muff in good-bye and they were off, the empty carriage following behind with the luggage.

But even on that quiet road people had gathered to say good-bye to the beloved doctor who was leaving them. They cheered and clapped as the trap went by as if royalty had been visiting the town, and windows that had been closed for Christopher's funeral were opened wide on that frosty day as his patients leaned out to wave, while on the pavements small children threw sprigs of myrtle and rosemary up into the trap for his bride.

On the platform Charles waited for a moment to shake hands with Benson. "I know you will look after Dr. Annerley as you have looked after me," he said, as a crisp banknote changed hands. "And look after Whitestar as well. He's too old to take to fresh pastures now, but he knows the streets of Saltbech and the lanes about it, and he will be happier in his own stable than in Edinburgh."

After Charles had seen the luggage safely into the guard's van and the train moved slowly out of the little town, he asked what Dinah had done with her wedding bouquet.

"I asked Janet to put it on Christopher's grave," she said smiling.

"But he tried to kill you—"

"He had twenty-four wasted years, poor dear, and I have so

much." Her eyes met his. "I could not do anything else but give him my wedding bouquet."

For many weeks after they had left, Charles's patients would appear at Dr. Annerley's surgery with small presents for Dr. Bellingham, and the request that he would be so good as to give them his address in Edinburgh.

Because in spite of being generally popular, and in spite of the fact that he took as great a care of them as Charles had done, there was for a time a feeling that persisted among his patients that they would be doomed to an early death if they had not Dr. Bellingham to write to in emergencies.

And when his elderly patients called for their bottles of medicine every Saturday night, although it was exactly the same medicine as Charles had made up for them, and Dr. Annerley wrapped the bottles every bit as neatly in white paper, with little dabs of red sealing-wax on top, it took a very long time before they became convinced that the medicine had the same magical healing qualities about it as it had when it came from Dr. Bellingham.

Let COVENTRY Give You
A Little Old-Fashioned Romance